CONCLUDING

By Henry Green

*

CONCLUDING

A Novel by
HENRY GREEN

LONDON
THE HOGARTH PRESS
1954

PUBLISHED BY
The Hogarth Press Ltd
LONDON
*
Clarke, Irwin & Co. Ltd.
TORONTO

FIRST PUBLISHED 1948
SECOND IMPRESSION 1950
THIRD IMPRESSION 1954

PRINTED IN GREAT BRITAIN BY
R. & R. CLARK, LTD., EDINBURGH

MR ROCK rose with a groan. Crossing to the open bedroom window he shone his torch out on fog. His white head was gray, and white the reflected torch light on the thick spectacles he wore. He shone it up and down. —It will be a fine day, a fine day in the end, he decided.

He looked down. He clicked his light out. He found there was just enough filtering through the mist which hung eighteen foot up and which did not descend to the ground, to make out Ted, his goose, about already, a dirty pallor, almost the same colour as Alice, the Persian cat, that kept herself dry where every blade of grass bore its dark, mist laden string of water. —Old and deaf, half blind, Mr Rock said about himself, the air raw in his throat. Nevertheless he saw plain how Ted was not ringed in by fog. For the goose posed staring, head to one side, with a single eye, straight past the house, up into the fog bank which had made all daylight deaf beneath, and beyond which, at some clear height, Mr Rock knew now there must be a flight of birds fast winging, —Ted knows where, he thought.

The old and famous man groaned again, shut the window. He began to dress. He put working clothes over the yellow woollen nightshirt. The bedroom smelled stale, packed with books not one of which he had read in years. He groaned a third time. —Early morning comes hard on a man my age, he told himself for comfort, comes hard. —How hard? Oh, heavy.

When he put the kettle on downstairs he did not lay out his granddaughter Elizabeth a cup because Sebastian Birt might be with her still, in the other bedroom across the landing.

Five minutes more saw him off to fetch Daisy's swill. It

was lighter already, but with pockets of mist that reached to the ground. Over his shoulders he wore a yoke. The hanging buckets clanked. He wondered if he should have brought his torch, but it seemed the sun must come through any minute.

He went slowly and was overtaken by George Adams, the woodman, going up for orders.

They did not speak at once, went on together down the ride in silence, between these still invisible tops of trees beneath which loomed colourlessly one mass of flowering rhododendron after another and then the azaleas, which, without scent, pale in the fresh of early morning, had not yet begun, as they would later, to sway their sweetness forwards, back, in silent church bells to the morning.

The man spoke. "It'll turn out a fine day yet," he said.

"Yes, Adams," said the other.

They walked on in silence.

"How's your wife, Adams?" Mr Rock then asked.

"Why I lost her, sir, the winter just gone."

Mr Rock said not a word to this at first. "I'm getting an old dodderer," he ventured in the end, sorry for himself at the slip.

"You're a ripe age now," George Adams agreed.

He never offered to help carry those buckets, the man reminded himself, because whatever the position Mr Rock had once held, this long-toothed gentleman did his own work now, which was to his credit.

"Yet I feel not a day older," Mr Rock boasted.

"It's my legs," the sage added, when he had no reply.

There was another silence. It was too early yet for the birds, or too thick above, because these were still.

"Nothing anyone can do for the bends," Adams said at last, out of an empty head.

At this instant, like a woman letting down her mass of hair from a white towel in which she had bound it, the sun came through for a moment, and lit the azaleas on either side before fog, redescending, blanketted these off again; as it might be white curtains, drawn by someone out of sight, over a palace bedroom window, to shut behind them a blonde princess undressing.

"It's not fair on one to grow old," Mr Rock said.

Adams made no comment.

"And how's Miss Elizabeth?" the man asked, after a time.

"Better, thank you," Mr Rock replied.

"She overtaxed her head where you put her out to work?" Adams hazarded.

"Don't they all?" the old man countered. He adored his granddaughter and, if it had not been for Birt, could have talked readily about her. "Same as those children up at the house." She was thirty five and they between twelve and seventeen. "Breakdown from overstrain," he ended, cursing Sebastian Birt in his mind, because, although she was not working now, she would never get well while she could meet that man, he knew.

"You'll find her a blessing to have at home. Somebody by you," Adams said in self pity.

—A blessing and a curse, the old man thought, then repented this last so violently that he could not be sure he had not spoken out loud.

"Why, that's strange," Adams said. "Did you hear summat?"

The sage looked blank at his companion. But it was too dark with sudden mist to read the expression on his face.

"I heard a call," Adams volunteered.

"I'm a mite deaf," Mr Rock answered.

"And I caught the echo," Adams insisted.

Which reminded Mr Rock of the argument he had had with Sebastian on this very point, not long since. "It would be from the house, then," he said in a determined voice, referring to the great sickle shaped sweep of mansion towards which they moved like slow, suiciding moles in the half light.

"It's the trees throw back the sound, sir."

"Yet if you face about, Adams, call away from the place down this ride behind, you won't get a whisper in return."

"I never heard that," the woodman said, politely disbelieving.

They walked on. Then the old man took the buckets off his yoke.

"I'll have an easy now," he announced, laying the heavy object by, to one side. He put the buckets bottom upwards, and they sat on these.

"You don't want to rush it when they're full," Adams said.

—I do this for Elizabeth, Mr Rock told himself, but out loud he exclaimed, "I hope I have more sense." His glasses were misted, fog still hung about, but the sun coming through once more, made it for a second so that he might have been inside a pearl strung next the skin of his beloved.

"It's what them younger ones have'nt got, sense," Adams said. —Elizabeth, Eliza, Liz, Mr Rock thought.

"And what age would you be, sir?"

"Seventy six come March."

"That's a tidy sum to be still carrying swill around," the man complimented him, and noticed it a second time.

"What would that be, again?" he asked.

Mr Rock did not answer.

"I thought I caught what I heard before, twice over," Adams insisted.

"Was there an echo?" Mr Rock asked, his mind adrift.

"Not that I reckon."

"They must have faced away from the house, then," the old man said, and let his love for Elizabeth, and fear that he might lose the cottage, sap what ability was left him. Then he tried not to start on this subject, but could not help it.

"Adams," he began, "how d'you hold your house?"

The woodman stopped listening to the woods or to Mr Rock. He took in what was being said, but he had heard it so often these last ten years that he barely paid attention. From habit he answered,

"The same as the rest. It goes along with the job to the estate."

"They'd like to have me away," the old man said.

"Well, I heard tell that you were goin' on your own, sir?"

"How's that?" Mr Rock demanded, turning his eyes full on Adams, with such a glare of alarm the man was startled.

"Why it might be just talk up at the house, like."

"What was?"

"Some up at the house has made out there was likely an honour for you," the woodman offered.

"Yes, and I don't doubt," Mr Rock exclaimed, with violence. "The paltry intriguers," he said. "But they did'nt tell you, did they, about the other?"

"I don't follow, Mr Rock, sir."

"It's the Academy of Sciences," the sage elaborated, boasting but frantic. "There's an election yesterday or today. If they elect me, I can spend the rest of my time in their Institute, or scientific poor law sanatorium, but I can't take my girl. Otherwise I may have some money, thank you. And then, of course, I can refuse. Would you hesitate in my place?"

"How's that, sir?"

"What's to happen to Miss Elizabeth?" he asked, talking as if to a servant in the days of his youth. "She's sick with her mind, Adams. Anyone can tell it."

"So you'll have the money, sir?"

"What do you think?"

"And good luck to you I say, Mr Rock."

"They'd like to have me out, this lot would, Adams," he said, calmer now. "It was'nt Mr Birt said about me, was it?"

"Why never in the world," the woodman answered. "Likely enough one of the girls only caught a word Miss Baker or Miss Edge let drop."

"Those two won't be sorry when my time comes," Mr Rock announced. "But I'll tell you. So long as she remains single I'll see they let her keep on at my cottage, the State I mean. I've some friends still in high places have'nt forgotten the services I rendered. Why, when the State took over from the owner, and founded this Institute to train State Servants, it was even in the Directive that I was to stay in my little place."

"That's right, so you've often said," Adams hastily agreed.

"Well then," Mr Rock muttered, and fell silent.

"There's gratitude," he added after a moment, "Throw him out in the street."

"That's the way things are," Adams agreed, glad to let the matter drop.

"But are you safe, man?" Mr Rock demanded.

"Houses are that short there's noone safe," Adams replied. Mr Rock was silent, for an entirely fresh idea had struck him. This woodman was a widower, living alone, and his was a five roomed cottage. This had never occurred to Mr Rock before. Perhaps because he never could remember Mrs Adams was dead. And as long as Elizabeth was alive he would not let her be turned out, not if he had to hang for it.

Then the cry came a third time, much clearer, so that even Mr Rock heard, and the double echo.

"Ma-ree," a girl's voice shrilled, then a moment later the house volleyed back "Ma-ree, mar-ee," but in so far deeper a note that it might have been a man calling.

"There's one been out on the tiles," George Adams remarked to make a jest, because he was relieved to hear just a girl hollering. But the sage made no comment. He had been struck by a second notion. What he asked himself now was, —could Miss Edge and Miss Baker, in order to get him out of the house, have set Birt onto Elizabeth, be in league with the man to break a poor old fellow down by simply driving his sad girl out of her wits? To have her straitjacketted even, muffled in a padded room?

Up at the great house Miss Edge switched on lights in the sanctum to which she had risen in the State Service, hand in hand with Miss Baker. It did not surprise her to find this lady not yet down.

Edge was short and thin. Baker, who hardly cared for early rising, fat and short.

Both, at this time, were also on separate Commissions in London, sitting Wednesdays each week, which necessitated a start that day very much in advance of the usual hour. On such mornings their breakfast was taken in this seventeenth century, grey panelled room, under a chandelier, on furniture which included two great desks set side by side, and equal to the authority these two whiteheaded women shared.

The panelling was remarkable in that it boasted a dado designed to continue the black and white tiled floor in perspective, as though to lower the ceiling. But Miss Edge had found marble tiles too cold to her toes, had had the stone covered in parquet blocks, on which were spread State imitation Chinese Kidderminster rugs. As a result,

this receding vista of white and black lozenges set from the
rugs to four feet up the walls, in precise and radiating perspective, seemed altogether out of place next British
dragons in green and yellow; while the gay panelling above,
shallow carved, was genuine, the work of a master, giving
Cupid over and over in a thousand poses, a shock, a sad
surprise in such a room.

In spite of summer and that it was dawn, there was
already a log fire alight as Edge moved across to draw one
pair of curtains, merely to look at the weather, or to lower
a window perhaps, she did not know, but the room in-
fluenced her to act on graceful impulse. She took hold on
velvet, which had red lilies over a deeper red, and paused,
as she gently parted the twin halves, to admire her hands'
whiteness against the heavy pile. Delicately, then, she proceeded to reveal window panes, because shutters had not
been used the night before, to disclose glass frosted to flat
arches by condensation, so that the Sanctum was reflected
all dark sapphire blue from electric light at her back
because it was not yet morning. She could even see, round
her head's inky shade, no other than a swarm of aqua-
marines, which, pictured on the dark sapphire panes, were
each drop of the chandelier that she had lit with the lamps
switched on in entering.

She also caught a glimpse of matter whisk across behind,
then dart back to hide. She turned. Held her breath, or
she might have screamed. And it was, as she had feared,
a horrid bat.

She made one dive for the wicker basket and put that
on her.

The anonymous letter she had torn into little pieces the
night before, now lay like flakes of frost on her white head.

She crouched down in case this new thing could flicker
up her skirts. And Miss Baker entered.

"My dear," Baker said, cutting the lamps off at the

switch, going across to the window which she opened. A light came through, so grey it was doomed, together with a wisp of mist. The bat flew outside at once. Whereupon Miss Baker turned lamps on again.

Edge rose, delicately took off the basket.

"If we could as easily rid ourselves of Rock," she said.

Over one eyebrow, caught in a mesh of hair, was a torn piece of paper with, printed on it, the word "FURNICATES".

"You have something on your head," Baker calmly told her.

Without a word Edge removed it, reread, and let the word drop from her fingers to spiral to destruction on the flames.

"What's for breakfast?" Baker asked. Edge looked at a wristwatch.

"They have five minutes," she said, referring to the ten girl students whose turn it was to do orderly duties, that is to wait on these two Principals. Then she slightly yawned. She began,

"Each Wednesday that you and I go up to Town," she said, "the weather we have here, Baker, is exquisite, truly exquisite. There may be black fog outside, just now, this minute, but we shall be cheated, dear. The sun will shine."

"I dread Wednesdays for that reason," Baker untruthfully agreed.

"And the day of the Dance on top of all," Edge mused aloud.

"Oh well," the other said.

"So much still to be done," Edge insisted.

"Least said soonest mended," Baker gave a hint. She moved over to warm her fingers at the blaze.

"If the whole routine is not upset already," Miss Edge complained, fidgetting with tableware. "Till we even have to go hungry up to our labours in London because they are going to Dance."

There was no reply.

"And such a day of it altogether, with the tamasha this evening" Edge continued. "Particularly now when at any minute we ought to hear about that dreadful Rock's election."

"Well Edge," Miss Baker objected. "I warned you, you know, last night. Did'nt I? Don't lay too much store. It may not eventuate."

"I cannot believe Providence will not provide the key after all that you and I have done," Edge argued. "You know what this means. Why, I have literally set my heart on it. And such a happy way out, dear. To go where he will be properly looked after, and we shan't have to see that granddaughter trail herself around."

"They won't take her, Edge," Miss Baker said. "Whatever happens."

Before Edge could answer, the door was opened by a tall girl with long golden hair, and who had been in tears. She was followed by another student bearing breakfast dishes and the toast.

"Why, Marion, where's Mary?" Edge broke off, for Mary had been so punctual in her attentions that these two ladies had let her wait on them out of turn, in fact almost without a break, so that she was readily missed.

"She's to go to Matron, ma'am."

"What's the matter with the child?"

"It's nothing, ma'am, I think."

"Will you tell Miss Birks from me I shall want to hear when I get back. We cannot have Mary away, can we?"

"What's for breakfast," Baker said again, getting with difficulty off a low footstool over by the fire.

"You have your especial favourite this morning," Miss Edge told her, after she had lifted the silver cover off a dish. "Kedgeree, my dear."

"And scrambled eggs to follow if you will just touch

the bell, ma'am," the girl who had been crying said, as, with her companion, she left the room, and the door gently, gently closed.

"Well, if it is scrambled I trust the bacon's crisp," Baker hoped, and spooned her kedgeree onto a plate. Miss Edge, however, did not seem able to settle down. She went over to the curtains, shaping as though to open these once more. But her dread of bats returned, so, lest there should be another nested within the heavy pelmet, she barely disturbed those folds with a forefinger, but peeped at the day as if by stealth.

"We are going to have such a wonderful morning," she announced.

"Come and take breakfast, Edge," Miss Baker said.

"I told you it would be, just the one day in the week we must go to Town. Oh, how really aggravating," Edge went on. "Baker, I wonder if you would mind? But it does seem rather stuffy here, now they've lit our fire. Could I trouble you to help with this window?"

While Baker came to lend a hand without a word, Miss Edge put long fingers up to her hair, as if to ward off another flittering animal about to be let loose. However the two ladies soon had the window open, and Baker went back to her place at table. But Miss Edge could not at once leave the scene spread out afresh. Because, with the coming of light, the mist was rolling back, even below her third Terrace, all the way to her ring of beechwoods planted in line with the crescent of her House; although, off to the left, where beech trees and azaleas came down over water, her Lake still held its still fog folded in a shroud.

"I love this great Place," she announced.

"You have your breakfast or you'll regret it, Edge."

But Miss Edge would not budge. She was moved. Then she thought she heard something.

"What was that?" she asked.   Baker plucked a fishbone from her mouth.

"I thought someone called," Miss Edge explained.

"Shall I ring for our eggs now?" Baker wanted to be told.

"Just as you please," Edge murmured. They did not command sufficient labour to mow the lawns, which, in the dew, over long grass, all down the three descending Terraces, had strings of brilliants garlanded now between the blades and which flashed prism colours at her from the sun, against a background of mist. "I love it," she repeated.

Fresh morning air flowed gently, coolly down from the window. She was about to move away, out of danger, when she was halted.

"There," she exclaimed.   "Did you not hear this time?"

"I did'nt," Baker said.

"I wonder," Edge murmured, hesitating. But Miss Baker cut her short. She insisted that her colleague must take breakfast, in view of the long day they both had before them. And at last Edge sat down, remarking that she would wait for her dish of egg.

"As I lay in bed last night," she went on, "I was going over the whole Rock imbroglio in my mind. You know, Baker, we are altogether crippled here without a proper furnaceman, while at the same time you and I are agreed that we shall never find a man before we can offer a cottage. And that means none other than this curious creature Rock."

There was a knock. A nervous Marion came in with scrambled eggs. Now that Edge was away on her pet topic she did not think to ask after Mary a second time, although she did break off so as not to speak of Institute affairs before one of the students. The moment the door was closed again, however, Miss Edge continued, still on the perennial subject,

"In the summer, when he no longer had his furnaces, the man could cut some of the grass. We might even get a few of the girls to try their hands at making up hay in their free hours to help the farms. In any case he could assist generally about the place, and, if we chose well, I do not doubt we could get some real assistance out of his wife, for the man must be well married. And that house of Rock's was built by the life tenant," which was their way of referring to the private owner of this estate, from whom the State had lifted everything. "Was actually built to that very purpose. It is a worker's cottage, Baker."

"After you brought this up the other day I had a look at our original Directive," Baker said, deliberately putting some egg on a plate which she laid in front of Miss Edge. "There," she said, "Now eat that up. And it lays down in black and white how, while Mr Rock's still living, he's to enjoy the house which the life tenant put him into. The State recognises a right in view of the past services."

"Ah yes," Edge answered, toying with a fork. "But yesterday I fetched through that Directive for myself, and there is precisely nothing in it about the granddaughter."

"Elizabeth Rock? She's in the Service," Baker objected. "She's on sick leave after a breakdown through overwork. You can't mean that a man's own granddaughter must'nt come home when she's ill."

Edge sipped at her tea. "It's Sebastian Birt," she said, in what was now a dangerous mood, over the edge of a cup, "the precious economics tutor. What doubtless goes on between those two can be a menace, dear, to our girls."

"Yes," Baker said, "that's as may be. But we're back to where we started ten years ago when we first came, Edge. The moment we're not allowed to choose our own staff, as under the present system we never can, we're in a dilemma over men like Mr Birt."

"But are you content?   After all, there are ways and means?"

"Edge," Baker replied, "you are simply not to allow this to serve as a pretext to eat absolutely nothing when we have a long day before us.   Do take your food now.   The car will be round in half an hour.   The last time we discussed the matter, and you went into methods to get rid of Sebastian, you had to agree with me that it would be difficult, while I considered it might be downright dangerous.   Now you bring the whole thing back to the granddaughter.   If you want to know what I think, then I'll tell you.   First, if we do get rid of him they'll send us someone who may be worse and, second, I have a feeling we could burn our fingers over master Birt."

"But it does so aggravate one, Baker; there is the cottage sitting up begging at me and I have set my heart on it."

"Well, Mr Rock won't live for ever, will he?" Baker asked, while she took a great bite off her toast heaped with marmalade and butter.

"I want action," Edge demanded.

"I don't know how you're going to get it, then," Miss Baker said.   "And there's this about Sebastian.   There's never come even a hint of trouble, the five years he's been here, between him and one of our girls."

"I am eating my heart out for that cottage, Baker."

"And all the while your stomach's crying aloud for sustenance.   Look.   I shall see Pensilby of the Secretariat of New Buildings at my Commission today, and I'll ask him if his Department would support a licence for an entirely new cottage."

"But new building does not come under that Ministry," Edge elegantly wailed.

Miss Baker then explained the acute approach to the official which had suggested itself.

"I see," Edge exclaimed.   "My dear, you are splendid,"

she said, which was praise indeed. But she was not the sort to let anyone rest for any length of time on such a note. She had been looking at the other curtains, and now she rose from her place to walk daintily across. She paused an instant, then, courage in both hands, she swept these back as dramatically as the scene disclosed shone on her now smiling eyes. Because, except for what still hung over the water, the mist was evaporating fast, the first beech trees away to the right were quite freed, her Park itself was brilliantly clear, the sun up, a lovely day had opened and, as she watched, a cloud of starlings rose from the nearest of her Woods, they ascended in a spiral up into blue sky; a thousand dots revolving on a wave, the shape of a vast black seashell pointed to the morning; and she was about to exclaim in delight when, throughout the dormitories upstairs, with a sound of bees in this distant Sanctum, buzzers called her girls to rise so that two hundred and eighty nine turned over to that sound, stretched and yawned, opened blue eyes on their white sheets to this new day which would stretch on, clinging to its light, until at length, when night should fall at last, would be time for the violins and the dance.

But Edge had caught sight of two specks. She looked again. Two men had come out from under her Trees. One was carrying a yoke with buckets, so she knew him. She cried out, in shocked vexation, "Rock flaunts himself."

"What?" Baker demanded, jolted by the tone used into looking sharply from her plate.

"Why cannot the man take the back way?" Edge asked in a calmer voice. "Must he trail across our beautiful front, even with his swill?"

"He's rather a favourite outside this room, you know," Miss Baker said, to moderate her colleague.

"Tomorrow I shall speak about it."

"Well, I shouldn't give a hint in the kitchen, Edge."

"Stumbling over our grass," Edge protested, when there was a knock. "Come in," she invited, triumphant suddenly. The girl Marion entered. She stood just inside the door. "Ma'am," she said, and swallowed.

"Yes, Marion?"

"Ma'am," she said, once more swallowing.

"Well?"

"It's Mary and Merode," and the child brought out everything, which was little enough, in a rush. "They're not there, and the beds not slept in."

Half an hour later, punctual to the minute, Baker left with Edge in the car for Town. They had a number of reasons why they should carry on as though nothing had occurred. What they had decided was, that the police must be casually informed, yet be instructed, at the same time, not to make a search.

Meanwhile Miss Marchbanks could question other girls in the dormitory.

There was no point in losing one's head.

The Dance must go on of course.

—Mary was such a steady girl, in fact they would not even consider it (although Merode had no parents), Edge had said speaking for Miss Baker, and that it was all a mistake, as they would find when, after their hard day, they themselves returned. In any case, the two girls must be together, which made for safety.

Baker had not been so sure.

But, as Edge pointed out, if they were to draw attention by staying down here to miss their Wednesday Commissions, they would look, when everything was cleared up by luncheon, as it would surely be, like nothing so much as old fools, or worse, yes, like a couple of old fools.

So they went. And two thirds of the students knew nothing whatever, at first, about the disappearance of these children.

Mr Rock left his yoke. When he came in alone by the outside kitchen door, he could just see Maggie Blain seated, in charge, at her kitchen table and beyond her, barely a part of one of the cookers. This was by reason of a great shaft of early sunlight which, as it entered one of the windows, shone so loud already that it bisected the kitchen, to show him air on the rise in its dust, like soda-water through transparent milk. It hid the line of girls beyond, fetching their own breakfasts at the other cooker. They were no more to him than light blue shadows, and their low voices, to his deafness, just a female murmuring, a susurration of feathers.

"The swill man," he called in a high cracked voice, bringing out the joke he had plied for ten years; anxious about his breakfast, because that depended upon Mrs Blain's present health and temper.

He felt it would be all right because she said, "Marion, a cup of tea for Mr Rock."

The girl and the old man came together over this, in the megaphone of light. When he was seated she whispered at him,

"You did'nt catch sight of Mary and Merode?"

He could not hear. "You'll have to speak up, my dear," he said, "if you want me to understand."

"As you came along?" she said louder, at a loss.

"There'll be time and to spare for secrets when the music's playin'," Maggie Blain told her. "Will you come along tonight?" she enquired of Mr Rock. He decided that she sounded hospitable.

"I'm past it," he said.

"Might do you good," she said grimly. He did not like that tone so well.

"And you?" he asked, then felt faint for lack of food, so that he had to close his eyes behind the winking spectacles.

"Me?" she said. "I'll be so rushed all day with work I shan't seek to be on my toes when the hour strikes." He took this to be a bad sign. And he had only had the cup of tea.

"Oh, you'll come to our dance surely, won't you Mr Rock?" a girl's voice called from the shadows. But he was not even going to consider now that the Principals had not invited him. It was breakfast he was after.

"You should'nt trouble about me," he said, with the one purpose in view. "This lady here's the one will have to bear the brunt," he said.

But it drew no response out of Mrs Blain. So he kept silent for a time. The whispering began once more. If he could have heard, past the glow from that hot tea which flooded his senses, he would have caught these sentiments,

"You did'nt?"

"I did."

"Oh, but you should'nt have."

"Why, whatever else was I to do?"

"But they'll turn up, directly."

"Mary and Merode?"

"I know, but all the same."

"There you are, you feel like me, like me, you see."

And all the while a line of girls fetched their breakfasts, served themselves, the sleep from which they had just come a rosy moss upon the lips, the heavy tide of dreams on each in a flow of her eighteen summers, and which would ebb now only with their first cup they were fetching, as his tea made his old blood run again, in this morning's second miracle for Mr Rock.

"It'll be a smashin' day," the cook said, heavily ironic.

—And why should'nt I come along, Mr Rock asked himself in an aside, because I could keep out of sight, and there will be a buffet.

"Not that I'll see much even if it does keep fine," the cook said.

—While I sit still, Mr Rock argued inside him, I shan't have to worry that I shall come upon Elizabeth and him round every corner, behind every palm; no, of course, there will be no palms. But he was famished.

"A holiday?" he asked out loud because, in that case, there might, at the moment, be less chance of food.

Several sang out together in answer.

"Why, this is Founder's Day," they announced. He had forgotten.

"Yes, I expect we spoiled the peace and quiet for you when they stuck us down in this damp den, ten years ago to a week," the cook pronounced.

"Pooled the diet?" he asked, not hearing.

One or two giggles came from the girls as they moved with their trays. But he was well-liked, and respected.

"I should'nt wonder you thought they'd let you live your life out in peace and quiet," Maggie went on, in a louder voice.

"How's that?" he said, catching it. "Plenty of go about me yet," he bragged.

"Come on, hurry now," Maggie called to the queue. She could not see this because it was beyond the sunlight. "Or I shall never get started," she explained.

"Yes, Mrs Blain," they dutifully answered.

"Heavy on you, too, with your girl sick," the cook added, condescending.

The old man wondered if she thought Elizabeth was a slavey, but what he jovially said was, "Well, I have'nt three hundred of 'em, have I?"

"Oh I don't let those be a bother, my goodness me," the cook replied. "No, all I meant was that a man your age does'nt want to be saddled to fetch and carry for others," she explained.

"I never permit a woman to be a worry," Mr Rock said, with decision.

"I don't suppose," Mrs Blain replied, sparing a glance inside her at the picture she imagined of the late Mrs Rock. "And then your granddaughter will wed and the place'll seem empty," she said, without malice.

"She's not there more often than not," he objected, in the sense that she was always off somewhere to meet Sebastian.

"But then she's not been so well," Maggie Blain agreed to defend Miss Rock, having misunderstood him.

"They overdo things at their age," Mr Rock explained, as though Liz were still a child, with all the time in the world before her for work, love, and marriage.

"Ah, there you are," the cook said.

"I would'nt have your family, nevertheless," the old man put in. He usually plied the one jest until he won his meal.

"They're good girls," Mrs Blain answered. She was in great ignorance. "Have you got the staff breakfasts up?" she called after the orderlies. At this half promise of food he felt his stomach gush digestive juices.

"We've taken them, Mrs Blain, and there's one over," Marion insinuated. "Mr Birt's had a night off." Mr Rock waited for the spare to be offered. He waited. Then, to his vague, wondering surprise, beyond the cone of light in which he sat and warmed his cold hollow bones, he gradually felt a tide of female curiosity flow up over him, so strong it was like the smell of a fox that has just slunk by, back of some bushes. He could not understand. If he had only known, this bit of news had been put forward, and some of the girls hung on the answer, to discover whether it was official and above board, the absence of Sebastian Birt under the particular circumstances.

"That's right," Mrs Blain said. "His name's struck off my list," and there was a sort of sigh came from outside the sunlight. The whispering began again. But it had given Mr Rock an uneasiness. Because he was certain Sebastian had been round to the cottage after dark. And now the snake was not even in next morning.

—Drat Mrs Blain, why could'nt she hurry his breakfast.

—How right, earlier on, not to carry the tea up to Liz, Mr Rock told himself, the fellow could only have been there all night, and somehow or other these girls knew, which must be one reason they did not propose to give him a bite of anything. He could go hungry now.

"But there's some don't trouble," Mrs Blain said, with so much suggested in her voice that Mr Rock, instantly apprehensive, decided in his own best interests that he would do better to ignore what was on the way, until he knew how grave it was.

"But there's some don't give themselves the trouble," she repeated, directly at him. He realised he would have to respond. He turned to her like a blind man.

"Going off up to London as usual this day of all days," she explained herself.

"Oh, Mrs Blain, it's the date the Commissions sit," said one of the embryo State Servants.

"I tell you I'm right sorry this minute for Miss March-banks" the cook continued. "All that goes awry will be laid to her door, and no argument," she ended, in a sort of hush about.

Most of the children were hanging on her words. She was aware, but in ignorance. She sought to improve on this. "God help her, poor woman, if she has'nt the decorations just so in quick time," she said.

The whispers began again.

"Is that the last of breakfast?" she called out, and the old man's heart beat wet in his mouth.

"I should be getting on," he said, to force matters.

"Don't disturb yourself, Mr Rock," the cook told him. "You're one who's never in the light, is he, girls? You'd better get your own now," she gave them leave. And with a sort of chorus of welcome and pleasure because they were hungry too, nine came with their spoons and plates of porridge, and their lovely, sleepy, but rather pimply skins, to sit alongside the famished, sweet old sage. None dared remind Mrs Blain of him. She was a terror for her rights.

"But you are coming tonight, Mrs Blain?" one asked.

"Me?" the cook demanded. "After I've finished the knick knacks for the buffet, which'll take me all day on my stoves?"

"You know you've got the best lot of orderlies on the whole rota to help you," they said.

"I'd never have agreed without," Mrs Blain retorted. "I told Miss Marchbanks. Give me Mary and the girls on her rota, I said, or you'll have a dead woman on your hands."

This statement had a greater effect than she could have expected. There was a sort of gasp round the kitchen, and at least three children, while Mr Rock blindly watched, pushed their porridge plates away. One or two even put what they felt into words.

"I don't think I'll come either, tonight I mean," the youngest said.

"How's that Maisy?" the cook asked. "Are you shy even of a bit of fun at your time of life?"

The girl would not admit it was Mary and Merode she had on her mind, that she feared the worst. But she blushed.

"To cook when the weather's hot turns my stomach," she explained, because Mr Rock's unseeing spectacles were

on her. The old man still did not know if he was altogether forsaken, whether, upon this, the dawn of their great
day, he was just to get the bare cup of tea.

"Now don't give me that, not at your age," the cook
coarsely insinuated.

"Oh Mrs Blain," they all cried out, while Maisy went
red.

"Because that's when you can say so," Mrs Blain elaborated with gusto. "Getting your man his Sunday dinner,
oh dear, openin' the oven door when you're in that
condition, and the hot smell of the roast comes."

"I can smell it now," Mr Rock suggested in great
ignorance, and smacked his lips.

They all laughed.

"There's expectant fathers' kitchens now," Marion announced, while the old man tried to reconcile himself to
the idea that he must go hungry. But the girls tittered, for
this that Marion had just put forward was one of Miss
Inglefield's more modern jokes in class.

"And I know how my fellow would have said, when
he was still alive, if I'd told him that, while my little Enid
was on the way," Mrs Blain announced, delighted. "Yet
what are you girls thinkin'?" she demanded. "Where's
Mr Rock's bit of breakfast, may I ask?"

"Oh Mr Rock," several cried out, got up, and at long
last hurried this over. "It was just . . ." Maisy began to
excuse herself, with intent to explain how upset she was
about Mary and Merode, but the cook would not allow her.

"It was simply you forgot," Mrs Blain interrupted.

Mr Rock, who deeply felt his position, begging, as it
seemed he had to, for this one meal per diem, next tried
not to have it.

"No thank you," he said. "This day I don't fancy . . ."
and began to get out of his chair.

"Sit you down, don't be awkward," the cook cried. "I

can't have my place treated cavalier fashion," she said. "You either eat a good breakfast or you may'nt move out of here in daylight. Then what would your Daisy say without her swill? There's a bit of bran as well, for Ted. You won't have that either if you can't do justice."

"And yourself, Mrs Blain?" he asked, then subsided in his place, mouth watering, glad.

"Me? I mentioned to my girls before you came. I'd rather not refer to that once more," she said with finality. Her stomach was upset. He nodded, old and solemn over the plate, with no idea of what she meant.

He ate.

He was greedy.

They watched in approving silence.

"I can't imagine what you'll think, Mr Rock, to forget you like we did," a girl lied, to cover her tracks.

"I don't," he replied, rather abrupt, but his feelings, at the moment, were directed to his stomach. Some of them feared he had been offended.

So they began to make up to him. They uttered little comforting remarks. He sat silent. With an old man's gluttony he had eaten too fast and he was, one might say, listening to the food settle in a cavernous, wrinkled belly.

"We all feel the same when we're on orderly duties, Mr Rock. We'd really miss you if you did'nt drop in of a morning."

"I think Daisy's sweet," Margot said.

"Will you ask me for a dance, Mr Rock?"

"They only played waltzes, too, when you were young, Mr Rock, did'nt they?"

"I think they might let us have something else besides," one of them put forward. "Like a tango," she said. "They still have those in the smaller halls."

"Enough's enough," the sage announced. Several of

the girls began to giggle. They were not to know this, but he was referring to his digestion.

"I think it a shame," Mrs Blain brought out, in a warning voice. But the younger ones could not stop, behind hands they had over their mouths.

"I don't know what's so comical, I'm sure," Mrs Blain said in reproof, and then the old man realised from their flushed faces that they were laughing at him.

"I should'nt pay attention," Mr Rock commented.

"Oh we don't," they answered, still giggling.

"To me," he said. They stopped. "I'm only on sufferance here, you know," he said, with a satisfied bitterness.

"Oh Mr Rock," they cried.

"I think it a shame," Mrs Blain announced, brightly. "Now then," she called out. "Let's get goin'." And in a moment the old and famous man was left alone at table, altogether blinded by increasing brightness, before an empty plate and a cup that was warm, behind a rumbling stomach, left to dread the journey back with full buckets.

When Sebastian Birt came into the staff breakfast parlour he found he was first. He did not look out on the bright daylight but under the dish cover on a hot plate. He took no scrambled egg.

He poured himself a cup of tea. He was sitting down to this when Miss Winstanley entered. He did not rise. He said to her, in what he imagined to be the manner of a State executive, for he was always in a part,

"Well, well," he said, rubbed hands together.

"Morning, Sebastian," she said. "It'll be a lovely day."

"So it is, so it is."

"But I thought you'd got off for the night," she went on, and helped herself at the side table, paying attention to how he acted.

"Could'nt fit it in, unexpectedly detained, these trade delegations from the North," he answered, to keep up the pretence. But he did not look away from his cup. As he was fat, and very short, he seemed a small boy. It was not at this that Miss Winstanley tenderly laughed.

"And is the guv'nor to let you come to the dance tonight?"

"There are, or rather were, two governors," he replied, this time, all at once, in the part of the sort of lecturer he was not. "The Governor of the Bank of England, abolished as such long since, then the governor of the local poor law institution, or poor house, known to each one of you, if not from personal experience, then at least by report, and a factor in our civilization that we have yet to eradicate." He raised his voice in mockery while he watched his cup. "To pull out by the roots," he ended.

"Edge?" Miss Winstanley prompted.

"The functions are so similar," he replied. "They may readily be confused. The best mind can fail to distinguish between Edge and the common or garden workmaster. Where similar functions are operated in dissimilar environments which may yet have factors common to both . . ." and here he paused, at a loss perhaps. This gave her time to put over,

"I know all that, but are you coming?"

"I should really see my secretary, let me just glance at my book," he replied, in the character of an executive once more. "I cannot be rushed willy nilly into appointments." A silence fell.

Then she thought of something.

"Look here," she said, "you put yourself down as not to want breakfast."

"Tchk, tchk," he answered, still the State manager. "What has my girl been about?" For the first time he looked slyly at Miss Winstanley. But she reached for the butter, and did not notice. When he went on, as he did at once, it was with lowered eyes once more. "They will allow themselves to be pressed. Not in a trouser press, ha, ha, I should hope not indeed. But they will lose their pretty heads over the telephone. When calls really begin coming in, they won't simply lay the receivers down off the hooks to have time to think, they will persist with answers till they get more and more flurried. Then the harm's done, the mistake is made, and I'm landed for an engagement I can't possibly . . ."

"But there is'nt a breakfast for you, Sebastian," she interrupted.

"I shall decline to take one of theirs, even if pressed," he answered, perhaps in reference to his colleagues who, this holiday morn, must be enjoying a long lie abed. "I know better than to get the wrong side of Mrs Blain," he explained, rather more soberly. Then he went on, back in the part once more,

"I always say, as a matter of fact I insist in the office, that we are all members of a team, helping others to help themselves."

"It's all very well, but there'll be a cup and saucer short, Sebastian."

"Well I can wash mine, can't I?" he demanded, falsetto now. "And my lipstick's lovely. It never comes off."

"You'd better," she said. "I don't use any, as you could tell if you looked."

At this moment, when Sebastian might not have known how to reply, for he was a shy fellow, Dakers, the law tutor, came in.

"Morning all," the man said. "Hullo Sebastian. I thought we were not to have the honour this forenoon.

D'you know I almost fancy it may eventually turn out to be rather a fine day."

"It's like this, Dakers," Winstanley said. "The lad here was detained. Calls on his time have been heavy of late," she explained, with malice. Mr Birt pettishly frowned into his cup at this open allusion to the hours he spent with Elizabeth.

"The guv'nor consulted me last night," Dakers said. He had not missed the implications in Winstanley's last remark. He had a particular sort of loyalty towards the young woman. He wished to warn them both.

"Edge? Consulted you? What on earth about?" Winstanley asked.

"Oh, she wanted me to run through the original Directive from the Ministry, which relates to the cottage held by our fabulous pensioner, Rock," Mr Dakers explained. Seated up to the table, he was now engaged in rather nervously rearranging the knives and forks on each side of a porridge plate.

"And which shelters his granddaughter Elizabeth," Mr Birt added, still with his highest falsetto, but which had an edge to it, a squeal of unease.

"The unremunerated opinion of a lawyer is not worth a rap," Dakers assured them, raising the spoon at last. "But I had to tell her, and, since noone else is here, I'll pass it on." Then he broke off to put some porridge in his mouth. "I don't think we have a leg to stand on. It's his for life," he said.

"How Machiavellian," Birt exclaimed shrilly. "You mean he can defy each and every one, the guv'nor included? Well, everything's perfect then, isn't it?"

"What I mean, and why I chose this moment, is that she'll cast about her to find some other way out, my dear fellow."

A grey line of milk escaped from a corner of his mouth.

He dabbed at it, as though he had cut himself shaving.

They prudently joined together to change the topic, did not refer to it again.

When Mr Rock got back to his cottage from the house he was tired and out of breath, because the swill buckets had been particularly heavy this fine morning. He noticed the postman had called and bent down with a groan to pick some envelopes off the mat. He always paid his small bills in cash with the result that his correspondence, which came to about half a dozen letters every day, was made up of complimentary resolutions passed by various scientific societies, letters from students, or maniacs, and so on; at least that is what Mr Rock believed, because, for some years now, this distinguished man had not opened a single one of the communications he received. Instead he always put them unexamined into a travelling trunk which was on the floor just inside the living room, and which he used for nothing else. He sat down on it today, looked at each envelope back and front because he expected to hear the result of the election. But there was no trace of an O.M.S. (On Majesty's Service; they had left out the His, long since, as being unworthy of the times). On the other hand there was a private letter which might be from young Hargreaves. But then, Mr Rock asked himself, what point could there be in finding out, it would not advantage him in what he termed his battle for the place, the roof here; and would'nt it rather weaken his resolve if he knew which way the election went? After all, his attitude was sound. More than that, it was straightforward, which could not be said of the cruel posturing taken up by those two Babylonian harlots, Baker and Edge up there, who schemed day and night, never actually to come out in the open because they knew very well they would never venture, but who, with a tireless industry, neglected their trivial duties to machinate against him, to play with his girl's reason even, and who fell so low as to work on her sentiments with truly Byzantine malice by the use of a tutor they had no wish to retain, or other pretext to expel, the lout.

—No, it would be folly on his part to break the rule of years, to open his correspondence just to satisfy a moment's panic. What he had done for the country was his monument, noone could steal that, even if they voted him to-morrow into the hunt kennels for broken down scientists. Because he was'nt going on a chain. Because he'd take the money instead, or refuse it. Besides he injured noone in the blameless life he led here. And an individual still had some rights under the State. And if he opened this letter now, learned whether or no he had been elected, he could tell the turn their conversation would take when he met Miss Edge at the dance tonight. By the way, was he going?

—Well, Mr Rock, she'd say, and am I to congratulate you, or some such phrase, the smarming harpy, after which, if he knew he had been elected, he would have to smirk thank you, yes, they've put me in, I'm delivered over to their charity now all right. Or, on the other hand, if they had not elected him, was he to eat humble pie, tell her that young men whose work he despised had not thought him worth the candle, after all he'd done. —Never, he told himself, never, he'd take the money, and then found he was actually opening the letter he had assumed to be from young Hargreaves, and which was'nt from the man after all.

"*Dear Sir,*" it read. "*Although I have not the honour of your acquaintance, yet due to the pride of place which science*

*occupies in the State, whereby she can work for the good of all,
I write to enquire . . ."* and the old man, who was breathing
easier for his rest, thrust the thing back into its envelope,
got off the trunk, opened this, and put the day's post onto
a mass of other unopened letters. Muttering, he stumped
off to his outhouse to boil the swill. He found he had no
paper with which to light a fire, came back, raised the lid,
took a fistfull of letters at random, and used these. He
employed the daily newspaper, which he never read, only
in the outside lavatory.

The fire was lit when he half heard a remark behind.
He turned round, saw his granddaughter, Liz. She was a
distracted looking woman and wore his winter overcoat
over red cotton pyjamas, with rubber boots.

"Morning Gapa," she said, as always to him, in an
exaggeratedly loud voice, "I think, you know, it's going
to be a lovely day."

"There you are, dear," he replied, and his sour old face
cracked into a grave smile. "Did you sleep all right?"

"Took me rather a long time to sink off and then it was
so tiresome, you know how things are, I awoke, I don't
know what time it was, oh about four in the morning,
and could'nt drop off again."

"Had'nt you better go back to bed then, dear," he said.
"I would if I were you. And I'll bring you up a bite,
directly I've done Daisy's swill."

"Oh but I had to come down at once, soon as ever I
heard the postman, I mean I'm so excited for you, Gapa
dear, today of all days this must mean such a great
deal . . ." and, as so often, her mind fell away in a wail
while she looked at him out of big empty eyes.

"Now what are you getting at?" he enquired, like she
were a child. His tone was goodhumoured, although he
knew very well what she had tried to express.

"Well, it's the dawn of the day after, is'nt it?" she said.

"When they had their meeting? I thought, that's to say I expected, well, I do think Mr Hargreaves might have written, just to tell, I mean. I'm so keen about this for you, there, of course."

"Why, so it is, I had'nt given a thought," he lied, and turned his back to stir what was in the pot.

"You mean to say you've put your letters away like you always do, this morning out of all, because it's important, you see, they might have had to write specially and you ought to answer. Oh Gapa," she ended. "Don't you understand?"

"Liz dear," he said, "there's little enough to upset anyone. They know me better than to write. And whatever the thing is won't make any difference. I've told you. Surely you remember?"

"You stand there and say that after all I poured out to you last night, what you want to tell me is that not a word, I mean absolutely water off a pig's back, no difference at all, that you did'nt even listen yesterday? Oh, you can be stubborn."

"Now Liz," he said. Tears came into his eyes, but she could not see because he stood averted.

"Look," the woman said, and meant it so much that she actually managed a connected sentence. "Would you allow me to get this morning's post out of your box?"

"You'd not find much, dear," he said. "I used them to light the fire."

"That's that, then," she said, not displeased. She liked decisions postponed.

"I should run along, dear, and have your rest out," he said, disappointed.

Liz did not move. "About tonight," she said. If he had watched, he would have seen an expression of satisfied guile pass across her face. "What are you, I mean, had you thought, will you go?"

"In the circumstances, yes, I think we'd better."

"What circumstances?" she asked sharply, for it would be too absurd if he imagined he must chaperon her with Sebastian.

"Why nothing," he said. "Only they might be curious, just now, if we did not put in an appearance. Though I'm too old for that sort of idiot jollification," he said.

"Oh, Gapa I am glad, that's splendid, because I was so keen, you see I'm so proud, proud to . . . you know, and I was afraid . . ."

"We're only on sufferance here, you understand," he pointed out, glad to ignore her genuine enthusiasm. He was aware of her desire to show him off, and, if he had remembered this in time, it might easily have prevented him coming to the dance.

"Dear Gapa," she said. "If you could only understand, I do so wish you'd realise, why there's noone, there could'nt be, and here of all places, why they'd never dare, what, after all you've done, oh it's too absurd?"

He did not reply.

"Did you see Sebastian already?" she asked.

"No. He had the night off," he replied, as though to keep up a polite fiction.

"He did'nt," Liz said. It was noticeable when she spoke of this young man, and even more so when in his presence, that she was fairly collected in her talk. "He slept over there, after all. He thought it would look strange to be away, you see, well not there, the day of the dance."

Mr Rock's jealousy and disbelief choked him before he could answer.

"He said he'd come over early," she explained.

"You get back into the house, then," he told Liz, all the more certain she had only come out to leave the way free for Master Birt to get off. "I'll see if I can't fetch you breakfast presently."

"But how about, I mean you've been up all this time, have you had some, oh, now Gapa, you can really try one so, what about you?"

"I'm all right. It's never hurt me to do without," he said, his self pity allowing him to forget what Mrs Blain had provided. "But you've been ill," he generously added, and felt tired.

"Hullo," she then exclaimed, in such a well known accent of pure gaiety that Mr Rock knew, before he could turn round. It was Sebastian Birt, in a neat brown suit.

"Hullo Sebastian," he said.

"And the light of their camp fires went out to meet the dawn," this young man announced, pretending to quote Herodotus, in a reference to the fire under the copper in which Daisy's swill was being cooked.

"You're up then," Mr Rock said, looked shortsightedly to see whether Sebastian was shaved and, when he found that the young man had done so, having to admit to himself, with a gloating reluctance, that the prating idler could not have spent the night in her bed unless, as was just possible, he had been slippy enough to bring his razor or depilatory with him. The worthless fellow would have had to do it on cold water though, which was very unusual in such a quarter, Mr Rock thought.

Meanwhile Elizabeth Rock, who had realised how unattractive she must look in her state of undress, was off back to the cottage. "Wait for me, now," she called, "I won't be a moment, really." And Sebastian, who did not answer, just stood there in a daze at the chance which bound him to these two strange people by the love he had for the granddaughter, the love, he thought, of his life.

"Well?" Mr Rock enquired, not for lack of more he might have said. Sebastian brought himself out of himself with a jerk.

"They've mislaid one of their girls," he mentioned as casual as could be, speaking in his own voice, as he almost always did to the old man.

"Who have?"

"Miss Edge and Mistress Baker," Sebastian replied, about to break into eighteenth century speech, but he checked himself. "In fact they're looking everywhere for a couple, a brace," he added.

"Bless my soul," Mr Rock commented, his eye on the swill. The news did not at once disturb him.

"And they've left Ma Marchbanks to hold the baby."

"How's that?"

"They've gone up to Town as per usual. Our misguided rulers have put both on separate Commissions which sit Wednesdays. Of course, they can't miss those."

"Good," Mr Rock said.

Sebastian barked a laugh. "What in general is good about it, sir?" he asked. "There's hell to pay up at the house."

"I always feel easier when those two State parrots are safe off the premises," Mr Rock said. "I don't know what they put in the food now, but these last few weeks I can't seem able to boil your swill."

"Preservative," Sebastian promptly replied. "For what we are about to receive may it be ever fresh," he misquoted in his falsetto, then immediately controlled himself. "Tell me, does she do well on it, sir?" he enquired with deference, as though Mr Rock might suppose the question to be sarcastic.

"So long as I'm allowed to keep the animal," Mr Rock nervously answered, "and I think I've a reasonable prospect. But if I were a younger man there's one thing I'd do." And he looked with savagery at Birt. He was in earnest. "I'd have a shot at this filth of a swine fever," he said. "Next to the system we live under each one of us nowadays, it's the curse of our time," he ended, stirring the swill once more.

There was a silence.

"You haven't seen Merode and Mary, then?" the younger man asked. He was anxious again.

"Me? No. Why should I?"

"They're the pair of students we can't find."

"So you said," Mr Rock admitted, horrified.

There was another silence.

"It's going to be a magnificent day," Sebastian suggested.

"When you get to my age you'll appreciate it."

"You mean the weather?" Sebastian asked, respectfully.

"Did you say 'end of her tether,' " Mr Rock demanded in a wild voice, thinking of Mary and turned to face the younger man who explained, "I spoke indistinctly again. No, I mentioned the weather."

"Oh I see," Mr Rock commented. "It's my ears," he said.

At this moment the swill began to boil with mustard bursting bubbles and, as a result, a stench rose from the copper harsh enough to turn the proudest stomach. Birt would have gone off at once but did not like to leave at a moment of awkwardness and incomprehension. Because, also, of his love for Elizabeth, he did not wish to antagonise the old man, so put up with the smell. Besides, he had promised to wait.

"At last," Mr Rock said, and came to Sebastian's rescue by moving away on his own. "Have you had breakfast?"

"Oh yes, thanks all the same, I had mine up at the Institute," Birt lied, so as not to saddle the sage with the need to prepare an extra portion. For his part Mr Rock showed no sign of what he felt as, with simplicity, he waited by the kitchen entrance for Sebastian to pass first. Even in this room Sebastian imagined he could taste the stink of swill. But just then Elizabeth entered, and the young man forgot in anxiously watching to find how she might be. Much could, as a rule, be told from the clothes she wore, from her manner when she set out.

"What's it to be?" Mr Rock asked, as he took a saucepan off a nail.

"Why Gapa," she said, eyes smiling upon Sebastian. "How sweet you are to us, but you must'nt bother, not on a day like this. I could'nt now," she said.

"Sebastian, you talk to her," Mr Rock suggested. The young man looked gravely at him.

"Don't think there's anything I can do, sir," he said with a sort of adolescent's smiling courtesy, out of place in a beak.

"Now Elizabeth . . ." Mr Rock began at once, but she interrupted.

"No," she said. "It's no use, I won't listen, either of you. Come on Seb, the weather's too good to waste inside." She took his hand, led him out. "Don't you ever smell anything besides your pretty students?" she asked in a low voice. "I believe you don't, and that's what makes you lucky," she said, as they turned into the ride by which Mr Rock had gained the big house earlier. It was noticeable how, when with her love, she no longer hesitated with her spoken feelings. "Darling, you're the luckiest man," she said, and sniffed fresh air.

"You're looking so much better," he told Elizabeth as they dawdled up the ride, holding hands. She was not tall like Winstanley, yet came head and shoulders above him.

"Oh Seb, I don't know that you'll ever forgive me; all my stupid hesitations," she said.

The sun, which was not high yet, came aslant between trees with a smoky light, much as it had through Mrs Blain's great window, and struck their blue shadows sideways.

"Most of it's my fault, I do know that." He spoke sincerely.

"Why no," she murmured back. "You're perfect."

"If we had'nt met," he said, "you'd never've had your breakdown, would you?"

"I might. You can't tell. Now I've had one, I know," she said. "Actually, I believe you saved me, my reason I mean."

"Oh Liz, it was hardly as bad, come now."

"That's how it felt," she answered. "And I've been such a fool all this time not realising my own mind."

He did not dare ask whether he was to understand she had at last decided what she wanted of him. His experience with her had taught Birt that she took refuge in a vast quagmire of vagueness when at all pressed. So, heart beating, because it was genuinely important how she would put it, he waited.

"Sometimes I wonder if you'll ever forgive," she began again. "Oh I can't imagine why you picked me out," she said. "I get frightened sometimes you won't ever see me the way I really am. But one thing I'm sure now. I worried so at the start. D'you think I'd better tell? Well, I will. It was about Gapa. He's very famous. You see, I thought it might all be because of him."

He again felt he must at all costs make her right. "What d'you mean?" he asked patiently.

"When you first showed an interest," she said. "Last Christmas. The time you began coming across the park to see us. Oh, for quite a long while I was sure you only did it to be by Gapa."

"Did you?" he said, indulgently.

She bridled, rather, at his tone. "Well, if you do want to understand I'm not so entirely certain even now, sometimes," she said.

"You're jealous," he said, trying to make it into a joke.

"Of my own grandfather?" she asked, and laughed.

"No, but I might be if he had a great granddaughter. That would be different, right enough."

"Liz, don't be absurd."

"Oh but I'm so much older'n you."

"Liz darling, we've been into this before."

"A whole eight years, Seb. It's not fair. When you're forty I'll have a Gapa head. Think of that."

"I have," he said, and sighed.

"There you are you see, you sigh, which is just what I mean," she pointed out. "And, if you're like you are now, what will it be when our time really comes. Is'nt it extraordinary? One starts out light as a feather, then everything gets difficult." Her voice was despairing.

"If you care to know, I can't abide him."

"Who?" she asked, for, in her distress, she had lost track of the conversation.

"Your grandfather."

"Don't be so ridiculous," she said in a most friendly way. "You know you dote on Gapa."

"What makes you say?"

"Why, it's in everything you do when you're together. Even if you're both just chatting, hard at it, your own voice drops you respect him so much and, poor dear, he's got to such a state of deafness he does'nt catch what's said."

"Do I?" he asked, guardedly.

"Noone has any idea of how they are," she explained. "And he adores you."

"Are you sure?" the young man enquired, not at all convinced.

"There you go, you see. The moment I tell, I can judge from your voice you're delighted. Oh darling, am I being very difficult, again?"

"Of course not, Liz, but I would like to get this untangled."

"Sometimes I can't imagine how you put up with me," she said, putting his arm in hers to press it to her side. "And who am I to be jealous of my own dear, dear Gapa if he is, even in part, the reason why you come over so often? Because I've a lot more to be grateful to him about then, have'nt I? Oh when I'm well again I shall make things up to him, you've no notion how much, and should everything go right, when I come through this, I'll make it up to you too, my darling, even if it takes me the rest of my life, and all my breath."

He kissed her as they walked on. "Don't take this so hard, Liz," he said.

"You're such a brute," she said tenderly.

"What's this?" he asked.

"To make me love you like I do," she said.

"That's my whole point," he took her up. "We can't help ourselves, can we? Things happen. When two people fall in love it's not their fault, surely? They can't help it."

"It must be the fault of one of them."

"How can you say that, dear?"

"When the girl is so much older, then she's to blame."

"You know I'm a fatalist," he said with an effort. "I don't know any serious economist who is'nt. It's an occupational risk with economists." He used a sort of bantering tone with which to speak of his profession. The trick he had with a conversation whereby he would bring it to what he considered to be the level of the person he addressed, was more highly developed when with Elizabeth than it was when he spoke to Mr Rock; in other company, it was the impulse which led him to do his imitations.   She was aware of this.   She did not approve.

"You say that just for me," she told him.

"I don't.   Why should I?"

"But you can't pretend about us, and that we know each other, was just luck," she complained.   "With all we might mean," she added.   "You cheapen it."

"Well to go on as we do is cheap," he said, apologetically.

"Oh you'll never forgive once all this is over, I know you won't," she cried out, then stopped so as to face him. He turned away in distress.   "Well?" she said.   "You see, you can't even look.   My darling, I'm so beastly."   But she stood on there, and did not kiss him.   Misery paralysed her.

"I'm so worried for you," he said at last, bringing out the truth.

"Because you're an economist, or why?   Because you think if it was'nt me then it might just as well be another girl?"

"Now Liz," he said.   "There was nothing further from my mind."

"What in particular are you worried about, then?"

"About your grandfather and you," he said, weakly.

"Why, what d'you mean," she demanded.   "He's everything, I worship the very ground he treads.   He works his poor old fingers to the bone for me.   Without him I don't think I could go on."   She, in her turn, swung round to show her back to Sebastian.

"Look," he said, "please be sensible," and his voice grated.   "I can't imagine what you suppose I'm trying to make out.   It's Miss Edge and Miss Baker's the trouble."

"Oh?" she asked, faced the man once more, with an expression of great vagueness.

"You're both of you a brace of innocents where those two women are concerned."

"My dear," she said. "You don't know Gapa very well if you think it. He's a match for two old spinsters!"

"He's not of this world, Liz," Sebastian objected.

"He's forgotten more of her twists and turns than you'll ever learn," she said. "There."

"I know, but so rash."

"Careful Seb, you can go too far, you know."

"I'm worried about this election. You understand what he is. He'll refuse what they offer, he'll simply disdain the whole thing."

"After what he's done for everyone in this country, I'd say he had a right to do as he liked," she announced, for her own purposes ignoring the fact that she had pressed her grandfather to a certain course only the night before.

"And I insist you can't, my dear girl. Noone can, these days."

"Don't be so absurd."

"But it's the State, Liz," he said. "What the old man will do is to wait till he's elected, then he'll refuse whatever they offer. And offend the powers that be very seriously. You know how he never even opens his correspondence."

"Oh but he does over important things," she lied, to re-assure herself. "Besides they would never dare, with men like Mr Hargreaves in the inner circles to protect the three of us."

"It's his age, Liz. Any man as old stretches back to the bad times. He's suspect just because of the years he's lived. They won't like it."

"Then they'll have to swallow their silliness," she said. "Why, he's famous, he's one of the ornaments of the State."

"Look," he explained. "In the class of work your grandfather did they're just lyric poets. After twenty five they're burned right out. He made his proof of his great theory when he was twenty one. And he's seventy six now."

"All the more wonderful then, is'nt he?"

"Yes, but don't you realise his idea is poison to the younger men, who think they've exploded it?"

"That's only jealousy."

"I still maintain it would be very dangerous for him to go on as if everything was just plain sailing."

"Oh, if you're going to lose your nerve now, my dear, what on earth, I mean can you imagine, of all the beastly things to happen . . . oh what will become of you and me?"

"There," he said, genuinely disturbed, "I've upset you and that was the last I intended, the very last," he added. But she was not done yet.

"And what's all this to do with Miss Baker and Miss Edge?" she demanded, recollecting the way he had opened the conversation. She caught him out. He could not even remember how he had brought these ladies in. So he kissed her.

Miss Marchbanks, with Mr Rock's Persian on her lap, sat waiting in the sanctum for one of the senior students, Moira. Extremely shortsighted, she had taken off her spectacles and put these on Miss Edge's desk as though, in the crisis, at a time when she had been left in charge, she wished to look inwards, to draw on hid reserves, and thus to meet the drain on her resolution which this absence of the two girls had opened like an ulcer high under the ribs, where it fluttered, a blood stained dove with tearing claws.

So that when Moira entered, and did not shut the door but stood leant against it, half in, half out of the room, dressed in a pink overall (this colour being her badge of responsibility over others), her bare legs a gold haze to Miss Marchbanks' weak eyes, her figure, as the older woman thought, a rounded mass softly merged into the exaggeration of a grown woman's, her neck and face the colour of ripening apricots from sun with strong eyes that were an alive blue, shapeless to Miss Marchbanks' dull poached eggs of vision, but a child so alive, at some trick of summer light outside, that the older woman marvelled again how it could ever be that the State should send these girls, who were really women, to be treated like children; she marvelled as Moira stood respectfully flaunting maturity, even her short, curly hair strong about the face with the youth of her body, that the State (which had just raised the age of consent by two whole years) should lay down how this woman was to be treated as unfunctional, like a child that could scarcely blow its own nose.

"About the decorations, Moira," she began, dismissing certain uncertainties with a sigh, only to find she was unsure even of what she was about to say. "A thought came to me," she said, then forced herself on, "a thought for the alcove. Fir trees, Moira," she improvised. "And you know all that salt they delivered by mistake, well we could lay that for snow on the branches. It's what they used to do in films. So cool for dancing. Because it will be hot today, I think."

"That would be lovely," the girl agreed with a low, lazy voice, the opposite to her looks.

"Then you do think so, Moira?"

"Oh, I wish you had the arrangements for everything, Miss Marchbanks. Only Miss Edge said it must be rhododendrons and azaleas. She wants huge swags, she said. What are swags, Miss Marchbanks?"

"Great masses, child." Marchbanks for some reason began to feel reassured. "Loot, you see," she went on.

"Well, that's that then. So you'd better take forty seniors to make a start."

"We have. And we won't cut the flowers, ever, not where they can see."

"It was just a thought," the older woman said. "Fir trees and waltzes. The snow for all of your white frocks as you go round. Rather a pity, don't you think? But come in or out child, do. Don't stand there neither one thing nor the other."

The girl laughed comfortably.

"You sent for me," she said. "We're so busy. We've been started ages. But please come and look, oh please. We want your advice particularly." At this she shut the door, came up to the desk. —They're incalculable, Marchbanks told herself. And up to yesterday I was so confident I knew their ways. Then her heart missed a beat as she wondered whether the child could be hinting.

"It's the fireplace," Moira said. "Very big." She stood close and absolutely still, to give the older woman, whose body age had withered, a full, wonderful, firm round smile.

"Well, we don't want to root up a whole rhododendron bush, and put that in," the woman gently said.

Then the girl leaned right over, stroked that white cat. She smelled warm to the older lady.

"Why it's Alice, Mr Rock's," she said.

"Every morning," Marchbanks agreed. "Every single day. You could'nt do without, could you?" she said to the puss, which Moira could now at last hear purr, which she could tell was in a cat's swoon.

"Is'nt it awful," the girl casually said.

"What d'you mean, dear?"

"Why, about Mary and Merode."

Marchbanks swallowed a gulp of the morning.

"Now don't be so silly," she said, in a bright voice. "But I do wish you'd each of you come to see me before you decide on some of your little foolishnesses." She looked in a dazzled way at the large, brilliant, smooth face bent over the cat. She began to drum the fingers of her left hand on Edge's table.

"What might'nt Alice be able to tell?" the child remarked.

"Now Moira, you know as well as I, they've simply gone off somewhere and the car's broken down most probably," Marchbanks said. "Besides we rely on you senior girls, you realise, before the bird is flown, so to speak, you know."

The younger woman did not reply. She went on stroking puss, which had opened huge blue eyes.

"Of course Miss Edge will be very cross with them when they get back properly ashamed of themselves," Marchbanks continued. "But I'll have a word with Miss Baker first. Why child, you don't know anything, do you?" she asked, with an uneasiness as shrill as Sebastian's in her voice.

"Oh Miss Marchbanks, we always tell you all," the girl replied.

"Then what did you mean about Mr Rock's cat?" the older woman said, and put on her spectacles.

"She might have seen them when she was coming over," Moira explained. Now that she could watch the girl in detail Miss Marchbanks no longer approved, and was even half irritated with the creature's blankness. —You could admire children when you were not in a position properly to focus them, she thought, because, soon as you had your glasses on, they were merely fat, or null, unless of course they were babies.

"You've a smut on your nose, child," she said.

"Oh have I? Thank you," the girl said, rubbing with a hand. "Well I must get along at once or we'll never get finished," she excused herself. "I know they'll be disappointed over the fir trees," she said, and backed away with a look of complicity about her nose. "It would have been too lovely. But some people, I mean . . . well . . . you know," she finished on an adorable smile of pure respect, then was gone.

There was a knock at the door. Upon being bidden to do so, Winstanley entered.

"Why come in, my dear, sit down," Miss Marchbanks said, and took the spectacles off again.

"I would'nt have bothered you, ma'am, today of all days, but I wanted to know if there was any sort of help at all I could give."

"My dear," Marchbanks said. "And less of this ma'am to me. I hold the position only for twelve hours, if I last those," she said. "No, I've just had Moira along, to find whether I could arrive at anything."

"Why Moira particularly?"

"It was just a thought. Such a pretty child."

"I suppose I must'nt ask, but . . .?"

"Not a word," this lady answered. "We're as we were except that I'm very kindly left in charge, and noone's to know lest it gets out. But I'm to use my discretion continuously, thank you."

"I would'nt put up with it," Winstanley said.

—How can the lovesick make such sweeping statements, Marchbanks wondered.

"Especially with the Inspector of Police," she went on without a sign of what she thought. "He's to come over because I'm not to tell him on the telephone. 'We must be discreet'," she quoted with irony. "I must'nt say to his face."

"But I know both girls well," Winstanley protested. "I can't imagine . . ."

"My dear," Marchbanks said, "what do either of us know?"

"Yes, quite. But . . ."

"My dear," Marchbanks interrupted a second time, "you're well out of this."

"You don't mean . . ."

"What I suggested was they should have fir trees in the alcove for the ball," Miss Marchbanks said, and put the spectacles on again. Her tired eyes were sharpened by lenses to a very light brown. Winstanley scanned anxiously for a hint of the inner meaning, but without result. "Adams is round here now," the older woman continued, "and it would'nt have taken him a whole morning to saw half a dozen over in the new plantation. But, so it seems, we are to continue with our traditional decorations," she ended, with a gesture of dismissal. "My dear, thanks all the same," she said.

"Oh I know what I meant to ask," Winstanley said, as she gave in, and went to the door. "Some of us, the staff naturally, thought we might have a swim in the lake this afternoon since it's a holiday. You'd have no objection? We'd keep to the end away from the weeds, of course."

—You think Sebastian will like you in your bathing dress? was what Marchbanks did not ask.

"I should'nt, not just today," she said with a look of resignation that silenced the agitated query with which Winstanley was about to take her up. The older woman sighed once the door was closed, and she was alone again. Who could say what might be in that water?

"Adams," she began, when in his turn the man entered. He interrupted her at once. While attending outside for the day's orders, Mr Rock's hints had preyed on his mind. He was beside himself.

"It would'nt be about my cottage, now would it, ma'am?" he demanded. "There's no question, is there? For I've a nephew over to me directly, with the girl he married in church. Can't find a place of their own anyhow. It's cruel this housing shortage, miss, I mean ma'am."

"Why of course not, Adams. Whoever gave you that impression?"

"You know the ways things are with a place this size. Nothing but rumours and buzzes about your ears the whole day, ma'am. Till a man can't tell what to believe, and that's the truth."

"But I only wanted to ask your advice, Adams."

"How would that be?" he enquired, putting on his dullest expression.

"You've heard of our two silly students? You must have."

"Me? I would'nt know the first thing, miss."

"Well, there's two of them gone, Adams, absolutely without trace. Of course, only temporarily. But can you imagine such deceit?"

There was a pause. Adams might, or might not, have been amazed. Then he said, in a voice of doom, "I pity those two lasses."

"Oh, you know, I don't think there's any necessity to be tragic," Miss Marchbanks said. "I'm sure not, indeed. I only wanted to ask if you had noticed anything."

"Me, miss? What should I see of them?"

"Why possibly they may have fallen into the habit of meeting strangers from outside in the grounds, perhaps?"

"There's been none like that, miss, or I'd have reported it, and double quick to be sure."

"I know you should. That's why I was so determined to ask. Then you have'nt come across them?"

"I can't tell one of your learners from t'other, miss," Adams said. "I've no call."

"Exactly," Marchbanks agreed, to humour him. "But you have'nt noticed anything unusual?"

"If I was in your place," the man replied, "I'd speak over the telephone with the station."

"Yes, I've done so, Adams."

"They can't have passed that way, then.   And the coach halt?"

"Of course," she patiently said.   "You don't imagine we've been seated idly by," she said, going over in her mind again the guarded, embarrassed enquiries she had made.

"Well, it's got me beat," he said.

"You see, I just wondered if you might have marked down some little detail, all over the woods in your day's work, and trained to be observant."

"I don't know about trained to be observant, miss?"

"Why yes, naturally, in the course of your duties. Foresters always are," she said, to flatter him.

"It's not me you should enquire of," he said, at last. "Some of the creatures will for ever hang around Mr Rock's place, any day of the week you care to name."

"I know," she said to encourage the man.   "He has those animals," and remembered the cat on her lap, the goose, and the pig, all white.

"Well, to my way of thought, Mr Rock's your money, miss, if you'll excuse me now, because if you've nothing special today I should get on with our logs for the firewood."

"There's just one matter, Adams," she said, and ordered fir branches to be brought up, in case room could be found.   Then she dismissed him.   At the door, however, he turned back.   "It's the overstrain, there you are," he announced.   "They overtax their strength," he said, and went.

A great beech had fallen a night or two earlier, in full

leaf, lay now with its green leaves turned to pale gold, as though by the sea. It had brought more vast limbs down along with it, so, in the bright morning, at the thickest of the wood, colourless sky was suddenly opened to Elizabeth and Sebastian above a cliff of green. The wreckage beneath standing beeches was lit at this place by a glare of sunlight concerted on flat, dying leaves which hung on to life by what was broken off, the small branches joining those larger that met the arms, which in their turn grew from the fallen column of the beech, all now an expiring gold of faded green. A world through which the young man and his girl had been meandering, in dreaming shade through which sticks of sunlight slanted to spill upon the ground, had at this point been struck to a blaze, and where their way had been dim, on a sea bed past grave trunks, was now this dying, brilliant mass which lay exposed, a hidden world of spiders working on its gold, the webs these made a field of wheels and spokes of wet silver. The sudden sunlight on Elizabeth and Sebastian as, arms about one another's waists, they halted to wonder and surmise, was a load, a great cloak to clothe them, like a depth of warm water that turned the man's brown city outfit to a drowned man's clothes, the sun was so heavy, so encompassing betimes.

"It will be hot," she said, as though stroking him.

"I love you," he said. She pretended to ignore it.

"I wonder what brought her down," she said. She might, from the tone, have had in mind a middle aged woman he'd seduced.

"Oh Liz, I do love you, and love you," he replied.

"Adams won't like this," she said, and turned with a smile which was for him alone to let him take her, and helped his heart find hers by fastening her mouth on his as though she were an octopus that had lost its arms to the propellers of a tug, and had only its mouth now with which, in a world of the hunted, to hang onto wrecked spars.

"Darling," she said in a satisfied voice, coming up to breathe.

"Help," another girl's voice then distinctly uttered, close to these lovers.   Sebastian felt Elizabeth go stiff.   Neither of them spoke.

"Help," it came again.

Sebastian stepped sharp away from his love.

"A snooper," he said with a little hiss.   "A Paul Pry."

"Who is it, oh dear . . .?"   Elizabeth called out.   She had at once put on her vagueness for protection in the circumstances.

"Help," the voice called once more, louder.

By this time both had gathered its direction, which was lefthanded to the deepest of the stricken beech.   Sebastian began to force his way through and, as Elizabeth cried out, "Now do mind, take care, it's your best suit," he had parted a screen of leaves that hung before him bent to the tide, like seaweed in the ocean, and his pale face, washed, shaved, hair cut and brushed, in this sun a bandit, he looked down on a girl stretched out, whom he did not know to be Merode, whose red hair was streaked across a white face and matted by salt tears, who was in pyjamas and had one leg torn to the knee.   A knee which, brilliantly polished over bone beneath, shone in this sort of pool she had made for herself in the fallen world of birds, burned there like a piece of tusk burnished by shifting sands, or else a wheel revolving at such speed that it had no edges and was white, thus communicating life to ivory, a heart to the still, and the sensation of a crash to this girl who lay quiet, reposed.

"What are you about?   Come off at once," Sebastian said, unaware that he had been shocked into a close parody of Edge upon his recognising Institute pyjamas.   As there were three hundred students he could not be blamed if he did not know the girl, although he was at fault in forgetting,

as he did until too late, because of the kisses, that there were
two young ladies absent or adrift.

"I must ask you to come away off," he repeated, like
Miss Edge.

"I can't, I'm hurt," she said.   After which she added, as
though terrified, "Oh Mr Birt."

"My dear girl, we can't have this," he said, clambering
down.   And then became confused.   Because her soft
body, stretched out, was covered only in thin geranium red
cotton, it lay with all grace and carelessness, the breasts
lightly covered and the long limbs, and he saw, so that it
interrupted his breathing, that she had mud on the white
of leg below the knee, with enamelled toes in sandals caked
with mud.   Sun, through the bright leaves, lit all this in
violent dots, spotting the cotton with drips as of wet paint,
and making small candle lamps of flesh.   Then he was re-
prieved, now that he was so at her side, for she reached
behind and brought out some nondescript overcoat which
she pushed over her middle.   A schoolmaster mind knew
she must have put this away at the back before she called.
Thus he was saved because she had made him suspicious.

"Can't you walk?" he asked, unkindly.

"Yes," she said.

"What is it, dear?" Miss Rock demanded.

"You're not to worry, I can manage," he shouted back.

"But what will, in heaven's name, what is it?" Elizabeth
insisted.

"Look," he said, to the girl he still did not know for
Merode, and in his natural voice once more.   "Hang on
to me."   He was frowning.

"I can manage, Mr Birt," she said, awkwardly struggled
up to turn a drooping back and shrugged herself into
the coat.

"But there must be some explanation," he said, in another
severe imitation of Miss Edge.

In reply she just walked out of the place she had made for herself, and this when he had laboriously climbed down to her. She was gone. He found a rent in his own trouser leg and scowled. Then went out after.

He came upon Elizabeth who was being her most warm hearted with the girl.

"Have my comb, sit here, let me button this up," she was saying, Sebastian imagined, so there might, for not a moment longer, be displayed in full sunlight that expanse of skin how like vanilla ice cream where one of her jacket buttons had come undone. So Elizabeth drew the coat about the girl who, from raised arms, snuffling, and with an absent, ceremonious look, combed out the heavy hair a colour of rust over a tide-washed stovepipe on a shore.

"Why, you poor dear, there, that's better," Elizabeth was saying to Merode, "well . . . I can't think . . . but we need'nt bother now, shall we? Seb, she must go back with us, it's too far all the way up to the house. We're only a few yards, really, from our little place," she said to the girl. "Then we'll get a cup of hot tea, I mean to put inside you, d'you think you can manage?"

There was no reply.

"You take her on that arm," Elizabeth ordered Sebastian. "Now lean on me, dear, d'you see, that's right, only a step," and in this fashion they started off to Mr Rock's, neither Birt nor Merode speaking so much as one word.

Meantime, some five or six of those who had been sent to collect azalea and rhododendron had wandered through the woods, had stopped here and there, braving wasps and bees and even a hornet to cut out great bundles of bloom and were overladen now, for, even with arms outstretched, the red and white flowers came half up over their faces; the gold azalea nodding next their gold heads, in all this flowering they carried like a prize. Although they were so burdened, they had decided to move on to see Daisy, and had arrived to stand by emerald nettles at the edge of her sty.

She lay, very white, on a froth of straw and dung which fumed to the warm of day. She was on her side and twelve most delicate fat dugs in pink struck out from a trembling belly in a saw toothed frieze. She had violet, malevolent small eyes under pink cornucopia ears. Her corkscrew tail twitched as though its few inches could reach, in a hog's imagination, far enough to plague the brilliant, busy flies on her white, dirt dusted flanks. She was at rest.

"Is'nt she sweet?" "Do look," "Oh fancy," they cried out one to another through a frond of flowers held to bursting chests, "There, doze Daisy," "Is'nt she a beaut."

Mr Rock came out of the cottage with two buckets of boiled swill. His eyes burned behind spectacles at this bevy of girls. And, when she heard his step, Daisy got up with a start and a heave to squeal with anticipation while her audience, crying out in the alarm they affected, backed from the now simmering pen.

But he did not feed his pig at once, because he had not gone three yards before he heard Elizabeth call 'Gapa,' and then there she was, tearing towards him, hair straight out behind, running with her legs extended sideways from the knees. The group round Daisy ceased to exclaim the better to watch the woman old enough to be its mother. And, in watching, they saw emerge down a ride behind Elizabeth the figures of Birt and the girl they knew at once for Merode. This set them off in whispers, as a cloud passes the moon, like birds at long awaited dusk in trees down by the beach.

While Elizabeth explained to her grandfather in a low voice, obviously with difficulty in making it plain, Merode and Sebastian drew near, and the child began to limp. When she was quite close to the others, who had drawn together, one of them cried out, gurgling,

"Why what on earth's happened to you, Merode?"

Whereupon Birt knew for the first time who she was, and doubted his wisdom in bringing her to the Rocks. He also knew he must keep Merode away from friends until she had made out her account; because there would be reports to be written to Edge, and beyond, and that lady was certain to say the girl had been given an opportunity to concoct the tale.

"Dear me what a crowd," he suggested to Merode, in Edge's accents. "Don't you think we'd better take you back?"

"My leg hurts so, Mr Birt," she complained.

"You never said," he expostulated shrilly, becoming even more like the Principal. "Where does it pain most? Tell me."

By this time the crowd of students was upon them.

"Why, Merode," they cried, "Merode, just look at you," and "What on earth have you done to get in such a state, Merode?" and they giggled.

Upon which the redhaired girl burst into loud, ugly sobs. She put up hands to cover her face.

Elizabeth hastened back to the group followed by Mr Rock, who had set his buckets on the ground. Daisy set forefeet on top of the timber of the pen, and, at the sight of that dinner laid by, redoubled the squealing, to do which there had to be opened a great pink mouth to make display of golden fangs.

"Now my dear, you must'nt," Elizabeth told the girl, and put thin arms about her. "Really not, you'll be fine. We're looking after you now," she said, with a wild look around.

"Oh is'nt it awful?" the child moaned.

"We'd best rush her up to the Institute," Sebastian suggested, in his common or garden voice.

"Whoever heard of such a thing, how could you, and in

her state," Elizabeth replied, leading this girl in the opposite direction, towards their mauve and yellow cottage.

"Now all you others hurry back then," Sebastian ordered, Edge once again. "How d'you think the decorations will get done if you stand here?" he demanded. They went off. One or two still giggled.

"They did'nt say a word, not a word passed between her and that lot, you're my witness," he continued in all seriousness, but in a low voice for Mr Rock, unconsciously imitating now the manner of his colleague Dakers.

"Witless?" the old man asked, and laughed. "They don't go by their wits at that age."

Sebastian was so agitated he could not find it in him to answer.

"You should know, whose work it is to teach the creatures," Mr Rock finished, went back to his buckets. At this moment Sebastian noticed the pig's outcries for the first time. It might just have seen the knife the butcher was about to use. He was disgusted. To get away, he hurried after Elizabeth and the girl, into the cottage.

They took Merode back to the Institute as soon as they thought she was a little recovered, and handed her over to Matron, who sent for Marchbanks.

"Miss Edge and Miss Baker's in London," Miss Birks told the child. "You rest yourself while I fetch a cup of tea," she said. "And dear," she added, "I'd pull myself together if I was you. In their position they have to make reports. There'll be a lot of answers they'll be requiring, to know how you came to find yourself with that Mr Birt, not to speak of the old prof's granddaughter." Merode opened her wet, red mouth, as though to explain. Then she thought better, and did not say a word.

"Why just look at you," Miss Marchbanks cried out the moment she entered.

The child was a sight indeed, lying in the surgery, on the couch covered in deep blue rubber with great highlights from tall windows, while she looked sideways over this older woman.

At the ends of her arms lying along her, she scratched with dirty thumbnails about the caked skin round the red nails of her third fingers.

"It's shock," Matron said, in a satisfied voice.

There was a silence. The girl did not cry, did not speak, just lay there, cautiously watching.

"Well I can't talk while you're in that state," Marchbanks announced, making up her mind. "Have you had anything to eat, at least?" But there was no answer. "It's shock," Miss Birks claimed again. "You'd better have a hot bath first," Marchbanks ordered, "and Matron will get you breakfast. Then we can have a little chat, Merode," she said, giving a sign for Miss Birks to follow so they could speak in the passage.

"I don't want anyone to see the child," Miss Marchbanks instructed, when they could not be overheard. "Not a soul, mind. Poor thing," she said. "It will go hard with her, I'm afraid, out and about the Park at night in those pyjamas."

"But you'd want me to call in Dr Bodle, naturally?" Matron enquired.

Miss Marchbanks pondered this. "You see," she replied, "it's not fair to ask a word in her condition. She must get herself straight, and then she can make an account. Because we don't want anyone to put ideas into her head. You know what girls are once they come together. Besides, there are the Rules. So my instinct is, not even

Dr Bodle, though, of course, a doctor's different. Nevertheless, not unless she has a temperature. Yet I leave it quite to your discretion."

"Very well ma'am," Matron said, and obviously found this unfair.

"Don't let her speak until she sees me. I leave that particularly to your judgement," Marchbanks ended as she made off, having regularised everything, as she thought, for the best.

Matron unlocked a door leading to the bath corridor and then shut the girl into a cubicle. "There," she said from outside. "Mind you have it hot."

"Yes, Miss Birks," Merode replied, quickly turning on water so there could be no conversation. For, in her perplexity, she had resolved she would say not a word to anyone, whatever happened.

Matron looked into the remaining cubicles to be sure there was no other child could get in touch with Merode, then left, locking the outer door into the passage. She said aloud, "Poor mite". After which she made her way to Mrs Blain, to see about something hot for the little wretch.

In next to no time the bath was run, with Merode stretched out under electric light and water, like the roots of a gross water lily which had flowered to her floating head and hands. This green transparency was so just right, so matched the temperature of the hidden blood, that she half closed her eyes in a satisfied contemplation of a chalk white body. She felt it seemed to sway as to light winds, as though she were bathing by floodlight in the night steaming lake, beech shadowed, mystically warmed.

Then came a loud whisper from somewhere, out of the
air. So that she covered herself with her hands, exactly in
the pose classic to plaster casts.

"Merode," it said, "Merode."

She was too modest to answer.

"I'm talking through the ventilator, you fool. It's
Moira."

When she realised she could not be seen, the girl uncovered herself with a shy smile, looked up at that black
grating in the wall.

"I'm only on the floor above" the voice said, "that's all.
Can you hear me?"

"Yes," she said, covering herself again.

"Then what on earth's happened?"

Merode did not say one word.

"It's made an awful stink."

"What has?"

"Why you and Mary cutting off like that. You did'nt
go down to the lake, did you?"

"No, why?"

"Because when Winstanley went to ask Ma if the staff
could bathe there, she said better not."

Merode began to be frightened once more. She kept
silent.

"Well you did'nt, did you?" Moira repeated.

"Can't you hear me?" the same voice went on, when
there was no answer.

"Are you all right?" Moira asked at last.

In reply there came a muffled sound of crying. In the
bath beneath Merode pressed the wet back of her hand to
a snuffling nose, under the light blue rubber cap almost
enclosing her hair which, in this light, was dark honey
coloured.

"Why don't be so ridiculous," Moira said. "You are'nt
to let those old women get you down, surely?"

Merode pulled herself together enough to say, "No."

"Then what did happen?"

"Nothing," the child insisted, in a trembling voice.

From above there came through the ventilator a low "Damn", followed by the echo of heavy footsteps, and a brief noise of scrambling as Moira made off fast. Then Merode was alone in warm silence. She rested. She almost fell asleep.

Later, when she was shown into the sanctum, Marchbanks still had the cat on her knee.

"Sit here where I can see you," Ma said, pointing to an armchair set opposite the two great desks in full sunlight that beat through the windows and was hot. The girl at once became dazzled when she sat down.

"Here," Marchbanks continued, getting to her feet with the cat in her hands, "I've put up with the lazy creature long enough, you take this." She made as if to lay Alice in Merode's lap. She carried the pet curled up as it had been lying, and she placed it just so, but with wide open azure eyes, over Merode's legs. But the girl did no more than move her blind hands to give the animal room, upon which, finding no welcome, Alice got up to stretch, jumped off, and left, tail in the air.

"You never stroked poor puss," Marchbanks remarked, sad to see her plan miscarry.

She got no answer.

"Whose is it then, Merode?" she asked.

"Why, Mr Rock's of course, Miss Marchbanks," the girl was shocked into replying. She had seen the creature so often out with him.

"Because Miss Edge and Miss Baker are away you must call me ma'am," Marchbanks said. "Now I'm in charge for the moment. Which is why I sent for you, dear."

The girl stayed silent, repeating inside her that she must never tell any of them anything.

"Did you see Alice?" Ma Marchbanks next enquired.

Once more Merode was surprised into an answer.

"Why how d'you mean, Miss Marchbanks?"

"Call me ma'am, Merode. Well now, she makes her way over the Park each morning to visit us, does'nt she? I think you may have come across her."

"Not me, ma'am."

"Dear, dear, how blind you children sometimes are. But there's no need to be obstinate, is there?"

"Obstinate?" Merode echoed. "I have'nt been."

"Then what are you now, child?"

"I really did'nt notice puss, ma'am."

"Well, what were you doing not to, dear?"

"But I might'nt have been there, might I?" Merode defended herself, while at the same time a voice, inside, told her she was talking too much, too fast.

"You never explained to me you were'nt in the grounds all night, Merode."

"But, ma'am, it was only I could've been in another part while Alice came by."

"Where were you, then?"

There was no answer. So Marchbanks tried again.

"Whose cat is that, Merode?"

"Why I said, ma'am. Mr Rock's."

"Then how did you happen to be found by Elizabeth Rock?"

"Alice was'nt there, I'm sure," the girl answered.

"You're distinctly aggravating, child, and today's sure to be so busy. I'm terribly rushed. How is it you don't pay the slightest attention to what I'm trying to put?"

Merode said nothing.

"It's not fair on one," Marchbanks continued, then brought it out suddenly, in her ordinary voice, "Where's Mary?"

To hear the name came as a frightful shock, and the student at once burst into more tears behind spread fingers which she splayed out over a bent face. At this reaction Miss Marchbanks felt her heart miss a beat, which gave her the old, sickening sensation she hated.

"Good heavens," she said in a loud voice, to reassure herself, "don't work up into a passion. There's nothing wrong, is there?"

She got no answer.

"When did you last see Mary?"

The girl went on crying, without reply. Miss Marchbanks would have left at that moment, to give her time to recover, but the child got a handkerchief out, which made the older woman think a lull was on the way.

"Then something is rather wrong?" she asked.

Merode did not respond. She seemed calmer.

"Merode, is it particular? Are you ashamed?"

"Oh no, Miss Marchbanks," the girl said, which somehow came as a comfort to both.

"Well then, matters must be all right," the woman said brightly. "So there's nothing you feel you can't tell me?"

Merode was mopping her nose by now. But she kept silent.

"You see, my dear," the older woman went on, to bridge the silence, "you are putting me into such an awkward predicament. You're no longer a child," she said, disbelieving this. "You know as well as anyone that I must go by rules just the way you have to. And the regulations I'm under are simply this. That when one of the girls we're in charge of doesn't tell the truth after she's broken her word, we must'nt even question her, and we're bound to report it.

And I have to make out a report which must go right away, straight up to the State Board in Government Centre, nothing can stop that. To do so would be an offence," she ended virtuously, and took a good look at the child. Merode was staring, with a completely blank expression, at the dado painted to resemble Roman pavements in perspective.

"Then I don't have to tell you the view they'll take up there of a serious thing like this, Merode."

"But Miss Marchbanks, what have I done?" the girl burst out.

"Now are you being frank with me, dear? You're not a baby. Indeed, after all, you're practically a grown woman, that's just the whole trouble. Because you must see you can't be allowed to career about outside, at dead of night, and in our pyjamas."

The girl said not a word, kept her face averted. Miss Marchbanks decided what she did'nt like was her not meeting one in the eye.

"Besides," she tried once more, "there's the two of you. Mary is'nt back yet, you know."

The child, she thought, seemed to turn to stone whenever Mary's name was mentioned. But now that they had the one uncovered, the other could hardly be far away. Yet there was Edge's parting shot. 'Safety in numbers, Marchbanks,' she had said. And 'if it was only the one I would telephone Headquarters at once with her description.'

"Think it over, Merode." The older woman had again suddenly decided there could be nothing terrible, that everything would be all right. Almost as though the child sensed this she at once rose to leave the room.

"No, sit down, dear, I have'nt quite finished," Marchbanks said. "What were you up to? Tell me."

"I don't know, ma'am."

"Now really, Merode, I shall get quite cross in a moment."

"It was nothing, ma'am, really."

"You'll let me be best judge, if you please," Marchbanks said.   There was no response.

"Come now.   Did you go out with a boy?"

"Oh no, Miss Marchbanks."   This, at least, sounded genuine to the older woman.

"Did you try to meet someone else, then?"   No answer.

"In other words it's simply, Merode, that you won't tell. Is'nt it?"

But the girl had come to be mesmerised by the black and white receding pavements.   No longer blinded in sunlight, her eyes had caught on one of the black squares, as that pyjama leg had earlier been hooked on a briar.   And while her horror at this interview increased, so the dado began to swell and then recede, only to grow at once even larger, the square in particular to get bigger and bigger till she felt she had it in her mouth, a stifling furry rectangle.   Then, when she managed to shake herself free, she cleared it out, but only for a minute.   After which this process began all over again.

"Do think," Marchbanks was saying.   "My dear, your whole future is at stake.   If you set out with such a mark against you, things being as they are these days, when you leave here you'll just have a job on the machines," she said, speaking the brutal truth.   "Because you should realise I can't help myself," she ended by falsely admitting.   "I'll do all I can, of course.   But, as you must get into your head before it's too late, there's Miss Edge and Miss Baker.   Oh well, if you really want to know, I'm most afraid of Miss Edge."

Merode could hardly take this in, trapped, as she now was, by one of the more frightening periods of the dado, that immediately before the black square would begin to swell, when the whole stretch was beginning to billow, as if the painted pavement was carried out on canvas which had started to heave under a rhythmically controlled impulse actuated from behind.

"Was it a boy?" Miss Marchbanks demanded, her confidence about to evaporate. Then she thought of the child's mother and father. For she had known this come off when all else failed.

"I must wire your parents," she said, as she got up to go over to the file, and hated herself for playing the ace. —But after all, she thought, I've my own position, my pension to consider.

"Why, you're an orphan," she cried out, delighted because she knew this would make a great difference with Baker, who had long been an acknowledged authority in State circles on the parentless. "And made your own way with scholarships, I see here. My dear child, you don't want to throw all that away on a simple escapade."

Merode had got her eyes off the dado and was better for the moment. She did not want her aunt brought into this. "But what is it you wish me to tell you, Miss Marchbanks?" she mumbled.

The lady sighed. "You're surely not expecting me to put the words into your mouth," she said.

"You've always been so wonderful to us, Miss Marchbanks."

"You're rather a flatterer you know, Merode."

"A lot of us call you mother, ma'am." She began to cry again.

"Ma, you mean, which is quite different. Now, come on now, we have'nt got all morning. And you want to go to the dance tonight, don't you? It's going to look so lovely, really it is, especially if I can work in a pet idea of mine about fir trees. Adams is to fetch some. Was it a boy?"

Marchbanks saw the girl had ceased crying.

At this sudden return to the main object, the child's attention had been forced back to that dado, although at first the squares stayed as they were. —What's the use? Merode asked herself. Let them tell it.

"I suppose," she said at last. Miss Marchbanks went back and sat down behind Edge's desk. She allowed herself a small, satisfied smile.

"Was it Mr Birt, by any chance?"

"I don't imagine," the girl answered, obviously in a daze.

"Or Mr Rock?"

No answer.

"Was it?"

The furry square on her tongue started to swell once more.

"I'd like to help you but you won't let me," the woman said. Merode began to cry again. This cut her off from the growing dado, but the rectangle was black with stiff hairs on her tongue.

"Listen dear," Ma Marchbanks said, as a trace of the child's panic passed over her. "You were only sleep walking, were'nt you? That's all, is'nt that it? So simple, you understand. It must be? Can you hear?"

There seemed to be some lessening in Merode's sobs.

"But where is Mary, then?" Marchbanks insisted in a great voice, upon which Merode slumped forward in a faint. As she rang the bell on the desk for Miss Birks, and started up out of her chair, Ma Marchbanks thought, —oh dear, to faint right away while I was questioning, how will that look, oh dear, but the poor child.

Mr Rock went out with the bran to summon Ted, his

goose. It was unusual for the bird not to be at hand, waiting. "Ted," he called, "Ted," in exactly the swill man's voice he had used to announce his presence in the kitchen, only louder. He turned this way and that, but there was no sign. Then he saw a sergeant of police push his bicycle onto the path from the road. The blue uniform gave Mr Rock a jolt. —Already, he asked himself, —so soon?

The old man's cottage stood, like the hub of a wheel, on a spot at which several rides met. As he watched the policeman he saw, out of the corner of an eye, his goose come in a rush, absurd sight, its neck outstretched, wings violently beating to help cover the ground it had never left. Sun now made the bird a blaze of white.

"Morning, Mr Rock," the sergeant said. "Might turn out warm," he said.

"Yes," the older man replied and then, as Ted came up hissing, the policeman walked round his bike to put this between the goose and himself.

Mr Rock threw balls of bran as if to sow dragon's teeth.

"She'll do you fine at Christmas," the sergeant said.

The sage, who had no intention of ever killing Ted, merely grunted.

"Did I hear you call her Ted?" the policeman asked. —So much a detective he should be in plain clothes, Mr Rock sneered to himself. "Because it's a funny thing," the man went on. —Would be, Mr Rock shouted in his mind. "Yes, very strange," the sergeant mused aloud. "We have a cat at home, a tom, and we call her Paula."

"Poorer?" Mr Rock enquired, in his deafness.

"Why how's that?" the policeman asked.

"I don't know," the old man answered, putting on an idiotic look, as he often did. He knocked the bran tin against a boot to clean it.

"What I was going to ask was, if I could leave my bike against your shed, thanking you Mr Rock?"

"Shall you be long?"

"I've to go up to the house, that's all."

"Then why not ride there?"

"I came this way," the policeman said.

"Who are you going to arrest in any case?" Mr Rock asked. He was being made garrulous by his dread for Elizabeth and the cottage.

"Likely they'll kick up a fuss when they see me," the sergeant answered at a tangent, and laid his bike down on the grass. "It's only a matter for a few enquiries, but Miss Marchbanks would have it the Inspector must come himself. Did'nt want another. But he's hard pressed, that man is. And of course he's not the only one."

"They've found the one," Mr Rock announced, as though he had been questioned. He was watching the policeman, from behind his spectacles, with the same idiot look.

"How's that?" this man enquired, carefully expressionless, eyes on a now peaceful goose.

"Close to here," Mr Rock said. "Hurt her leg."

"You found her and she'd hurt her leg?" the sergeant echoed, reaching into a pocket for what the older man was sure would be the official notebook, but which turned out to be his handkerchief.

"No," Mr Rock said, and warned himself that he should be careful. There was a pause.

"I just wondered," the policeman said. "The lady came so serious over our telephone how nothing should get about. Close by, was it?" His manner, all at once, Mr Rock thought, was no other than threatening.

"Yes," the old man agreed.

"Then, I'd best get on up, of course," the other said. "Take particulars," he added, but did not move off.

"There's another of their girls missed yet," Mr Rock

volunteered. "A nasty business," he said, with decision.

"How's that, sir?" the sergeant asked, mildly this time, giving him the courtesy because, after all, they did say he had been someone.

"Well, if you live on a place you take part in the day to day affairs," Mr Rock said. The goose, having finished what there had been, made off, wagging its tail.

"Ah, news gets about," the policeman agreed mistakenly.

"You come to feel part of it," Mr Rock corrected.

"Still missing, eh?"

"They have a dance tonight. This has made them nervous," Mr Rock volunteered.

"How come, sir?"

"They're to celebrate the Anniversary of theirs. Only natural."

"As to that, Mr Rock, I could'nt say. And it was you found the one?"

"Mr Birt, who is a tutor, did. Together with my granddaughter. There's a holiday today, they were out for a stroll before breakfast. Brought her back here," Mr Rock explained quite freely, because he knew this would be eagerly reported later. "Gave her a cup of tea," he added, to make it all seem most harmless.

"You gave her a cup of tea?" the sergeant echoed in a blank voice. Mr Rock did not bother to correct him.

"Tea," he agreed.

There was a pause.

"Well then, if I could leave the old bike, I'd best be on my way over," the policeman said, having missed his cup, and made off. He left the machine where it lay on the ground. Mr Rock noticed, with a dreadful reluctance, that its uppermost pedal still revolved.

Not long after, and several hours before the usual time on Wednesdays, Baker and Edge were driven back into the Park in their little red State tourer, which hummed up the main Drive at twenty miles an hour. A cloud of white dust attended it, was always at a respectful distance, following behind.

"I love this Great Place," Miss Edge shouted to her companion as though the lady were as deaf as Mr Rock, then put her face out of one side. With the colour of the car, with the driver, a stout woman in black livery, and the smallness of the back and its occupants, then with the great sun beating stretched earth as a brass hand on a tomtom, they seemed no less than wicked, up to date fairies in a book for younger girls who had just started reading.

But it was not entirely in search of malice that Edge scanned the now high, almost unbroken ramparts of flowering rhododendron which whisked past in vast, red and white splodges, it was not, say, for a sight of decapitated frogs the artificial cherries, which matched the car's paintwork, bobbed and scraped to either side of her black London hat, nor could it even have been for the perfume of those eunuch scentless flowers that her thin nostrils opened and shut like a rabbit's, and little blue eyes, continually darting sideways to catch up with the car's speed, found no repose or a girl's face anywhere on which they could read the answer to the question she dared not put, —where was Mary, where Merode?

She turned back to Baker.

"I hope they have at least got ahead with our decorations," she said.

"If they've had time," Miss Baker dryly answered.

"I was watching to find if they might have cut any on **this exquisite** Drive," Edge excused herself. "I had blamed myself for telling Marchbanks they were to take care, when they robbed nature, that it should be where we could not see. For you know how it is, Baker. Usually one has only to suggest what must not be done to find it carried into practice far quicker than any order, however sensible my dear, but there."

"It'll always be so, till such time as we can engage our own staff," the other woman said. Edge made a face at the driver's back, and another at her colleague.

"I know," Miss Baker replied. "But there's no secret after all." What she had in mind was that, in any case, the staff, for their part, as they knew very well, could not leave either, at any rate not without scandal. Everyone was frozen in the high summer of the State.

"Well, as I invariably insist," Edge said, to change the subject, "whatever our duty has called us to in Town, this glorious Place repays a thousandfold on our return."

"It's a help today certainly," Miss Baker commented.

"You know I can hardly believe it yet," Edge wilfully misunderstood her. "Both Commissions cancelled and not a word or hint reached us. The thing is preposterous."

"We still have the training of them, Edge."

"I trust it was not one of our girls to skimp her duties in such a disgraceful way."

"There's worse, there's what we left this morning," her colleague said, coming out with it.

"Now, Baker, if we had not been reasonably certain how that little mystery would clear itself up by luncheon," Miss Edge expostulated, again grimacing at the driver's back, "we could never have travelled all the way to London." At this moment she caught the driver's eye stolidly watching her make faces by the mirror that was aimed to catch the cloud of dust behind their rear window, but which reflected as faithfully the features of any passenger in Edge's seat.

"I can't help being nervous, dear," Miss Baker admitted.

"Evershed," Miss Edge said sharp. "Do pray watch where we are going."

When they drew up outside the house Edge found her mouth was dry. Accordingly she went straight to the sanctum, ordered two cups of tea over the telephone, and asked for Marchbanks to come along at once.

"Why ma'am," this lady said, after she had knocked and been told to enter, "there's no trouble, I hope." She stood before the Principals sipping tea behind their desks.

"Trouble, Marchbanks? That is what we are back here to find."

"But we were'nt expecting you till after five."

"Which will have to be gone into when I have time," Edge said, then was so good as to relent. "The sittings were cancelled. Whether the fault that we were never told lies at this end is another matter. Now, have you any news?"

"Merode's found, ma'am. She's resting."

"Resting?" Edge cried out incredulously. "Is she hurt then?"

"Not exactly, ma'am."

"Marchbanks, there are no two ways about this incredible affair, is she hurt or is'nt she?"

"She complains of her knee and she fainted," Marchbanks replied. She started to twist fingers together, when Baker interrupted,

"Would'nt that be one of my orphans?" she asked. When told it was so, she closed her eyes.

"Then the other cannot be far then," Edge continued, with greater confidence.

"There's no sign of Mary, ma'am."

"I dare say not, but mark well what I tell you. If the one is found it will not be long before the other puts in an appearance, as though nothing had occurred."

Miss Marchbanks breathed a sigh of released suspense.

"When did she faint, I wonder?" Edge enquired, almost gay, now, in the relief it had become to have learned that one at least was back.

"While I questioned her, ma'am."

"Ah," Miss Edge said, "ah," as though she suddenly noticed something dirty in the corner. Nevertheless she left well alone for a time. "And what does Dr Bodle say about her condition?"

"We have'nt had the doctor in," Marchbanks explained, shifting her feet.

"You have'nt had him in?" Miss Edge cried, and her voice rose. But Baker most definitely interrupted.

"I told you that child was an orphan," she said, eyes still closed.

The other waited for a moment to see if her colleague had more to say. When nothing came she proceeded,

"Well, you must summon him at once, Marchbanks. And while you were about to question her too? We have our Directives, you know. And he should, perhaps, have been in the room with you all the time. How will it look if they hold an Enquiry?"

"Yes, ma'am."

"Tell me, where is the child now?" Edge enquired.

"Oh, Matron's on guard, ma'am. She's locked safely in."

"That is one thing to be thankful for, then," Edge announced. "But who found her, Marchbanks, or did she just come on her own out of thin air?"

"Elizabeth Rock and Mr Birt I believe, ma'am."

Miss Edge glanced sideways at Baker. In that lady's sightless condition there was no way of telling how much she understood.

"Did you hear that, dear?" Miss Edge asked. "It may be significant."

"Can't say I see a great deal to it," Baker muttered, after a pause. Thus it came about that the doctor was not called. Miss Marchbanks was under the impression Miss Edge would do this, and that lady had believed she had only to give an order to be obeyed.

"And what about the Inspector of Police?" Edge went on.

"Of course I rang him at once, ma'am, but he seemed rather occupied. However he said he would be up in no time."

"Has'nt he made an appearance, then?"

"Not yet, ma'am."

"Well, perhaps that may turn out a good thing, although it strikes one as feckless of him, does it not?" Miss Edge turned to Baker. But her colleague had still not opened her eyes. Then she spoke.

"And Mary? She has a father and mother I'm certain," Miss Baker announced, getting to her feet to reach the file. To do so she had to look where she was going, and, when she stumbled, they realised she was in tears. Upon which Edge made a face at Marchbanks so much as to hint, —pray take no notice.

"What did I tell you?" Baker asked. "Parents living apart and in Brazil," she read out from the card she held, openly wiping tears off her cheeks with the back of a hand.

There was a silence. After a moment Miss Edge arrived at the conclusion her friend's virtual collapse was best ignored.

"But, come to that, how was it?" she began again on Miss Marchbanks, who turned a horrified look round to her. "What induced them to act like little thieves? Is there a man in this, Marchbanks?"

"Why I'm sure there's nothing missing, ma'am. No-one's reported . . ."

"Please," Edge interrupted, with a weary gesture. "I

never said anything of the kind, did I? Who got at them, then, and planned it all? Have you found this out yet?"

"I was careful not to press too closely ma'am. . . ."

"And she fainted," Miss Edge again interrupted.

"She was very tired, I think," Ma Marchbanks said with dignity. A loud sob came from Baker.

"There is no need to lose our heads," Miss Edge rebuked her colleague, although she addressed the underling. "Rather it is a moment to keep what wits we have about us. As to being tired, the doctor will see to that, no doubt. The question I asked was quite simple. Is there a man in this, or not?"

Marchbanks, had certainly begun to lose hers.

"Yes," she said, almost at random.

"I thought so," Edge said, satisfied almost to jubilation. "And has he any connection with our Mr Rock?"

"Careful dear," Baker implored, with a trembling voice.

"But we must know, you know we must." Edge said. "Well, has he?"

"I'm sure I can't tell. I don't imagine so," Miss Marchbanks told her, with obvious resentment.

"You can't tell, you do not imagine, what is this?" Edge echoed.

"That's how things are," Miss Marchbanks said, happily hating her Principal.

"But why? Surely you can see? Why, Marchbanks?"

"Because she fainted just when she was going to tell, ma'am."

"Where is the girl? I . . ." Edge was beginning, when Baker broke in.

"Thank you, Marchbanks, I'm sure you've done all that was possible, you can go now," she said, and Miss Marchbanks walked straight out. As she closed the door she heard Baker, pleadingly, start to reason with Miss Edge, "Now dear," she said, "now dear, in our Directives . . ."

"The OAFS," Miss Marchbanks spat aloud in the passage, to relieve her feelings, the first moment she was out of earshot. "Oh, the oafs."

Moira came out of a ride into the small open space before Mr Rock's cottage. Its hideous mauve and yellow brick was swamped in shade, marked out by sunlight, for the beech trees were tall but not thick together hereabouts.

Sun lit up blue smoke, spiralling out of the chimney for two full yards in this stillness.

She could not see the old man but heard a chopping of wood within the trees, and moved towards the sound, knowing it must be him for he was the one to work round here.

"Hello," she said, confident she was the favourite, when she came upon Mr Rock in shirtsleeves, clumsily using his hatchet on a block.

He straightened up. The old face cracked into a real smile. She saw he was not wearing teeth, also that he could do with a shave.

"Well?" he asked. She came close, to let him take her in.

"Why don't you use the tree Mr Birt found Merode under?" she asked.

"Not dead enough," he said.

"But you'd have more wood. You are silly," she said, while he examined her youth. It made him think of a ripe plum, on a hot day, against green leaves on a wall.

"Mr Birt found her. There's a laugh," she began again. They stood watching each other comfortably.

"How d'you look so cool?" he asked.

"He would," she said about the finding. When this drew no comment she went on in a lazy way,

"Because I'm not hot, not yet, silly. I don't wear all the clothes you do," she added, shifting the position of her hip.

He had a fallen branch to cut into faggots, and he set to work once more.

"Let me help," she said, though she made no move forward. When he did not answer, she repeated, "Let me." —He's a hundred if he's a day, she said to herself.

"Just leave an old fellow get on with what he's about," he said.

"All that wood's for Daise, is'nt it?" she asked. "Well, I'm not stopping anyone."

"Yes, for Daisy's swill," he answered. "To boil it. Too many won't trouble, which is the cause of so much of this filthy swine fever."

She nibbled at one of the azaleas in her arms. She knew she made a picture, but he paid no attention. She waved away a bee.

"Have you seen your cat?" she enquired.

"No. She's all right I trust?" he said, not looking up.

"Oh, in her glory," the girl replied. "At the Institute, of course, with Ma Marchbanks. She'd better look out for herself, though. The Marchbanks may'nt know it, but Edge and Baker's back."

"Are they . . .?" he asked, and drew himself up to his full height, but checked his tongue in time. "Why, what about my animal?"

"They don't like pussy cats, those two, do they?" she answered.

"Two faced, cats are," he said, watching her closely. She took a whole azalea right into her mouth. "Cupboard love," he said, and wiped his spectacles.

"Why should'nt I, if I want. They taste good," she

said, after she had got rid of the flower into a hand and dropped it behind her back.

"Not you," he said. "Cats."

"What's cupboard love, exactly?" she asked, knowing full well, but to cover herself.

"Greed, that's all."

"You are queer, Mr Rock," she said.

There was a pause while he put his spectacles on once more.

"Have they come upon the other girl yet?" the old man enquired, getting on with his task. "Or why have they returned?"

"Mary, oh I know where she is," Moira told him.

"Where's that?" Mr Rock quietly demanded.

"She's down under water in the lake of course," the girl said.

"Is she now?" this old man commented, but did not look up from what he was at. "Have you been to see?"

She gave a small, affected shriek. "Me? Who d'you think I am? Oh, I simply could'nt."

"Then how d'you come by your information?"

"That's easy," the girl said. "Winstanley asked permission for the staff to bathe as today's a holiday, and Ma Marchbanks said better not, because Mary was drowned in it."

"When did you learn?" he enquired, selecting another stick to chop.

"Why everyone's heard." A silence fell.

"Where's George Adams at work?" Mr Rock asked next.

"He's to fetch the pine trees she wants round the Hall for tonight. We're to put salt over to look like snow. Only Miss Edge won't be so keen. Why?"

"Because in that case I should have thought he would be better employed if he dragged the water," Mr Rock said. He was watching the girl now.

"Oh Mr Rock you are dreadful, really," she cried out. "The horrible things you think."

"Dear, dear," he said, and bent down again. There was a pause.

"What did you make of it when Mr Birt found Merode?" she once more asked, with a giggle. He made no reply.

"She told me all," she went on. "You see, they'd locked her into the bathrooms so she could have a good cry, you know what a tremendous cry baby she is, but there's a grating on the floor above, or there's two, one above and one underneath. Anyway Matron has'nt discovered yet, so I was able to get on to Merode."

"Moira," he said uneasily, "you'll grow up an old maid."

She laughed out loud. "Me?" she said. "I don't think," largely understating this. "Why, Mr Rock?"

"Because you will."

"No, why?"

"All this chitter chatter."

"But I'm only explaining what happened, are'nt I? No she, that's Merode, confessed up she'd gone out at night to meet him. Lots of the girls do."

"Oh? Go out to meet Sebastian Birt?" His voice was sharp.

"Oh, why Mr Birt specially? But they do at night."

"But how do you know?" Mr Rock asked. The jealousy he felt over this man obscured his judgement, so that he was not sure what to believe.

"That's easy," the girl replied. "He said he was off to London last night, for the holiday, then stayed after all."

"Who told you? Was it Merode?"

"I said, did'nt I? Marion's senior girl at orderly duty today, and Mrs Blain said so. Which reminds me. You must'nt keep me here to pass along the news the way you are. I'm due back in the kitchen. I might tell you it's hard work jollying Mrs Blain, with all she's got on."

"Why do you say Miss Baker and Miss Edge are back?"

"Because I saw them come up the drive.   Is that good enough for once?   But they did'nt see me, no thank you."

"Well, well.   They missed a sight then, did'nt they, Moira?"

"Oh you are dreadful this morning.   Now I'll ask you a question.   Where's Dan?"

"Who?"

"I mean Ted."

"The goose?   She's fed.   It was a good thing I had plenty."

"Why, how's that?"

"Because she's down by the water, this minute, if I know much of Ted," Mr Rock said.

She gave another little shriek.

"Mr Rock that's foul," she cried.

"Grubbing about," he added.

"I shan't stay if you're like this.   All you ever want is to give me creeps," she said.

"You'll stay," he countered.

"Why, how's that?" she repeated, making no move to depart.

"You told me you'd have to get back a long while since."

There was a pause while she pouted.   But he did not bother to notice.

"Will you come to the dance tonight?" she asked, in a small voice.

"I might," he said.

"Because, if you did, I'd sit one out with you."

"That's a more sensible suggestion than saying you'd spare me a dance."   He chopped harder at the branch.

"Because, if you did, I might even give you a kiss," she continued.   The chopping stopped.   But he did not look up.

"There's an absurd idea," he said loudly. "If you want to know I've completely forgotten about it."

"I mean what I promise," she insisted.

"All I intended to convey," he said, frightened and embarrassed, "was, thank God, I've reached an age when I've long since forgotten everything to do with all such nonsense. Now do you understand?"

"No," she answered.

"Then why not?"

"Because I bet you have'nt really," she said. He went on with his work rather fast.

"Well, well," he tried to pass it off, uneasily.

"I don't know what else a girl can promise," she suggested. He let this go.

Then she began again. She dropped her voice to a whisper, so that he unwillingly stopped work to catch what was said through the disfiguring deafness.

"Now this is really secret," she informed him. "Have you heard about Mr Adams?"

"Look, Moira, I'm not here to chatter with students."

"Oh, if someone does'nt want to listen, I can't make them, can I?"

"All right," he said. "There's no need to be forward."

She inferred from this last remark that she had his blessing.

"There's some of the juniors meet Mr Adams of a night time. If we could only find which, we'd put an end to that, double quick."

"Who's we?" he asked, surprised into going on with it.

"Why, the seniors."

"Miss Baker and Miss Edge don't know, then?"

"Those two old pussies," she protested. "They'll never learn what really happens here. But that's why it's so silly your saying what you just did. You and he are the same age, anyway there can't be more between you than there is between me and one of the juniors."

"You're out of your mind, child. I'm old enough to be the man's father. And in any case, I don't like this."

"I'm sorry," she said, with an extraordinary look of innocence.

"That's all right. I've forgotten all about it," he repeated severely. But he straightened his back, and took off the spectacles once more, to wipe them.

"Then you will come to the dance tonight," she announced.

"I might," he said. "Will Miss Edge and Miss Baker be in attendance?"

"Of course. They've come back already, like I told. Anyway they only go up for the day, Wednesdays. No, they had to come home in a rush because of Mary and Merode. And when we gave them all the start we could."

"What?" he protested, laughing at last. "If this is any more of your nonsense then I don't want it, that's all."

"Well you see," she said, "Mary was almost forever on orderly duty. Edge said she always was so neat. Marion's the senior today and when Mary did'nt turn up, because I promise I never heard a word about Merode till later, Marion asked what she should tell the old grumps. And sure enough Edge spotted Mary was'nt there at once, so Marion told her like I said, that Mary had gone to Matron."

"I don't understand a word," he protested more cheerfully still, and went back to his work.

"Oh, you are dense," she cried. "D'you know while I stand here to pass the time of day with you my arms are simply dropping from all these branches for the dance?" She was indeed a lovely sight as she stood before him. But he laughed once more.

"Then you'd better rid yourself," he said.

"You are in a dreadful mood today. Goodbye for now," she said, and went off, happily pouting.

"Now dear our Directives," Baker said as Marchbanks left the room. "Be careful, do dear. You said yourself the child should not be crossexamined."

"But, Baker, she has not been crossexamined, has she?" Edge cried out, and pushed the saucer away with its empty cup. "If she has, this is the first I have heard."

"Her parents are not living, dear. If they hold an Enquiry they'll call it crossexamination."

"Oh, it does so aggravate one, Baker. Because she holds the answer to Mary's whereabouts."

"Wherever the poor child may be, with her parents away in Brazil, she can stay for a while yet," Miss Baker said, dabbing at her eyes with a handkerchief, rather in the same way that Mr Dakers had patted his mouth at breakfast.

"Why, what on earth do you mean?" Miss Edge protested. "You are surely not going to suggest . . .?"

"I suggest nothing, dear," Baker insisted in a tired voice. "All I say is that Mary can't have got very far, unless of course she has a conveyance. We left instructions about the station and the coaches, and now you have a policeman to see you. No, we must remember the poor mite was sick."

"I know nothing of it," Edge objected. "Her name is not down on Matron's list."

"But don't you recollect, dear? It was you who asked what had happened to Mary at breakfast, and Marion told you she'd gone to Matron."

"So she did," Miss Edge exclaimed. "That puts an entirely different complexion on the matter. In fact, when

I come to consider, I cannot understand how Marchbanks
has not been able to drag the wretched girl back to us
already. So unnecessary, too, to send for the Inspector.
Because he will need some good reason to explain our
bringing him up here. The staff simply will not take in
what I keep drumming into them about undesirable
publicity."

"We have'nt found her yet, dear."

But Edge had now gone to the opposite extreme, was
overconfident. "Why," she said, and left her desk to go
over to the window, "the whole affair is a mare's nest,
something tells me." Miss Baker had also risen. She
moved over to the telephone.

"And such a shame," Miss Edge continued, holding on
to folded curtains at either side with both hands, to face
a bright prospect as though crucified. "What a very real
shame to torture our nerves in this glorious weather, just
when the old Place is at its own great best."

"Madam here," Baker said into the receiver. "Would
you have Marion sent along at once."

The child must have been expecting it, for, in next to
no time, there was her knock on the door.

"Marion," Miss Edge asked, as though Baker had tele-
phoned on her instructions. "When did Mary go to
Matron?"

"I could'nt say, ma'am."

"But you told us at breakfast, surely you recollect."

"Yes ma'am."

"When did you see her last then, child?"

"I did'nt see her, ma'am."

"You did'nt see her?" Edge echoed, an ugly note in her
voice. "Oh but, excuse me, you must have. You told
us."

Marion stood in silence. She looked guilty.

"You mean you connived at this disappearance, Marion?

Just when my sixth sense had led me to ask you where she was. You say now she never went to Matron?"

"They told me she had, ma'am."

"And who was that, pray?"

"The other girls, ma'am."

"Then you never even saw her this morning?" Miss Baker asked, white about the lips once she found her fears confirmed.

"No ma'am."

There was a silence. Edge came away from the window, went right up to the child.

"You can go now, Marion," she said. "But we shall have to see you later about the whole wretched business, once we have got right to the bottom of it. I fear you may not have been quite straight with us, child."

"But I . . ." the girl began, raising limpid, spaniel's eyes to Miss Edge, and that were filling with easy tears, when the lady broke in on her.

"Yes, you can go, Marion," she repeated. "Perhaps you did not quite catch what I said?"

A call to Matron told them she had not seen Mary since last night.

"If you would manage the Inspector I'll just have a word with Matron, I think," Baker informed Edge.

"I shall get rid of the man," this lady agreed, with decision.

When the sergeant came he mopped his brow.

"Such lovely weather we have had, and it continues," Edge said, as she took him by the hand. "Tell me, would you like a glass of beer after your long ride?" she asked, for she had not reached the position she now held without learning the ways of this world.

"Thank you, ma'am," the sergeant accepted. He sat down before the two desks, one of which lay vacant. His face was traditional, the colour of butcher's meat. When she had ordered his ale over the telephone, she asked,

"And how is my friend the Inspector?"

"Ah," the sergeant said. "He was put out, there you are. He asked me to make his excuses, ma'am."

"Yes, the paper work does not grow less, does it?"

"There you are," the man repeated, in agreement. Edge bit her lip with impatience to be rid of him, for she felt there was so little time, and then, at that very instant, a scheme began to form in her mind. "It's not often he gets outside," the sergeant ended.

"Now, this is your beer," Edge announced brightly as one of the juniors on orderly duty carried it in. "Wonders will never cease. They have not forgotten the opener. Time was when a great Place like this brewed its own. You prefer yours in draught, perhaps? But then those days are not missed, not as we are now," she said, with fervour.

He hastily agreed. Behind his big, blank face he wondered once more. He took a pull at the glass. As might have been expected, the beer was flat.

"Which way did you come? It looks so beautiful today, I think," she said.

"By the back," he answered, and wiped his mouth with a handkerchief in such a manner that, for a moment, she wondered if it could be to hide a smile. "I saved a half mile," he said.

"Oh so you came along by Mr Rock's, then?" she made a sure guess, at her most affable. "What a wonderful man for his age."

"He is that," the sergeant said.

"And I dare say you saw some of our dear girls," Miss Edge went on. "At their search," she said, then pulled herself up. "Seeking out our decorations," she explained. "You could not be expected to know, of course, but today is our Anniversary, and we are to hold a little jollification for the children. Oh, noone will come in from outside," she assured him. "Just a small private gathering and, naturally, we have to dress the premises. So then, because we take pride in what has been entrusted to us, I gave the strictest instructions that they were not to cut the blooms where this could make itself felt, because at the present glorious season, down here, to see is to feel, sergeant."

He had a vision of six hundred golden legs, bare to the morning, and said, "Yes, ma'am." At the same time he had not forgotten what had been hinted on the way, and saw one pair of dripping legs.

"Yes," she agreed, "today our routine is disrupted. But that was not why I needed the Inspector."

The sergeant waited.

"No," she said. "The fact is, Miss Baker and I are made really anxious by what we have noticed in the Press these last few weeks. Up and down the country, sergeant, there have been such distressful cases, so horrible, so inhuman we think, because we have discussed the thing, naturally, though not outside these four walls, of course. I refer to all this interference with young girls, sergeant."

—Ah, now we are getting somewhere, he thought to himself. Although it was not to be quite what he expected. "Interference madam?" he asked. But she seemed not to know how to proceed.

"Oh hardly anything really serious," she went on. "Though I always maintain the indictable offence is encouraged, or perhaps provoked would be a better word, by the other party." Here she paused once more.

"By the complainant?" he prompted.

"Exactly," she said. "You will realise that it is a little difficult for me to express myself, how delicate . . .," she said, leaning back in her chair, smiling at him defiantly. "But we have noticed so many cases, up and down the land, where girls have been stopped by strangers. And here, it so happens, we are particularly vulnerable. I mean by that, not only our old tumble down Park walls, which are a positive invitation to itinerant labour, but our Mission here which, from the very nature of it, focuses attention upon our little Pursuits."

"Tramps," the sergeant broke in, not quite caught up with her.

"Because we are Trustees, you understand," she went on, after a short silence to give him time. "We stand in the shoes of our students' parents, it is a very real trust which the State has put upon us here, and, as Its Servants, we should not leave a stone unturned. . . ." She seemed to search for the right phrase. He watched as she closed her eyes. He waited. "After all, prevention is better than cure," she brought out at last, smiling at him, bright and sharp.

"What exactly did you have in mind, miss?"

"It was more a premonition, sergeant. But Miss Baker and I experienced what we did so acutely that we decided to talk it over with the Inspector. I suppose we felt in need of advice as much as anything. Because we particularly noted in the papers that it always seems to be the older men, I mean of a certain age."

"Have you anyone in view, ma'am?" the sergeant asked. The drift of her remarks had not escaped him.

"But I have just told you," she said, with another bright smile. "Our Park wall that we rightly cannot get the labour to have repaired. Anyone can step over."

"You feel you would like a watch kept?"

"I hope I have more sense of the urgency of the times in which we live," she replied, with a slight show of indignation. "No," she went on, "we are aware how you yourselves are short staffed also. And of course it is not our girls," she said. "In that sense they are above reproach, absolutely. They are hand picked. As you realise, it is a privilege, a reward for preliminary work well done, for them to be sent to us. No," she wound up, leaning slightly forward while at the same time she took her eyes off his face, " to tell you the truth, we did wonder if you might have information of any characters locally."

He thought for a moment. Then he decided he must pretend he did not understand.

"What characters, miss?" he asked.

"Well, men of an age," she said, " I mean really old men," she said, "who, from what one hears and reads, are more liable to let themselves collapse in that disgraceful way." Then she sheered off. "If I may refer to what is common knowledge, how in the course of your duties you take particular stock of the inhabitants of your own district," she went on with almost a sneer, " then what I am getting at is this, that you should warn us of any such sinister person. Forewarned is forearmed," she said, and gave a really brilliant smile to hide her mounting irritation.

He hesitated.

"We've been fortunate round about," he said at last. "I don't think there's been a case of the kind you mention for some years past, ma'am."

"But then, will there never be?" she enquired, assuming a discouraged voice.

"Ah," he said, "now there's a question."

Upon which, her point made, she changed the subject, and, not long afterwards, politely dismissed him.

Winstanley, hastening along a ride, came to where it crossed another. She looked to the right, saw Sebastian with Elizabeth Rock. They were standing within each other's arms, alternately kissing their eyes shut against an azalea in full flower half fallen across the ride. This mass of bloom in the full sunlight was almost the colour of Merode's hair in her bath, a slope of deep golden honey with its sweet heavy scent and a great buzz of bees about; caparisoned with primrose yellow butterflies, some trembling spread wings, some clapping theirs soundlessly together, some tight closed.

"Hey, you two," she called, but then, as she began to approach, and like wings, they came apart, though still holding one another by the hand, she felt such a distress she halted. —It was long since she had been kissed like that, and sometimes she wondered if she would ever be again.

"I was just on the look out for you," she continued, in hopes that she had not made a fool of herself, and shown what she felt. But they seemed as dazed as the noisy insect life around, which droned and shuddered while these flowers trumpeted the sun.

"Miss Edge and Miss Baker are back," she said. The others came slowly to her. —Beastly woman she's fairly drunk with him, she thought.

"But I'm off," he objected, in what he imagined to be cockney, yet hesitantly, as if he had not entirely found his feet, " I've got the day off, lidy, I'm not 'ere, you 'ave'nt seen me." And this moment he chose to wink, to cajole her not to speak of what she had just witnessed. She was immediately more than disgusted.

"That excuse would do if this was an ordinary day," she replied. "But there's a bit of a shemozzle on, my children. As you may have heard."

"What's brought them back so bloody soon?" he asked, keeping up the part he had seen fit to choose.

"I was wondering if you'd caught what I said," she remarked, stubbornly.

G

"Why you don't mean, you can't be trying to explain, what is . . . it's about Mary, is it?" Elizabeth asked, with dread.

"Oh no, there's no news. It appears their Commissions were postponed, so they came rushing back again, that's all. Evershed says she'll have to cool their car off like a horse. But they've held a staff meeting and you can guess who it was noticed you were absent."

"But gor' love a duck, guv'nor, I'm not on today, I'm tellin' yer."

"I spoke up to tell her, and then that silly ass of a prisoner's friend, Dakers, asked if he should go to find you, even went on to say he happened to know you had slept in after all. But it passed, anyway for a time. The thing is, my lad, I think you ought to put in an appearance."

"That goes for the two of us, then," Mr Birt said in a last attempt to keep up his attitude. "I seen you dashin' about the grounds."

"I made my excuses prettily," she answered, again with some impatience. " There's one of the girls still loose, after all."

"Oh it's my fault," Elizabeth broke out in a wail, while Miss Winstanley observed, not for the first time, how a person's lipstick, when it was smudged half way to her nose, wounded the whole face like a bullet. "We took what's her name back, you see, then we thought, well it was only natural really, my grandfather's all alone, I had to get dinner, so the thing is, and of course we did'nt know they were coming, we just began to walk along but as a matter of fact it was my fault. I know I'm silly but you've heard, haven't you, I haven't been really well, and I asked Seb to see me to the cottage, so foolish when you come to think, as though it was dead of night, in time of course, but then I have been made rather nervous. What I mean is, we none of us know, do we?"

"Don't you fuss, my dear," Mr Birt said in his natural voice, which Winstanley heard so seldom that she was not sure to recognise it, "I'll take you, then I'll nip along and go on duty," he ended, lamely.

"Look Sebastian," the other woman said, "If I were you I'd get there right away. Make some excuse to show yourself."

"But gor' love a duck, what went on, then, at their extry special meeting you're so wrought up about?" he asked, returning to his best cockney, which he knew only from books.

"It was old Edge," Winstanley told him. "Studying her as I have to I think it was to set her mind at rest. Baker's not much in a crisis. She wanted our support, or so she said. If you ask me, I think she just had us all in to explain what she intended not to do. In other words, to cover herself by being able to say she'd had a staff meeting to discuss 'this unprecedented occurrence', and that we'd all decided, in an ad hoc committee, to proceed on a certain course."

"Which is?" he enquired, in his ordinary voice.

"Why to do nothing at all," she answered. He came out with a disgustingly high, screamed laugh. " Seb," Miss Rock protested sharply. He broke off at once.

"Well Sebastian, I don't know what else they, or we, can be about. They can't set the girls on to search," Winstanley said. She was distressed. "Well now we're not sure what they'll find, are we? We don't want general hysterics. And they've told the police. Dakers has it for a fact the roads are to be watched within a radius of twenty miles. The sergeant left an hour ago after he'd seen Edge. Besides I believe Merode's told some story which does'nt sound too improbable and is reasonably reassuring." Most of this was false, if Miss Winstanley had only known. The child had said nothing. "But you'd better make a show. I would if I were you. We're all to keep our eyes sharp open, she says."

"I won't ask what else I'm a'doin' of," he commented, "an' in their Park into the bargain, where it will likely do most good," he said.

"No Seb," Elizabeth Rock spoke out. "You're not to . . . I can't imagine why . . . it's so silly after Miss Winstanley's been so kind. Go back at once, I'm sure Gapa would say that, yes, at once, don't clown."

"Look here, let me walk you back," the other woman offered.

"All right then," Birt said, and went off fast towards the Institute, without another word.

"I have'nt been quite well, I had a breakdown at work," Elizabeth told Miss Winstanley, as they set out along a great hill of rhododendron twelve foot high with flowers the colour of blood, and the colour of the flesh of bathers in open air in sunless country. Winstanley, as she bent her head to listen, took her companion's hand in hers as a sort of tribute to this woman's being drenched with love. But after a few yards she let go of that hot hand.

"Would you like my mirror?" she asked, and rummaged in her bag.

Lunch at the Institute this day was cold, to allow Mrs Blain time to prepare the buffet for their dance. The students waited at long linen covered trestles for Miss Baker and Miss Edge. The noise of their talking was a twitter of a thousand starlings.

The hall in which they took their meals was that used whenever there was an entertainment. The tables could be removed, were lightly constructed, as also High Table, on a dais at which the staff were served, and which could be taken to pieces although built to a massive, shining, mahogany front. Behind it, neatly stacked in a great pile or pyre on the floor, was a mass of cut azalea and rhododendron the seniors had gathered to decorate the room later, but in time for their gramophone when this was set to endlessly repeat one valse.

When the staff filed in, Edge and Baker bringing up the rear, that clatter of conversation stilled as, with a rustle of a thousand birds rising from willows about a warm lagoon, the girls stood in silence to mark the entrance. Then, after Miss Edge had been last to sit down, the three hundred budding State Servants, with another outburst of talk as of starlings moving between clumps of reeds to roost, in their turn left to collect plates of cold meat and vegetables ready laid out in the kitchen.

"Ah Marchbanks," Miss Edge called out above the bustle, "I see they have not neglected our tamasha." She was looking at the mass of flowers.

"I'd thought pine branches with salt," that woman answered with a blush. "So cool, in this hot weather, for the Dance. A soupçon of snow" she elaborated.

" Indeed," Edge said, unenthusiastic, while conversation, for the moment, became general around High Table.

"In their white dresses," Marchbanks explained, painting the picture.

"I hesitate to think what our Supervisor would say," Edge objected, referring to a Government Inspector whose visits, in order to check up, were exhaustive and unannounced.

"Yes, there is that of course," Marchbanks agreed.

"What a time they are being, Baker, with our luncheon," said Miss Edge. And her confidence was now such that she continued, having for the moment forgotten, "What can have happened to Mary and her girls?"

It was Mary whose privilege it had been to serve them, each day almost. Right from the very first she had shewn such diligence.

Miss Baker winced. Once more she closed her eyes. There was a noticeable pause.

Winstanley offered up a topic to bridge the awkwardness.

"Ma'am," she said. "Have you ever thought of Chinese pheasants for our grounds?"

"Chinese?" Miss Edge enquired.

"The plumage," Winstanley explained. "A perfect red and gold. They are'nt any trouble either, they live off the land."

"I seem to remember Mr Birt telling us there was no such thing," Edge expatiated, with a glance of malice at this man.

"Ah," he said, bowed in her direction, and assumed a close imitation of Mr Rock's party manner which they could all recognise. "We admit of no domestic animal as self sufficient under the State. But it would certainly add a touch of Babylonian splendour to the walks."

"It might startle his goose," Edge objected with a knowing look. All laughed at this allusion, Sebastian Birt excessively.

"They need no attention, ma'am, for sure," Winstanley insisted. "They roost in the nearest tree, and feed off acorns."

"Like cats and pigs then," Miss Edge said, with a smirk benign.

"Where I was brought up there used to be a black and white farm," Baker announced. "A half timbered place, piebald horses, black and white poultry and so on."

"I often wish I had been reared in the country," Edge

said, throwing a bright smile at her colleague to mark this lady's return into the fold of conversation. "Sometimes I wonder if our girls appreciate how fortunate they are to find themselves in magnificent Parks and Woodlands."

"Oh they do that, I'm sure, ma'am," came from Marchbanks.

"And someone like Mr Rock, again," Edge pursued, her eye on Sebastian Birt. "How truly privileged."

There was another pause.

"The amenities of urban life in sylvan surroundings," the young man said at last, still with an exact imitation of the sage.

"More, I think," Miss Edge said. "Indeed I fancy that taking Youth, as he has it round him now, and in this beautiful great Place, one of the State's ornaments, a veritable crown of Jewels, a man could be expected to live out his life at rest with himself, and the world."

"But it must depend on one's physical condition. There can be no comfort in age as such," Winstanley, who loved an argument, objected.

Miss Edge looked gravely at her. "In that case," she said, as though to refer to incurable illness, "there is another alternative. The State looks after its own. There are Homes of Repose for those who have deserved well of their Country and who, with advancing years, find the burden of old age detracts from the advantages of a life of quietude they have been permitted to lead at large." Sebastian squirmed. She saw this, then turned to Baker, who looked woodenly at her in warning.

"There are great mercies," Miss Marchbanks said.

"And great responsibilities, Marchbanks," Edge corrected, upon which she swept over the hall of students with an imperious slow swing of her eyes. She did not, at once, go on with what she had been about to say, for here and there, below, she could perceive a mood she particularly detested, and which today she could not have after all that had occurred, girls whispering. She was unable, of course, to hear this. But it was the heavy heads leant sideways into one another's hair, the look of couples as though withdrawn upon each other, in one word, the air of complicity, which startled and digusted Edge.

"A community at peace within itself," she went on, but her attention was no longer directed onto those immediately around, "can well be a corrective," and then she saw how many of these whisperers seemed to watch someone at High Table, "can canalise," she said, in wonder —could it be Sebastian Birt? "will influence all those who come under the sway," she continued haltingly —but no they seemed intent on someone or something beyond, "must bring out the best," she said, then realised it could only be the mass of flowers, "can but . . ." she continued, and there she stopped. Her colleagues, who turned in surprise, saw Miss Edge go pale. —It was one of these deadly rumours had taken hold of the students, the Principal knew, was spreading through their ranks in poison. She pulled herself together. "Can but turn all those who come under its influence upwards and onwards to the ideals, to the practical politics, that is, the High Purposes of the State," she ended in a forced rush.

She blew her nose, then, to hide her face a moment. —What idea could it be had taken hold, she asked herself?

"The greatest good of the greatest number," Sebastian echoed, in a peculiarly servile manner.

"I think your suggestion about these Chinese pheasants excellent," Baker said to Winstanley, with a nervous eye on Edge, who, at that precise instant, rose up from her place. She went slowly over towards the mass of flowers. The staff's anxious conversation covered the guv'nor's halting step. But they began to keep their girls in view also, and could see those who whispered fall silent the better to watch Miss Edge. Then, when this lady reached the pyre of azalea and rhododendron, which towered well above her head, and which must at once have assailed her with its burden of hot scent, one child even rose to her feet she was so curious about Miss Edge, only to be brought back by a neighbour tugging on her skirts at which she subsided, rosy cheeks covered by blushes, and in a fit of giggling which she managed to choke off too easily, too soon.

It was uncanny for Edge to leave her place at mealtime. But, having found little at fault with the pile of blooms, not even a nettle, she came back as though nothing were the matter. Only, once she was seated in her chair again, she fairly glared out over the students.

"The scent's so strong it quite puts one off one's feed," Miss Baker remarked, to offer Edge a motive. She pushed her plate away untasted.

"My dear," Edge said, almost as though from a dream. "This excellent cold roast beef! You surely do not propose to forgo your luncheon?"

But she paid no real heed to Baker's antics. It was the girls. That whispering had spread once more. Several, like her colleague, had ceased to eat. Fifty or sixty, even, sat heads bent, their thick hair, dark, gold or red hanging across eyes which, behind this warm screen, watched the flowers, or watched herself so Edge sensed, as well as whatever else it might be had attracted them, unfortunate children, and that drew sharp jewelled eyes this way, and muted voices.

On a sudden Edge felt deathly hot.

"Are all our windows open, I wonder?" she asked. Dakers half rose from his chair, which was entirely unnecessary because their table on the dais was raised well above the three hundred heads beneath.

"It's stifling," Baker agreed.

"No, I'm sure they're wide as can be," Miss Marchbanks said.

—The eyes, Edge asked herself, and then came over deathly cold.

Because she knew, now.

—It could only be the body under the flowers, a corpse.

"Sip some water, dear," Baker suggested.

"The early start," Marchbanks murmured, while Sebastian was on guard as though to see the hag die before his eyes.

Then Edge made a stupendous effort and came through.

"What?" she asked. "Yes of course," she said. "Yes, I daresay they may be a trifle overpowering." Then she began to address herself under her breath. —Mabel, she murmured, Mabel, pull yourself together, this is ridiculous. After a short time she looked guiltily over the girls and was relieved to find they did not appear to have noticed, indeed they already seemed to talk more freely.

"Azaleas can bring on hay fever," Miss Winstanley suggested.

"And pine branches asthma," Edge said, rather wild, not yet herself quite.

"Oh I don't think Adams cut any in the end," Marchbanks protested, intolerably nervous and sensitive at one and the same time.

"It was the salt," Miss Edge explained at random, recovering poise. She fanned herself with a handkerchief. "The Supervisor would never pass it."

But, as often as her thoughts turned to the absent Mary, who, she knew well, could never be under those flowers, they reeled away back to Mr Rock and his granddaughter Elizabeth.

"Mr Birt," she began once more. "You have seen our sage this morning. Has he news of his election?"

"I believe not," Sebastian said, in rurtive embarrassment.

The girls were filing out to fetch the sweet. Miss Edge felt rejuvenated.

"Strange," she exclaimed. "It was yesterday they sat, surely? I made certain I would hear at the Commission, only to find we had been cancelled. I set great store by it for him."

There was a silence. The staff waited to have their plates removed. Edge took a sip of water.

"Because, you know," she went on at large, "he is too old to live the life he does. He needs help here," she explained.

"Amazing the things he did," Miss Baker put in, and a look passed between her and Edge. The subject was dropped.

"Marchbanks, I do not want any of the decorations touched before I am ready to supervise all that myself, directly we've had tea," Miss Edge ordered, and then at once felt almost completely well again. What she had been through she saw now as just a moment's weakness.

"The great thing is, ma'am, they're to all intents and purposes practically self supporting," Winstanley began once more.

Because Miss Edge had just asked herself if the horror Rock could have sheltered Mary she was startled.

"How do you mean?" she fiercely enquired.

"The Chinese pheasants."

"Yes, I had gathered that," she lied. "But the point occurred to me, how would they do in winter, in snow?"

"Oh, ma'am, I'm sure they must be hardy. Why, think of the giant panda," Marchbanks said.

"Yes, there's another black and white animal," Miss Baker agreed.

"But the bran," Edge announced. "We came across that only the other day. Did we not, dear?" she asked Miss Baker. "Oh, I make no bones," she went on, raising her voice so that the staff, and in particular Sebastian, should not miss the implications. "Mrs Blain has her little preferences, perhaps we all have, and in any case I do not want this mentioned away from High Table. But it seems she has a weakness for his goose, which, to my mind, is nothing less than a danger. A blow from one of its great wings," and her voice rose so that the nearest students heard, even stopped eating their cherries the better to listen, "one blow, in one of its savage tempers, and the miserable bird could smash a leg."

"You don't suppose, you know who . . ." Miss Baker began, in an obvious reference to Mary and Merode, when Edge interrupted her.

"My dear," she said. "No shop at meals."

"They might need a little grain," Winstanley admitted.

"And how so?" her Principal demanded.

"The Chinese pheasants, ma'am."

"Of course," Edge replied, who had, in fact, forgotten these decorative birds. "I do not deny the wheat. But there lies my whole difficulty. If Miss Baker and I are exercised in our minds over this matter of our Supervisor and the bran, and really it is peace at any price these days, for I do not suppose we shall mention it in the kitchen," she sneered, knowing full well that her remarks would be repeated to Mrs Blain, in all probability by Sebastian Birt, "I do beg leave to question the wisdom of additional food at certain seasons. We already have an unofficial cat," she added, not looking at Marchbanks, no longer afraid.

"But ma'am," Winstanley said with tact, "it's swans, I'm certain."

"What is?"

"That break a person's leg with their wings."

"I'm sure Alice does'nt get anything," Miss Marchbanks interjected. At just a momentary glance they could, each of them, see that she had flushed with rage.

"Quite, Marchbanks," Edge said in a soothing voice. "I never even suggested it. We all respect . . . there can be no question . . . Well, in a word, it is Mr Rock's white Persian, and who is there can stop a cat making free with the Grounds?" She seemed almost embarrassed. She was still not quite herself.

"She never even gets a sup of milk while over here, it's a shame," Miss Marchbanks said. She could not let the matter drop. Miss Edge gave her a small bow.

"But a goose is not much less large than a swan," Edge went on, turning to Winstanley. "And consider the power they must have in their shoulder muscles for long migratory flights. I know some of my girls are simply in terror of the bird."

Sebastian Birt cleared his throat, as though about to speak. But Edge glared at him, and Baker gave such a glance of doom that he did not have the heart. Then Miss Inglefield made her first contribution.

"Grace, ma'am," she said.

"Good heavens," Edge exclaimed, verifying the fact that all the girls had finished. "Whose turn is it, Baker?"

"Yours dear, I think."

Upon which Edge rose, and, with her, all the staff, and each one of the students. When the noise had subsided Miss Edge brought the session to a close with a shout of two prime, immemorial words.

"Thank you," she cried in a great voice, looking brilliant.

"Thank you, ma'am," they all replied traditionally, and luncheon was over.

THE buzzers went for tea.

It was five o'clock. Most of the students were on their beds, after waiting in queues all afternoon to iron the cotton frocks they were to wear that same evening, for the dance. These first floor dormitories overlooked the Park, with tall windows brilliant in summer sky, as the variously bedded girls lay yawning, stretching, happy to take time because today they were allowed half an hour in which to be down for tea.

Panelling around the walls was enamelled in white paint, as also the bedsteads with pink covers, the parquet floor was waxed and gold, two naked Cupids in cold white marble, and life size, held up a slab of green above a basket grate, while white and brown arms were stretched into the tide of late afternoon pouring by; a redhead caught fire with sun like a flare and, out of the sun, eyes, opening to reflected light, like jewels enclosed by flesh coloured anemones beneath green clear water when these yawn after shrimps, disclosed great innocence in a scene on which no innocence had ever shone, where life and pursuit was fierce, as these girls came back to consciousness from the truce of a summer after luncheon before the business of the dance.

For already shadows were on the creep towards this mansion.

Beech trees were pointing fingers out along the quiet ground. Day was committed to night; the sequence here is light then darkness, and what had been begun in this community under the glare of morning, is yet to be concealed in a sharp fresh of moonlight, a statuary of day after sunset, to be lost, at last, when the usual cloud drifts over the full moon.

"Has'nt it been hot?" a girl's clear voice announced.

—How warm it had been, Miss Edge shaped five words without a sound as, at the noise of the buzzers, she turned on a chaise longue across which she was stretched in the sanctum. Then she sat up straight. How could she have dropped off, she asked herself, with Mary missing yet? She reached out for the telephone and spoke to Matron. No, there was still no news. Then, as her head cleared and she moved a dry tongue about her mouth, she felt more than ever this temporary disappearance must only be an escapade; that, at all events, their little Fiesta, as she now termed the coming entertainment, could not be cancelled at the whim of a single student who, in a moment of jealousy perhaps, had hidden herself from some adolescent qualm, thus laying their Institute open to the Grand Inquisition of a State Enquiry, and the horror of Reports.

Meantime the lovers, Sebastian and Elizabeth, were asleep in that same corner of a fallen beech found by Merode, and to which they had returned. They lay under lace of gold, through the hush of an afternoon's fine heat, at rest in one another's added warmth, in a peace of sleep.

Her tangled head lay on his arm, her left hand between the tutor's shirt and jacket. She stirred, and it woke him. When he moved, she came awake in turn. She yawned, and her tongue, too, was coated. She said, "Oh darling, it's cooler." She kissed his sticky cheek. Then she sat straight with a jerk.

He lay on his back, wore a sulky expression.

"Good heavens," she went on, "Here we've been snoring, is'nt it awful, and all the while that poor girl's lord knows where, dear. What d'you think? Is'nt it awful?"

He gently said, "Don't fuss."

"Yes but I've got to think of your position, have'nt I? I mean it's no use to make pretence that what Gapa calls the Babylonian harlots just are'nt here, is it? Particularly when they've got it in for you, darling."

"The child's probably back now," he murmured.

"Why be beastly about her, Seb? I expect, you know, she could'nt help herself, poor soul. Driven to it, don't you see, by something or other, would'nt you say?"

He raised himself. He kissed her. Then he looked at his watch.

"Tea," he said, and got to his feet.

"Well we did search about, I mean before, did'nt we?" she asked, scrambled up, and tried to smooth her slacks, at one and the same time.

When she heard the buzzers, Ma Marchbanks took a wet towel off closed eyes and let her hand fall back, which still held this towel, over the far side of the armchair. She had a splitting headache. She had been backwards and forwards in the Park through blazing heat of afternoon, and now her head drummed with sun, roll upon roll of pain behind the eyes to cauterise her brain. And she could not ignore that scene she had had with Adams.

She'd come on him at such a curious spot, the clearing by the New Plantation, where he was seated in a sort of hut, which she did not recognise, that seemed to be made entirely of old doors, and which, if behind a dwelling house instead of out in the open, could have been taken by anyone for the outside privy back of an uncultivated garden of a few wild, gay, separate flowers.

"Adams," she'd said, as she thought secure in his sympathy, for they had always got on well, " Oh Adams I am so worried." Just that. And he'd answered with a really rude voice, "It's what every man and woman living is heir to, miss." "Which does not make anything easier,

H

does it?" she'd replied, and wondered if he spent every afternoon like this, not chopping trees. At that he had come right towards her, away from that hut or whatever the thing was, and, when all was said and done, likely enough he would have acted much the same whatever she said, but he'd cried out in the revealing sunlight, and she had seen he was shaking, "Why do you keep on at me, the lot of you?" he had shouted, looking dreadful, and it was then she'd remembered he had lost his wife. "Adams," was all she was able to reply, "you are not yourself," and had walked off. But, after this, she'd searched too fast, she reminded herself to excuse the headache, had looked everywhere at twice the speed. One or two parties of girls were out as well. It showed the right spirit. And there was the haste, the haste she'd used, dashing empty handed to and fro, after she'd met Adams, must have brought on this ghastly head. But she knew the time was not now, with Miss Edge in her present mood, to dare not to put in an appearance at tea, down in the Hall.

Tremblingly, therefore, Marchbanks got up to dash cold water on her brow.

Mr Rock had been doing his kitchen out all afternoon, at work with an old man's painful slowness. Then he'd brewed himself a cup and left the pot, in case Birt and Elizabeth came, parched, in from their ploys about the grounds. Now he had lit a pipe, and gone to his pig. He leant against the sty to watch the animal laid down, in shade, with feebly twitching ears and an occasional weak grunt, given over to the heat and comfort of summer.

Mr Rock, as well, had thoughts for Mary; now and again considered whether he should not take a turn round the lake, in case the girl was floated three inches under water; and his excuse for going, if he was seen, or if he made the discovery, would of course be Ted, his goose. —For that child had been driven to desperation, he told himself, there was never a clearer case, he'd eyes in his head, he had noted for himself the overwork other children were already whispering about. Had'nt he the example of his own granddaughter before him? It was savage the extra hours they made Mary do in their kitchen just because they liked the way she served a plate, and all the while driving her on to those final examinations, with that power they had, and which was now revealed, or, so he feared, proved, of life and death.

Back in the great kitchen which the sun, now in another quarter, no longer cleft as with an axe, so that the cookers were visible and shimmered no longer, where windows, opened wide, let in a breeze which, fanning between more trestle tables set high with sandwiches and cakes, carried for some unexplained reason a smell of lemon, Marion sat beside the girls on orderly duties, at rest after the preparations for the Dance, their work finished, side by side over cups of milk coloured tea with an exhausted Mrs Blain.

It was all grey and white, then golden confectionery, and pale, tired, faces.

"Where's my Mary now this great while?" the cook demanded. "I declare I've been so rushed I never missed her."

"Why Mrs Blain," one of them answered, "have'nt you been told?" The others, dead beat, looked with open distaste at this girl. Only Moira pricked up her ears, who had done the least all afternoon.

"Noone bothers to inform me whatever," Mrs Blain said. She sat over the kitchen table, her chin propped on a hand. "But I won't have Miss Edge in here, she well knows. Baker's different. As you'll not have appreciated maybe, I never had an order for what I'm to get ready this evenin', not a word. If I've done what I have on my own responsibility, it was for you children. But I've had a feelin' nag all along at me. I'd something or somebody short, only I could'nt seem able to set a name, and there you are, it's that girl."

"Did'nt you hear?" Moira asked, after a silence. "She lost her Dolly."

"Now don't speak riddles, thank you," the cook objected, not knowing what to make of this, and deaf to some gasps the child's remark had provoked round the table.

"That's right enough, is'nt it, you others?" Moira appealed, but had no answer. "She always was a one to cry," she said. Mrs Blain fastened onto this.

"She always was a worker, if that's what you mean," the cook announced. "Has she had to go home, then, and in haste?"

"I expect," Moira said.

"Oh why will they make mysteries in this perplexed establishment?" Mrs Blain wearily accused Miss Edge. "When there's a death in the house and a girl has to haste back to comfort her old parents, well, it's natural, surely? As you would do well to remember, Moira. I'm sad to hear this news, that's all, and I can't tell why I was'nt told." She took a sip out of the cup.

Moira made some remark to a neighbour, in order to change the conversation.

"But I don't see what call there was for you to pass remarks," Mrs Blain went on to the child. "I'd go your own way and let others follow theirs. You can't tell how close they was together. Death comes like that, my girl, in every home, as you will kindly recollect next time you sit to my table."

Moira blushed. There was awkward silence.

"Say nothing, do nothing, but with a helpin' hand for them's in need," Mrs Blain ended, with satisfaction.

The cook was not a woman to allow herself to be contradicted, or even corrected, in her own kitchen. Accordingly they could not tell Mrs Blain, or at any rate not yet, not all at once.

Sebastian and Elizabeth came back to the cottage for tea and, as they passed the pigsty, there was no trace of Mr Rock. When they entered the kitchen he was not there either, nor in the living room where the sage kept his letters unopened in a trunk, because Elizabeth took the precaution to look see. She knew he would not be upstairs.

"But he's left the pot, is'nt that sweet?" she said. "And done the room out, which is so dreadful. He does make me ashamed."

"I don't know," Birt said. "He's old."

"But that's exactly it, darling," she objected, while her young man switched off the electric kettle.

"When they get beyond a certain point they do as they please," he said, still in his own voice.

"What a lot you know, Seb. At your time of life."

"Well you can't force him to act any different, can you?" he enquired in self defence. "It stands to reason he'll keep himself occupied. You must'nt let his managing the housework be an upset. You've been ill. There'll be plenty of time when you're better."

"But I'm not ill now," she said, almost as though to ask his opinion.

"Of course not." He refilled the teapot. "Sit down," he said, as if he owned the place. "Do you want to eat, because I'd have thought today too hot for food? I feel liverish after the afternoon."

She looked round and round the kitchen, without a word.

"But one thing you might say to him," he began. "Liz, are you there? About this Mary." She seemed not to pay the slightest attention. "I've an idea he's being tempted into error."

"My love," she said unexpectedly, in a contemptuous voice.

"You must listen, dear," he pleaded, but she seemed taken up with all the work done by the old man. "After so many years they get fixed in their notions," he continued. "If you and I have grudges, likely enough we'll cultivate enormous ones later, like goitres over our back sides to weigh us down, dear. And I'm sure now, he's out to make a cardinal blunder."

She glanced at him, lit a cigarette, looked away again.

"He'll report this girl's disappearance, sure to," Birt went on. "He's not said a word, of course, but I can even tell who he'll report to, Swaythling. So he can get his own back on Edge."

"And why should'nt he, if he wants?" she asked, at her most practical. But she got up and stood by the low window. Her lover saw she drooped.

"It would be fatal," he said, with increasing embarrassment.

"Look, Seb, will you understand, once and for all, I won't have a word of criticism of Gapa, even?"

"But this is not criticism, dear. If you watch someone stumble away into fast traffic, just about to be run over, you don't stand there and not take action, do you?"

She started to write her name on window glass with a forefinger that left no trace, making the trapped blue-bottles buzz.

"Dear," she said sadly, "you don't love me, you can't."

He got up at once, came to her side. But she turned from him. He stood helpless.

"You can't," she repeated, in a wail.

"We were'nt talking about ourselves," he pointed out.

"He is me," she said.

"Then listen to this, Liz please, I beg."

She moved off to the door, watched the copper in its shed. Because she had not walked out right away he felt it was safe to continue, yet was so nervous he fell back on the voice of the sort of lecturer he was not, and which he did not often use when with her.

"Consider for a moment our whole position here," he said. "A complete community related in itself, its output being what is, of course, the unlimited demand for State Servants, fed by an inexhaustible supply of keen young girls. Staffed, as well, by men and women who are only too well aware they can be replaced almost at a stroke of the pen by the State, from which there is virtually no appeal. In fact, we have here a sad bevy of teachers lying wide open to be reinvigorated, as it would be called, by new blood of which, worse luck, there is only too plentiful a supply in the Pool."

Still with her back towards him she laughed. "Darling, you do do it well," she said. He thought, —anyway she seems to listen, and was encouraged to pursue the matter.

"It follows," he proceeded, "that for the present an equipoise can be claimed here. There are, naturally, individual tensions, what one might describe as instances of disintegration or even of centrifugal action, whereby certain appear, now and again, to be flung out into the periphery of outer darkness. In other words we do not always agree between ourselves. Nevertheless I claim that we have a general measure of contentment in spite of what are, no doubt, inherited differences of outlook. To sum up, we exist together to earn a living by teaching others how to gain theirs. By and large we go about it in peace, and so I claim that there is what I can call a condition, which is to say a self compensating mechanism, in, or of, equipoise."

He paused. He was about to lose the thread. She said no word.

"But an incautious movement towards the centre," he went on with an effort, "towards the shaft upon which our little world revolves, that is to say upon the State which employs us at our main function, that of spinning like tops on our own axis," and here he gave one of his cracked laughs to point the jest, "can only fracture the spinning golden bowl, the whole unit, and bring the lot to nought, in other words, reduce us to the lowest, the unemployable."

"What is it, dear?"

"He's worried about this cottage, Liz," Sebastian replied promptly, but in his own voice.

"If he's worried, then he only is about me. I do blame myself," she said.

"Oh no, he's not," he said. Then Birt lost control. "He's past the age," he rushed on. "Besides he's ending, dying on his feet, I tell you. More than ever capable of some incredible folly."

"Don't be absurd, please," she said, and walked out in the sun in a sweat, as if she had been dowsed with cold water. He followed.

"Why, you don't mean he could have been upstairs all the time?" he whispered.

"There you are," she said, then turned on him in the sharp light. "You're terrified of Gapa, you all are, every one of you, and quite right. He'll do what he thinks fit, so he should. They've been at you about our house, though I don't know exactly how or what, and I don't want, I would'nt stoop so low."

"Justice," Sebastian began almost to shout. "Old men have no idea at their age. They're too old."

"But darling I'm sure I did'nt say a word, even, about justice."

"Yes Liz, but that's the essence of what we're discussing, surely. He's got his teeth into some injustice he thinks they've done this student, he will talk too much with the children you understand, and he's out to make trouble. But the bad part is, don't you see, he'll do it in spite of our cottage."

"It's me he wants to protect, it's me he loves," she said, showing signs of great agitation which he was too excited to notice.

"Yes, yes, he is, and that's why, and . . ." he answered in a jumble, but she burst into tears and hurled herself at him. She forced herself on his chest as he stood there, arms hard around his neck.

"Oh Seb darling, why do you frighten me so?"

He clutched her, speechless.

"If you love me like you say you do?" she went on.

He held her tight, as though to crush the fears out.

"Forget it," he said. "This girl's disappearance has bowled me over."

She relaxed a trifle in his arms.

"But you said yourself Gapa was too old, and had to be let do what he wanted."

He stiffened.

"Why, you don't mean he really has anything on with this Mary?" he asked.

"Of course not," she said. "You must be mad. At his age? Really."

"It's all very well, Liz," he said, and relaxed his hold. "They do, you know." Then he put on the lecturer's voice again. "There have been regrettable instances," he intoned. "We have only to recollect the Police Court cases in the old regime."

"Stop that, Seb. I won't have you go on like it about

Gapa. He's worth the whole lot of them." But she gave him a Judas kiss on the mouth.

"I love you," he mumbled, against lips which were thin as grass. He drew back. " No," he said, " Baker's all right. It's Edge is the trouble."

"They have no men," she said of these spinsters.

He winced. He even squirmed. But she did not notice.

"Baker can, and will, listen to reason, but the guv'nor's a real terror," he brought out at last. He took her hand. They wandered over to the sty. "She'll stop at nothing. She'd a light in her eye at lunch which made me uneasy, I can tell you. And to say what she did into the bargain."

"All right then, what did she say?" Miss Rock asked in a tired, bored voice.

"Oh not in so many words," he answered. "But it would do no harm at all to watch most conscientiously. She'll fight."

"What about?"

"To win her own way, of course. D'you suppose he could ever be persuaded to accept this election if it comes?"

"So that you can take over the cotttage?" she asked with extraordinary perspicacity in a small, languid voice, while she glanced at him.

"Hullo, what's this?" he said, halted in his tracks.

"You're not being open with me," she said, and did not meet his eyes.

He knew this was so, but could hardly admit it. He had also to bear in mind that she must be spared shocks.

"I am," he protested. "Darling, we've not kept things from each other, have we?"

"You must remember Gapa's everything, Seb."

"Everything, Liz?"

"Well, after all he's done, when he's worked his fingers to the bone, and his discoveries from the time he was young, I do think he's entitled to lead his own life from now, I mean we owe it to him, don't we, and if you loved me, darling, you'd see it that way too. I mean if he's good enough for the State, for them to let him and me live on here, then I don't see we've a right to tell him whatever it is might suit us at the moment."

"But darling, they will offer the election. The State will."

"Who said they would?"

"Miss Edge heard, Liz. When she was up in Town. This morning."

"You don't mean to say you've talked over Gapa again with that woman?"

"Of course not, dear. She just mentioned it at lunch."

"So that's what you've been at, then?"

He stayed miserably silent.

"Don't let's mention them even, any more," she said, as though she had made up her mind this was all a stupid misunderstanding. She kissed his cheek. "Shall we go down to the Lake?" she said.

"Oh, not there, Liz, I'd want to bathe," he extemporised. "They've put out an order against that on account of the weeds."

"All right, where? The beech tree?"

"Back to our private beech, Liz?" he agreed, nervously. She kissed him twice. "Dear me," she said, very shy all of a sudden. "You have become loving." And they made off, hand in hand once more.

The staff, as well as the students, were allowed half an hour in which to be down for tea today, nevertheless it was unprecedented for Miss Edge to be the ten minutes late she was, and still more so for her to be faced with the fact that many of her colleagues could be even more unpunctual than herself. There was no sign of Marchbanks, which was, perhaps, to be expected after the ridiculous misunderstanding that had been uncovered about not calling the doctor, but Miss Baker was absent, and, most significant of all, Sebastian Birt had not put in an appearance, which was inexcusable after what had occurred, and, for that matter, was still going on, perhaps.

Because they still had no news of Mary.

Edge literally itched to get to grips with Merode in spite of the rules and regulations, but now Dr Bodle had seen her at last, he'd forbidden even the simplest questioning, an injunction which Miss Edge would have been inclined to ignore, or forget, only Baker rather lost her head, had grown quite insistent. The thought of a girl laid by in full possession of her faculties, with a key to the whole mystery, protected even from points her own mother should put by the too hasty opinion of this fool of a medico, angered Miss Edge so much, now she had drunk some tea and felt restored, enraged her so deeply that, from the dais, she turned another terrible look on her charges, and several were caught in the middle of huge yawns; the soft, brilliant wetness of their pink mouths, and shining pearly teeth, being struck at her glance to pure enchantment, under wide, astonished eyes.

"Can Dakers and I help with the flowers afterwards, ma'am?" Winstanley asked.

"Thank you. I really feel I can manage," Miss Edge answered. She glared around. There was one good thing, she told herself, the girls were no longer at their whispers, there were none of those stares as at luncheon. But, on the other hand, the atmosphere was lax. They sat over tea as if washed out.

Next she examined her pile of blooms.   Was it imagination, or had these in some way settled?   But surely not by their own weight?

How absurd that, at lunch, she had had this feeling the child was underneath.

And certainly the flowers were fading.

She took another glance at the students.   No, they showed small interest in High Table.   They entered by dribs and drabs, lazily, slack.   Miss Edge clenched her thin fists.

She sent a frightful look at the gigantic, repeating gramophone, dumb in a corner.

"Has it been overhauled?" she asked at large.

"What is that, ma'am?" Winstanley questioned.

"Why, the music for our Ball of course," Edge replied. "We do not want to be suspended, so to speak, by a breakdown."

"Oh, the old thing's in a good mood now, ma'am.   We tried the records as late as Tuesday."

"A mood, Winstanley?   Will you arrange for the car to go at once over to Bradhampton to pick up Edwards, that is his name, Edwards?   Then he can give the mechanism a thorough doing."

"Your car, ma'am?" Winstanley said.   "But Miss Baker's taken that."

Edge felt her heart lurch.   —Hermione take the car and not say a word?   What was this?

"Dear, dear, where is my memory?" she lied.   "The truth is I have so much before each of these Festivities I sometimes wonder how I shall get through.   Then you might send word, and he can come up on his bicycle." —Like the policeman, she thought.   But Baker must have something up her sleeve which could only have to do with Mary.   How disloyal not to have mentioned it.

Miss Edge once more began to feel nervous.

She looked about the great room. By good fortune none of the girls seemed to watch the pile of blooms.

"Did she say when she would be back, then?" she asked.

"Miss Baker, ma'am? She's upstairs, resting."

"I distinctly understood her to tell me she had to run over somewhere," Edge lied again, to save her face. But she let all the anguish she felt sound in the voice she used.

At this precise moment one of the orderlies brought her Principal the post. A letter, marked O.M.S. in great black capitals, was addressed to her personally, and she opened it at once.

"*Dear Miss Edge*," she read, "*I am directed by Majesty's Secretary of State Swaythling to inform you of the following, reached by the Secretary's State Council as conclusions, and with which he is in agreement. He intends to implement these conclusions by means of a Directive to be issued as soon as possible.*

(1) *That, generally speaking, there is insufficient opportunity at present for those girls under tuition for State Service, through-out the various Institutes, to take part in practical management.*

(2) *That, for this purpose, it is advisable they should be provided with pig farms.*

(3) *Under the supervision of their Principals, students should run such an undertaking themselves, co-operatively, but in strict conformity with all Directives as may from time to time be issued by Majesty's Minister of Agriculture to professional pig farmers.*

Finally: It is anticipated by these means that students will avail themselves of the opportunity afforded to learn from practical experience the day to day problems which arise in Administration.

Bearing in mind the need for stringent economy which obtains at present, your suggestions as to how this scheme can best be set in motion, together with those of your colleague, who should have received a similar communication by the same post, can be addressed to me, so that I have these on my desk not later than today week.   Your fellow worker.   John Inglethwaite."

Miss Edge was quite pale when she had finished.

One of the juniors seated below the dais said, to make conversation with an older girl,

"Gosh, will you just look at Edge now, again."

"She's not so bad," the senior tolerantly answered. "It's your first summer here, I suppose ?   She's always a trifle nervy before the dance.   But she'll be very different once we're under way."

Edge folded the communication from Inglethwaite and laid this on the table.   She pressed the flat of a thin, open hand down over it.   She was breathing heavily.   —Pig- . sties all over the wonderful Place? And the Stench? There were times, indeed, when one's ultimate loyalties were tested.

Not a scrap of help could be expected from Baker, who would find the whole idea quite practical; no, Miss Edge decided, no, her colleague would just remark . . . 'how quaint, how black and white.'

She looked with anguish about the great room in which they were to dance.   It had been The Banqueting Hall, burned down in Edwardian times.   When the owner rebuilt he had replaced a vaulted roof of stone by oak, and put flat oak panelling eight foot up the walls, all of which, including a vast bow window over the Terraces, had been varnished a hot fox red, then, at some later date, treated with lime, until the wood turned to its present colour, the head of a ginger haired woman who was going white as her worries caught up, in the way these will.

But Miss Edge's glance, now, was seeking the familiar, she sought comfort in what she had known so long, there was a long appeal about her look.

"Oh, we must give them a good Time," she said aloud. "It shall be a real Success."

A younger girl turned under this gaze to another, and whispered,

"I bet Edge is a bit inside out to do with Mary."

"Why, whatever for?"

"Have'nt you heard? There was a telegram to say the sister Doll was badly ill at home, and she was to go at once. Muriel had it from one of the seniors, who was there when this wire came. Rotten luck, on the night of the dance."

Her friend said, "I thought I had'nt seen Mary today," and went on to speak of the time she'd had to wait before she had been able to iron her dress.

An evening air, entering cool by wide windows, wafted the scent of that pyre of flowers to Miss Edge, reminded the lady that she had not yet had her stroll, that there could be no leisure for that now, with all she knew she had still to do. At the same time it carried a small buzz to her sharp ears. She at once looked more closely at the azalea and rhododendron. With a great rush of horror, she realised the whole pile of blooms was alive with blue-bottles.

For a moment she thought she might faint.

She looked again. She forced herself to admit that, at first glance, she had exaggerated. There were not as many as she had thought. Yet the scent was distinctive, sickly. So what did this new frightfulness portend? And how could they ever dispose, now, of this huge mass of blooms? While the whole idea, that there must be the body underneath, was unhealthy, morbid, too absurd, would she have to face it, after the girls had made these flowers into great swags of fragrant colour at her direction on the walls, would it be that buzzing flies might stay round the bouquets, turn all to decay and desecration?

Her mouth and throat burned dry. Try as she might, she could not swallow. She picked up the cup of tea with hands atremble, but before she could bring it to her lips, she retched.

She supposed there was noone who had not noticed. She looked about, clinking the cup down. And not a soul seemed to have seen.

—How idiotic to start an illness at this juncture, when she would get small help from Baker, goodness knows, and with the Dance upon them. But she swore she must protect her Girls; they should never know. It was Founder's Day. Everything must proceed, and in due order.

At this moment she saw their little red State tourer come up the drive past these Banqueting Hall windows, attended by its cloud of dust. A middle aged woman, on whom Miss Edge had not set eyes in her life, sat alone in the back. The worst was, if this should turn out to be some new plan of Baker's, she could not ask who in the world might the creature be. Then Edge wondered whether Mr Rock had a younger sister, or perhaps it was even Elizabeth's mysterious aunt. She watched the staff, but they seemed to pay small heed.

Mr Dakers entered.

"You are not last," Edge said, at her most gracious, in an allusion to Marchbanks and Sebastian, the intense curiosity making her feel livelier already.

"My apologies, ma'am," the man replied. "I do not know how it can have happened."

"You need not insist," she assured him. "Founder's Day is one occasion in the year when we may all relax. Until evening, that is, when the real business of our holiday commences, with music, with the first waltz." She smiled in a friendly manner. And the smile stayed frozen on her face as Marion entered from the direction of

I

the Sanctum. The child had been in tears again. She
bent to Edge's ear.

"Miss Baker says, ma'am," she whispered. "Can you
spare a minute. Mrs Manley's just arrived."

—Manley, Edge asked herself as she rose, Manley?
Why Merode of course. Merode Manley. Oh, what
devilry was this?

When Edge came in Baker was pouring a cup of tea
for the woman. She remarked, "Dear, this is Mrs
Manley, Merode's aunt."

"How d'you do, Mrs Manley," Edge said, while she
took her hand, "I'm sorry we've had to bring you all this
way," she added, so as not to admit ignorance of her
colleague's intentions.

"How d'you do," the woman replied. "But I still don't
quite understand," she said to Miss Baker.

"I was just explaining to Merode's aunt the predicament
in which we find ourselves," Baker suggested diplo-
matically, because it was quite on the cards this woman
might give trouble. She had the air of a determined
creature. "There is nothing the matter with Merode,"
the Principal went on. "On the contrary, we've always
found her so helpful, have'nt we dear? But I must say, in
the present circumstances, we hardly know what to decide."

"It is Miss Baker, is'nt it?" Mrs Manley addressed
Edge's colleague. "Then I'd be so grateful if you could
tell me what this is all about. You say she is quite well?"

"Yes, Mrs Manley, I'm glad to assure you the doctor's
given a clean bill. But the truth of the matter is, she was
out most of last night."

"Who with?" Mrs Manley asked sharp.

"Another student," Edge replied, as quick.

"A girl?" Mrs Manley enquired, turning what Miss Edge decided was a hostile look upon her.

"We have no male students here," Edge spoke out severely, so much as to suggest that a joke in bad taste had been cracked.

"And the other girl is not home yet," Miss Baker explained.

"Yes, I see," Mrs Manley said, not in the least apologetic.

"So we were wondering if you could help," Edge announced, as though her colleague and herself had hatched a curious plot.

"I wonder if I could see Merode?" the woman asked, but in a hard voice.

"I think that would be best," Miss Edge agreed.

"But, dear, the doctor," Baker objected. "He said she was on no account to be pressed. And we have our regulations."

"Surely the child's own aunt . . .?" Mrs Manley asked.

"She was in pyjamas," Edge interrupted, as if this explained all.

"Well of course, since it was at night," the strange woman said.

"Do have another of these cakes. We rather pride ourselves on them," Miss Baker offered, and it occurred to Edge that, everything considered, this particular aunt and guardian was having a fine tea. Did they have nothing at home, for them to eat so enormously whenever they came over? Was it fair to the girls in the holidays?

"Thank you," Mrs Manley accepted. "No," she went on, "had you said Merode wore her day things, then I would have been worried."

"She has torn the leg," Miss Edge pointed out.

"But you told me she was not hurt."

"The trouser leg," Edge patiently explained.

"On a briar, because it was dark, no doubt," the guardian answered, and again showed relief in her tone of voice.

"Oh, it had occurred to us this thing might have been worse," Miss Edge commented, at her most dry. Baker gave a glance of warning.

"We wondered if we could put our heads together," she said in a conciliatory way.

"I'd like a word with the child first," her aunt insisted.

"Of course," Miss Baker said. "The only trouble is the doctor . . ." and she did not finish her sentence.

"You surely did not get me over to forbid my seeing my Merode," Mrs Manley objected, and appeared to harden.

"There are also our regulations," Baker pointed out, in embarrassment.

The relative snorted.

"All the more reason, then," she said, starting to get her gloves and bag together.

"I think what my colleague tried to explain, without having to cross the i's and dot the t's, is this," Miss Edge announced. "You cannot, of course, be familiar with the Directives under which we carry on our work here. They are designed to protect us, as well as the students, from day to day inconveniences that may arise where a community of young people exists."

"But you are not going to tell me this happens commonly, Miss Edge."

"In the ten years we have been here, I do not know when we have had someone over at such short notice," the lady answered, then waited. When there was no retort, and she had given Baker a look to express her disagreement at the summoning of what had turned out to be a recalcitrant witness, Miss Edge continued,

"We are fronted by an entire scaffolding of Reports. In certain circumstances we are obliged to render a Report of behaviour to our Superior Authority.   And, if we are to do so, the most stringent Rules obtain.   Access to the party concerned before she has given an explanation is rigidly excluded.   I cannot see her, my colleague even cannot do so, noone can intervene before she has given her own story."

"Then why have me over?"

"We thought it the human thing," Baker interjected, miserably.

"But what's behind this, what has she done?" Mrs Manley complained.

"There's a man in it, I'm very much afraid," Baker muttered.

"No really Miss Edge . . ." the aunt began.

"Miss Baker," Edge corrected, as if to dissociate herself from the line which was being taken.

". . . I can't accept that," Mrs Manley went on, with a look of venom at Edge. " Only sixteen, and not ever a hint of the kind at home."

"We sometimes notice with families . . . where the parents are no longer together . . ." Baker uttered in a faint voice, mixing Mary with Merode.

"Their orphans wander about the garden at night in pyjamas?" Mrs Manley asked, and actually laughed aloud.

"Miss Baker has written the standard work on this difficult subject," Edge said, thrown back on the defensive.

"Well I don't know that my husband would'nt agree with her," the woman announced in what could only be termed a fruity voice.   "But you and I realise it's hardly usual, don't we?" she had the impudence to ask Edge.

"I am afraid we shall not see eye to eye," this lady said, while Baker made a gesture of weariness.

"There's a whole history of such cases," she explained.

"I've no doubt," Mrs Manley agreed, conscious perhaps that she had gone too far. "And of course I'm grateful to you for the chance to put our heads together," she added with what was, to Edge, an altogether offensive familiarity. "But I have the right to see my ward at any time, I hope?"

"Of course," Miss Baker said.

"Yes," Edge put in. "The question is, how not to make it harder for her."

"In view of your rules about reports, you mean?" the aunt enquired.

"Just so."

"Oh well, Miss Edge, I hope it won't come to that, indeed not," Mrs Manley answered, in such a way that the lady felt this relative was in full command. Then the aunt tried a shot in the dark. "But I do feel I have a right to learn how it was you came to the conclusion there might be a boy in it, before I go up to see my niece," she said.

"She told Miss Marchbanks," Baker explained, quite unaware.

"Exactly," Mrs Manley said. "But did she write out an account?"

"Oh no," Baker replied, with signs of distress because she saw looming ahead the awkwardness that Merode had fainted. But Edge could see further. She was on tenterhooks.

"Then this Marchbanks person questioned her?"

"Yes, and such a distressing thing occurred," Baker hurried on, regardless. "The dear child fainted."

"Fainted?" Mrs Manley echoed, in a voice of horror. It was then that Baker saw the pit she had dug for herself.

"Oh, not what you think at all," she said pettishly. "It was what made the doctor diagnose shock."

"Third degree shock," Mrs Manley snorted. Edge had to keep herself from clicking her fingers together she was so exasperated.

"Really, madam, I cannot have this," Baker said, with great firmness, rising to the occasion. "I asked you here to have a quiet talk about what was best in the child's own interest, and you make suggestions as to our competence. Perhaps I should remind you that the State, when It delegated Responsibility to my colleague and myself, gave us a large measure of protection, or latitude if you prefer the word. I asked you over because I felt that was the human thing to do. If you insist you must see your niece before she has voluntarily made her explanation, then my Report shall go in and I'll note the fact in what I have to write, which may go hard with her. After all, I can lay claim to some experience."

"There is one of our students missing yet," Edge added, white of face.

"But what d'you get out of your girls if you won't allow anyone to go near 'em?" Mrs Manley asked, in a humble voice. Baker, at this point, was misled.

"My dear Mrs Manley," she said, back at once to her most expansive. "We are not like that with our children. There is perfect confidence."

"And if they won't talk?"

"Well then, that is very difficult, is'nt it?"

"But Miss Baker, who is this Marchbanks?"

"Our deputy. We both have to go to London Wednesdays, and while we are away she takes our place. We have complete faith in her, is'nt that so, Edge?"

"Of course," Miss Edge agreed, showing in her voice the disapproval she felt at the line their little talk was still taking.

"And, in spite of the rule you have about interviews with your students, she was brought before Miss Marchbanks?"

"She was found hidden," Edge interrupted, finally taking charge.

"Then who hid her?"

Miss Edge answered with a prolonged shrug of the shoulders.

"That's one point on which I'd like to see Merode, of course," Mrs Manley said. "But this woman interviewed the child?"

"Certainly not," Edge objected. "When Merode was discovered she was brought before our deputy, as she would have been before us if we had not been obliged to be elsewhere."

"She was asked no questions?"

"Miss Marchbanks has thirty years in the State Service. I am confident she would never betray her Trust."

"But excuse me, Miss Edge, you have'nt answered my question."

"I have some regard for accuracy, madam. Since neither myself or my colleague were present . . ."

"And yet my little girl fainted?"

"She blurted something out about a man and then she fainted," Edge agreed.

"You see, it is just this point that I find so difficult to understand," Mrs Manley appealed to Baker. "What man? Where is he? If she volunteered what she did, why don't I know about him? And in her pyjamas, too."

"But my dear lady, it is precisely why we asked you to come over. Merode has been simply splendid the whole time she has been here. We just wondered if she had given any indication in her letters?"

"There is one of our girls we cannot account for yet," Edge repeated, in a warning voice.

"But I've had not a hint from the child," the aunt protested. "She's always been so very happy with you both. Of course, I don't say she has no secrets from me. I know

I never told my mother a word, and I don't expect any different from my poor sister's girl." Edge sniffed audibly, but was not noticed. "Yet I'm sure, if she'd fallen under the influence of an older child, then I'd have had at least an idea."

"And there's been no sign?" Baker asked, hoping against hope.

"Not one," Mrs Manley answered. "But I'll tell you a perfectly simple explanation of the whole affair."

"By all means," Baker encouraged, dubious to the last.

"Sleepwalking," the aunt announced, in barely concealed triumph. And Miss Baker was so flabbergasted at this forgotten echo of the dawn that, without more ado, she took the woman up to Merode at once.

Edge did not stay to argue. There was no time, she felt. As soon as Baker had led the woman out, she herself hurried off to get the decorations done because, now they had decided to hold their Ball, it must be the most successful ever. The girls simply must enjoy themselves.

She found a number of her charges waiting, unconcerned, by the side of that horrible pile of blooms.

She concentrated on Moira, in whom she had sensed almost an antagonism these last few weeks.

"Here we are, dears," she cried out gaily, at her most genuine. It would be enough, in a day or two, to think of the implications with Merode's aunt, when they came to write out their Report.

"Moira, will you take the satin ribbon out of that drawer and divide it into twenty-one inch lengths? You will find scissors at the back. Then you must cut it

square, with two v's afterwards at each end. Be as neat
as you can, child. Tie the branches in bundles. Now the
others," and she approached the pyre with a distaste they
did not seem to share. "We'll have you parcelling bundles
up." She flicked with a long handkerchief at the blooms,
was relieved to find no flies. They misunderstood the
gesture. "Oh, we sprinkled with water to keep fresh,"
two or three sang out. "We've put sheets of paper round
to save the floor," they added, and then scent from that
mass of flowers came over her again. She was heartened
to find this sharp as wine, now day was cooler.

"How will I tell the inches?" Moira enquired, while her
companions attacked the pile.

"Hurry, Moira," they called. "We'll catch up in no
time."

"Marion, fetch the steps," Edge ordered, relieved that
the senior had recovered from her last bout of crying.
"Judge the best way you can, dear," she said to Moira, and
thought —I must have been poorly at lunch, it was the
heat, forgetting she had felt so bad at tea. "Busy as bees,
aren't we?" she added aloud, standing dead still in the
midst of commotion, while that heap of lovely blooms
was robbed and diminished by her charges.

When several swags of azalea had been tied in neat
bows, Miss Edge led a short procession down, through
evening sun, to the alcove which looked over descending
Terraces towards the trees beyond, —the blessed, dear
prospect. She closed her mind to Mrs Manley. After
she had given directions, she stood at one of the windows
and lovingly, sun in her eyes, watched the Park. Until
she remembered.

"Oh my dears," she called out. They turned beaming
faces which she could not see for sun, for this was the mood
in which they most liked Edge. "We are going to be
allowed to keep pigs, have you heard?"

There was a descant of small cries.

"But where, we have'nt been told, of course," Edge said, her wrinkled face back to the prospect. "How shall we hide them?"

"Down by Mr Rock's, I'd say," Moira proposed, because she would then see more of the old man.

"Not a bad idea at all," Miss Edge approved.

"And he could look after ours," Moira went on. "He's done such wonders with Daise."

"We shall have to think about that," Edge objected, showing signs of reluctance. "The idea is you should manage everything yourselves, under supervision of course."

"Oh, what a good plan, ma'am," they said, although several, if she had only known, were no keener than their Principal. And this lady did not disclose her fears. Why should she?

"We shall go into everything," she promised.

"When will it come about?" one of the girls asked.

"All in good time," Edge answered. "Now back with you and fetch more bundles, or we shall never be done." She was, for the moment, left alone with Moira.

"He really would be best," the girl informed Miss Edge. "He knows everything about them."

"I'd not tell him so, if I were you," the guv'nor said, certain the child would rush to do it if advised against.

"Why not, Miss Edge?" Moira asked, and went beyond what was permissible when she omitted to call the Principal madam. However Edge contented herself by merely saying,

"Think."

Blind sun, three quarters down the sky, was huge to the right. A soft breeze swayed curtains. Miss Edge regretted her walk, which she usually took about this time. She could have gone by the old man's cottage to prospect for a site to place the pigsties, up wind of course.

"He has ideas about himself, you know," she added.

As they were still alone for the moment, Moira thought she would make the best use of her chances.

"Is that right, ma'am, when they reckon Merode's aunt's here?" The scissors went snip into the ribbon, shiny, primrose yellow.

"Why yes, Moira," Edge answered, then screwed her eyes up against the sun. Was that Mr Rock, or not, afar off there, skirting the beeches to get down to the Lake?

"Is she all right again?" the child asked, about Merode.

"There's never been anything the matter, not so far as I know," Edge replied of Mrs Manley, aloof and absent. For it was Mr Rock after all. Much worse he was deliberately exercising his animal. How intolerable, if she had taken her stroll, to have come upon him driving the slobbery pig.

"But is'nt it strange about Mary, ma'am?"

Miss Edge barely heard.

"Moira," she said. "You have younger eyes than I. Look over there and tell me what you see. Is that Mr Rock? And what has he got with him?"

The child collected her face into an expression which the old man, had he been present, would have found adorable in the effort to pierce the slanting sun, which turned her skin to coral, her red hair to live filaments.

"Why how sweet," the child exclaimed. "Yes, it is him. He's taking darling Daise for a run."

The others came up, then, with bunches of red and white rhododendron.

"But not loose, dear?" Edge protested.

"Oh, she's absolutely safe, is'nt she?" Moira appealed to her companions. "Why Mr Rock's often let her out while we've been there, when she's stayed so busy and well-behaved."

At this moment there was the sound of a motor car engine. Coming or going? The Principal looked left, then right. Almost at once their little red State tourer came down the Drive, its cloud of dust not yet martialled but already falling in behind. Mrs Manley was seated in the back. She looked straight ahead. By some trick of the light, perhaps, her face was purple.

"That's Mrs Manley, is'nt it?" Moira cannily enquired.

"She's been to see Merode," a child said.

"I'll bet she asked some posers," yet another suggested.

"We'll have to hasten if we're ever to get through," Edge propounded, and saw, or thought she saw, that Mr Rock had stopped to look. Their car, so soon invisible to Edge, must have just been entering the Trees. For a cloud of dust now lay afar, at the Drive's opening, and was a delicate pink.

The old man seemed to stand fast, the better to watch.

The decorations for Founder's Day were already traditional, although the Institute had been open for only ten years. In consequence there was no need for Edge to give orders, her presence was designed to preclude innovation, such as the fir branches Marchbanks had so foolishly suggested. Hooks were fixed permanently in the walls at proper intervals, and the work of tying azalea and rhododendron to hang head downwards in separate, glistening great masses went on apace without Edge having to give a thought to the proceeding. Indeed, despite a renewed preoccupation with Mr Rock, she was already conscious of a glow within her at the prospect of so much that would inevitably please, and which was to be enjoyed and enjoyed; when the trees' shadows crept at last over the mansion, and then there was moonlight; when Baker, with herself, in front of all the students dressed in their clear frocks, could sway out in one another's arms at last to open everything to that thunder of the waltz.

She had dismissed from her mind each carking memory of the Manley creature. The die was cast. They were to go on with the Dance, any other course would be unthinkable. So she was happy in anticipation, culpably at rest. She could even forgive the sage his sow.

Accordingly she had, at first, no qualms when she heard a child back at the pyre exclaim, "Why, whatever's this?" And paid no heed to the giggles which followed. But when, in the girls' chatter, she caught one say gleefully, "It's the living spit of Mary," she did turn, then, with a sickening premonition of the worst, to have the quick comfort to realise they had found what was only a short, small object. Yet she moved down upon them at once. "What's this?" she demanded, horrified by the agitation in her voice. The students parted. And she saw, and it gave her such a frightful turn she straightaway fainted, a rabbity Rag Doll dressed gaily in miniature Institute pyjamas, painted with a grotesque caricature of Mary's features on its own flat face, laid disgustingly on a bit of mackintosh, embowered by these blooms.

When Edge came to, she was laid out on her chaise longue in the Sanctum. Miss Baker ministered with smelling salts, while Marion stood at a cut glass bowl in which were cubes of ice. The late sun caught these with sufficient force to distress Edge, and she closed her eyes once more. The minutes passed.

"It's been so hot," Baker said finally, with vexed accents. Miss Edge looked at her, and again had to turn her face from the intolerable insistence of salts on top of light. She even squirmed in protest.

"That's right, dear," came Baker's voice. "Now rest."

Upon which, Edge raised a hand to her hair and looked about. She fastened on Marion.

"What a remarkable thing," she said, not without effort.

"Don't give it another thought," Miss Baker ordered, bright as the day outside.

"But did you see too, Marion?" Edge enquired. The girl seemed so weighed down by guilt, almost as though she were in for another bout of crying. Her Principal noted this from a vast distance of lassitude, which allowed her to ask questions out of a calm, almost intellectual curiosity.

"Yes, ma'am. Oh, I have it here."

"Plenty of time, Edge," Miss Baker warned. "Now, would'nt you like Dr Bodle?"

"So foolish of me," Miss Edge lied to the child. "I thought it was a . . . a dead rabbit," she said in anti-climax, voicing the secret, known throughout the Institute, that she had a terror of rabbits dead. "And then I did realise, only too late, too late." A tear began to roll from each of her blue, old eyes. "I'll never forgive myself," she ended, in a small voice and a hiccup.

"Nonsense," Baker said, "It's the heat. You're over-strained."

A silence followed, while Miss Edge pulled herself together.

"But was there, really, a Doll?" she asked. Her colleague turned away, anguished. Miss Edge did not notice.

"Oh yes, ma'am. Someone in the kitchen said she'd lost hers."

"Someone said . . .?"

"Who was that, then?"

"I can't remember exactly. But she did know Mary had lost it," Marion explained.

The older women could not disguise the fresh shock this was to them. Miss Edge sat bolt upright even.

"Who?" Baker gasped.

"Mary, ma'am."

"No, but who informed you?"

There was another pause.

"I can't seem to remember, quite," the girl told Baker.

"Well," Miss Edge said, better already now that she was following a cold scent. "Suppose you go up to Matron and inform her from me that you are to stay with her until you do?"

"Oh but ma'am, and the dance?"

"It will come back before then. Yes, run along, Marion."

The moment the door was closed on the girl, Miss Edge burst out,

"Were there Pins in? Had it a painted Heart?"

"My dear," Baker expostulated. "This is practically no more than a golliwog."

"Oh my heart," Edge said. "How terrible."

"Now, I'm sure it is'nt what you think," the other tried to comfort her colleague. "This is all a mistake."

"I knew, right through lunch," Miss Edge insisted.

There came a knock on the door.

"Come in," Edge cried, trembling, and sat up straight again.

"I thought I ought to tell you, ma'am," Marion said, as she sidled in, "But I just remembered I heard Mary got a wire. She's gone home."

"Gone home?" the two Principals burst out. "When?" Edge demanded.

"Mrs Blain told us there was a wire to say the sister was sick," Marion announced in a shocked voice.

"Did any telegrams come last night?" Baker asked her colleague, because all communications to the students were read before being handed over.

"You can go to Matron now, Marion," Edge ordered.

"And remember, not a word about any of this to the others. You still have something to tell us, child."

As soon as the girl was out of their room Miss Baker got on the telephone to Marchbanks. The reply was that nothing had come for Mary in the past week.

"She could have stopped the postman," Baker suggested.

"My dear," Edge said faintly, "I still cannot believe it, and now this terrible Doll in her image. At her age too."

"Then what d'you really think?" Baker asked, her voice trembling.

"The Lake," Miss Edge insinuated, almost hoarse.

"Oh no, not that, dear."

"You see, Baker, I understand now why Rock should have been on his way down."

"Last night?"

"No, just a moment ago, with his pig."

"With his pig!"

"In South Eastern Europe, Hermione, they are used for tracking."

"But listen," Baker announced, "this is too mysterious. The child's alone in the world, except for her parents living apart in Brazil. She has nobody to send wires."

"Are you sure?"

"I looked up the card this morning, don't you remember?"

"Then it must have been a man," Edge said, from the depths.

"No, I don't think so. I'll tell you why. They may simply have invented the whole tale."

"Oh, Baker, what is the matter with the Police that she cannot be found?"

"They have just made it all up," Baker insisted.

"We must cancel the Dance, there is nothing else for it," Miss Edge then said.

But her colleague was on the house telephone again.

K

She found out the postman had not been yesterday, after the second delivery at lunch time.

"And she laid our tea, that was the last I saw of her, Edge. There was nothing, then, not in the way she looked."

"That is as may be," Miss Edge replied. Like a spoiled child, she put her face away from Baker along the back of the chaise longue.

"Of all our children she was the truthfullest, dear," Miss Baker continued. "They are good girls. It's some misunderstanding."

"I blame myself, now, that I went to London," Miss Edge announced, but in stronger tones.

"What else could we have done? We can't have a hue and cry, dear."

"You think not?" Edge asked coldly.

"Well, not yet, can we? We don't know much for sure."

"What did that ridiculous Manley woman say after she had seen Merode?" Edge demanded, at her driest.

"My dear, I so regret ever having called the creature over," Miss Baker protested. "How wise of the State to lay down that the girls must be held incommunicado after serious affairs like this, until they have written their own account."

Miss Edge listened in silence, thus forcing her question which was a reproof.

There was a pause.

"Still sleepwalking," Baker confessed at last.

"And Mary?" Edge insisted.

"Nothing to do with Merode, naturally," Miss Baker replied in a bitter voice. "I blame myself," she volunteered.

Her colleague did not help in any way. Still holding her face averted, she began a cold silence.

"But I do feel, dear," Baker tried once more, "that it

would really be unwise for us to cancel our arrangements, at any rate before we learn the truth. It will go so much the harder with the child when she does turn up."

Edge sniffed.

"After all," Miss Baker went on, in a soft voice. "How does a dolly alter matters? We were going ahead before we came across that, weren't we? What d'you think?"

There was a longer pause. Then, from the same remote position, Miss Edge was so good as to say,

"Let me see it once again."

When she had the thing in a hand, she did not raise her head but laid the Doll out along the chair back, on a level with her eyes. Its limbs were intolerably loose, as before rigor mortis. The flat, white, miniature, flannel face of Mary was, of course, unwinking, and Edge saw the eyes, the mouth and nose had been drawn with blood red lipstick. But her heart grew lighter as she began to believe it was not, after all, altogether like the child. Yet she held the thing elegantly over a cushion, with a kind of high bred weariness. At last she said,

"You know this could be Merode, or even Marion."

"D'you think?" Baker asked, with hope.

"You understand they are too old, Hermione, for dolls?"

"But, Mabel, are they? We've known it here, you know."

"There is just this about the pyjamas," Edge went on. "Merode was found in hers, I recollect. It may only be a stupid prank."

"That is certainly an angle," Miss Baker said with rising spirits, as ever the optimist.

"I might confront the child," Edge suggested. She sat up, laid the Doll on her lap.

"Oh but Mabel, don't you consider you ought to rest? You must remember you've had a turn, quite apart from our directives."

"I feel somehow the whole future of this beautiful Place is at stake, dear," Miss Edge answered. "Of course, I would not say a word to the girl. I might just go into her room with it."

"But how d'you feel?"

"I am quite all right, thank you, Hermione."

"Then in that case," said Miss Baker, to whom it had become imperative to escape, "I was thinking I'd just run down by the Lake. It would ease my mind."

Edge made no reply. She picked up the Doll by its short neck, and left, staggering a little.

As Mr Rock drew near the water he was more than ever sure it had been a mistake to bring Daisy. She was not ringed, and, now that they had moved once more under the beeches, she kept turning last year's leaves with her snout, also the ground beneath, but so slowly and with such loud delight that they hardly progressed forward; and the ends of sticks of sunlight, pointed down from high trees, moved across his pig's flanks like pink and cream snails, then over his own face in little balls of warmth.

There were even moments when Daisy actually knelt, and all was still.

—He would never get her home, he knew. She would have to be left to make her own way back at meal time, but there had been no other excuse to go down by the water, and someone had to after the poor girl, because those evil ninnies, whose absolute power so absolutely corrupted them, were too muddleheaded, or imperious, to see what must be done in merest human charity. Ted, his goose, covered a deal of ground each day, besides he had no call to look for her, and then pigs, as was well known, possessed a sense of smell which might come in handy amongst thick reeds. Imagine not organising a search as soon as they had learned, the fabulous Neroines, already tuning their fiddles before the rout, the fireman's ball.

He wiped his forehead with the back of a hand, after which he polished the spectacles. He clucked at Daisy to encourage her, then found that he had come into full sunlight, and could see the lake at last.

On the side by which he was approaching, water was dammed well up above ground level, a white mirror almost to the level of his eyes, and out of which grew rushes, pink and green, with willows and other smaller gray bushes everlastingly leant over their several likenesses in a faint lakeside, sunlit smell of rotting, for perhaps all of three times seventy years.

He reminded himself that he should not come out from the shelter of the trees, must not be seen. Daisy would be his eyes.

At the scent of the lake she suddenly trotted forward, burst through a little undergrowth with a great amount of noise and, while he stepped back into concealing shade, she halted at the brink, nose up, ears folded forwards over violet eyes, and with deeply heaving flanks, by which Mr Rock assumed she must wish to challenge, or had sensed, someone on the further bank to whom, in her startled whiteness, she might seem his goose, he thought, if the person had not got his or her right spectacles.

All was still, not a bird moved, but the sun was already turning edges of green leaves red, and soon it would be time for russet pheasants roosting.

Meantime Miss Baker, going down to this lake another way, for all her fat moved silently to come upon the

sergeant seated on a log in the traditional attitude, a high
helmet on the ground at the side, mopping his brow with
a red, bandanna handkerchief.

She was much settled at the sight of him, took it for
proof that Edge, when that lady interviewed the man,
had counselled his keeping an eye upon the place.

"Why sergeant," she said, therefore, in an arch voice,
"this is a pleasure I must say's entirely unexpected."

He jumped as though he had been shot.

"Why Miss Baker, ma'am," he exclaimed.   Getting up
he replaced the helmet with a guilty movement.

"It has been warm, certainly."

"It has that," the man replied.

"Take a few steps with me," she invited.   "And to
what do we owe this pleasure?" she asked, as he fell in
at her side.

"I was up at the house this noon, ma'am," he answered.

Baker did not know how much her colleague had given
away, but she, like Miss Edge before her, would never
be so injudicious as to disclose that what one of them did
could be without the consent, and full agreement, of the
other.

"I don't fancy there's much in all this," she said about
the disappearance.   He kept in mind Miss Edge's hint as
to men of a certain age and replied,

"I'm right glad to hear you say so, ma'am."

"Really?" she asked.   "You've some information that
has'nt yet reached us, perhaps?"   She was overconfident.
She was so sure that all would yet be well.

"Not us, we have'nt," he said.   But he considered these
two women were not being straight with the police.
It was why he had returned to what he called 'the
scene.'   So he added, "Then you've a student still missing,
ma'am?"

Baker did not realise that her colleague, when she

talked with the sergeant, had, as usual, pursued a devious course.

"Why yes," she answered. "Well, after all," she went on. "What does one mean when one says missing?"

This struck an answering note in the sergeant's head. At the station much of their time was taken up with young women adrift, who, after fourteen days, returned brown and happy from a fortnight with a boy by the ocean.

"You've got something there, ma'am," he agreed.

"It's a question of degree," she elaborated.

"I wonder if I might put a question, ma'am?" the policeman said, his doubts back again. "What does Miss Edge have in view?"

"I'm afraid she's very worried, sergeant."

"On what grounds, miss?"

Baker then made the mistake of taking the man for a fool.

"Why because we have a girl absent, of course," she said.

"Strange Miss Edge should never mention the disappearance, when she had me along only this morning." Baker's heart fell. The sergeant had spoken quite disagreeably. It was now obvious that one had to be careful with him. Oh, what had her colleague been about?

As warily as possible she began to explain the danger of Reports, and how fatal these were to a girl's chances if they had to be written. "In their own best interests we leave it to the very last, except for impossible cases, of course. To tell you the honest truth, as one State Official to another," she tried to humour him, "in nearly every instance we manage to forget to make one out, sergeant."

"Yes, ma'am, we also have reports to render. And it goes hard with us if there's a fatality we don't know all about, almost before it's happened."

"A fatality?" Baker echoed, with a wail.

"To a manner of speaking," the policeman said, in a low voice.

At this moment they came within sight of the water and Daisy, from a considerable distance, saw them first. She gave a warning grunt, which made Mr Rock look twice. He then noticed Baker with the sergeant, and again had the unreasoned impulse that he must explain his presence, for which he could not, he felt, account by merely saying he had taken Daisy for a stroll. So, instinctively, and with the swill man's yell, he called out "Ted."

Because he faced the great house, the echo volleyed back at him, "Ted, Ted."

"Good heavens, what was that?" Baker asked.

"Man shouted," the sergeant said, his eye on the middle distance.

"It was a man, was'nt it?" Miss Baker quavered, to be reassured.

"I do believe it's Mr Rock, miss," the sergeant replied, in a careful voice. "Indeed, if I'm not much mistaken, he has the porker with him."

"He may have found something," Baker objected.

"In such case, no doubt he'll sing out again."

"But should'nt we go over at once, sergeant?"

"One moment, ma'am, if you will allow me. I just wanted to put a question regarding Mr Rock."

"Yes?" Oh what had Edge done?

"Does he see much of your girls, ma'am?"

"He lives on the place, you understand," she said.

"How did that come about?"

Baker then gave Mr Rock's history, in some detail, to explain his presence, and added what she knew of the coming election to an Academy of Sciences or State Sanatorium. The sergeant was left with the idea that Mr Rock was joyfully packing up to leave.

"I see, ma'am," he commented, heavily non-committal.

"Now, since he has'nt called a second time, shall we go over?" And they started off.

It was not until they were half way, that the policeman was certain of the pig.

"He's got his sow along after all," he confirmed.

"Good heavens, not his pig, surely?" Baker echoed Miss Edge, afraid the sergeant might be referring to Elizabeth.

"He'll have his work cut out to drive her home when he wants," the man said, with satisfaction.

In another few minutes they came up to Mr Rock, who stood his ground. Daisy fled a few paces, and squealed in what was perhaps simulated horror. And Baker gave a small gesture of distaste, which did not escape the sage.

"Good evening, sir," the policeman said. "Just the weather for a stroll."

"So I notice," Mr Rock innocently answered, but Miss Baker's heart began to pound.

"We fancied we heard you call, sir?"

"Only after Ted." Baker noticed the pig watched them with disrespect, thought it seemed to hold a muttered conversation half under its breath, judging by the petulant squeaks which issued from that muddy mouth.

"Now she's not disappeared, I hope, sir?" the sergeant asked, in fat jocular tones.

—When a man, such as he, becomes civil it is just the moment his type wants watching, Mr Rock told himself. But the truth was the sergeant had come only for a look around, in which he felt could not indulge with so many present. Also he was parched for a cup of tea, and had been of the opinion that Mrs Blain was an understanding sort of woman who knew better than to offer a glass of flat beer, this had been his thought as Miss Baker stole up on him.

"Disappeared?" Mr Rock echoed. "I know nothing."

"That's good," the sergeant answered absentmindedly, his eyes to the ground.

"They stray," Mr Rock added, and once again agitated Miss Baker. "According to their age," he added.

"Yes," the sergeant said, as vague. "Well, if you'll excuse me now, I'll have to get on, miss," he said, to the lady's surprise. And he went off without another word, left her flat.

"The Law," Mr Rock tried the Principal out, looking full at her with, behind their spectacles, his enormous, magnified eyes.

"What a shame in this beautiful Place," she agreed, quick as quick.

"Makes you wonder."

"I never wonder, Mr Rock. I take things as they are," she corrected him.

"Daisy," he exclaimed and, indeed, she was nowhere to be found. "Excuse me, Madam," and made as if to move off, stumbling a trifle.

"One minute," she said, in the voice of authority he so hated. "Is she safe?"

"Who are you asking?" he fiercely demanded. She did not understand.

"This is your pig, is'nt it?"

"Daisy?" he enquired, and, extraordinary man, she could see he now actually laughed at her. "Would'nt hurt a fly." She unbent a trifle.

"Yet, you know, where I was brought up in the country, on a black and white farm," she lied, "where all the animals were that, you understand, well, I shall never forget, but I was out to pick apples one day and the pigs were loose in the orchard. It was rather thundery weather, so I had my mackintosh, which I left below while I was up the ladder. But I suppose I must have been pre-occupied, because they ate it, every scrap."

He bowed. "Madam," he said, "never fear, we are not in for rain the next few hours."

Blushing with humiliation, she turned on her heel and left without another word. —Really, she thought, the man must be malevolently hostile.

As Baker tramped back to the great house along a ride, fanning herself with a dock leaf, she came to within sight of the fallen beech. She did not know, but the sergeant had not preceded her by many minutes. Neither of them could tell this was where Merode had been found, or they might have stopped to investigate. It was lucky for Sebastian and his Liz they did not do so, because these two were lying stark naked in one another's arms, precisely at the same spot in which Merode had been found. For Elizabeth saw how it was with her lover after he had come upon the girl lying stretched out in pyjamas. And now, a second time, Liz had taken him back to wipe off the memory of Merode, on this occasion by cruder means.

As the policeman was coming by, Sebastian and his Liz had lain stark, scarcely breathing for fear they might be uncovered. Then, as Baker minced past, apparently tracking the sergeant, it was far worse, more than the cottage depended upon their not being caught, and Sebastian had nearly burst a vein in his forehead. Yet, before the Principal was out of earshot, Miss Rock thought of the expression there would have been about the Principal's nose if this lady had come upon her lover as he now was, which jolted Elizabeth into such a loud, gurgling laugh of cruel, delighted ridicule, that it sent Sebastian wooden with horror.

When she heard, Miss Baker, her blood run cold, looked back the way she had come, like a hen, at night, watching behind for a fox. She did not stop to investigate. It was all she could do not to break into a trot. —Oh, she thought, our beautiful Park seems suddenly full of vile cross currents.

When Edge got to the door behind which Merode was locked away, she still held the doll by its thick neck. She paused before she entered, and tried holding the thing by its middle. But that was ridiculous because, with no backbone, it simply flopped. So she took a blunt hand, and this would not do, for the head, when released, hung sideways. Finally she cradled it on one arm like a baby, turned her key in the lock without a sound and crept forward, not waking Merode, whom she found astride her chair, asleep.

She put the dolly on Merode's lap, under the child's dreaming head which lay, with all her hanging hair, over crossed arms along the chair back. This small weight woke the girl who, when she first opened eyes, saw what she dizzily took to be Alice, exactly as Miss Marchbanks had offered the animal curled up at rest. But in a second she realised, and sprang to her feet.

"Oh," she cried out. "Not puss."

Edge stood there astounded.

"Merode," she said, to warn the child, in fairness, of her presence.

"Oh ma'am," Merode gasped.

"What has so frightened you, dear?" Miss Edge demanded.

There was no reply. The girl kept looking back at Edge then away to the doll on the ground.

"Pick it up, won't you, Merode?"

The Principal was relieved to find the child seemed able to do so reasonably quick. She had feared there might be something about the absurd doll, after all.

"Put it over there, dear," she said. "Now tell me, what is this to do with a cat?"

"I was dreaming, ma'am."

"What about?"

"That Miss Marchbanks had given me Alice."

"Mr Rock's cat? But why, Merode?"

"You see, she did, ma'am, when I saw her after I was brought in."

"Hardly hers to give, was it?"

"No, she put puss on my lap, ma'am,"

"And then you fainted?"

"Oh that was later, ma'am," the child said, quite collected.

"So the animal did not frighten you," Edge pointed out. "Is this doll yours, Merode?"

The child winced. "No, ma'am," she said.

"Look at her well, dear. Whose is it, in that case?"

Merode swallowed.

"Mary's, ma'am."

"Are you quite sure now? I should have thought a big, grown girl, would be too old for such things."

"The others did laugh at her," Merode said unwillingly.

"I expect so," Miss Edge encouraged. "And did she mind?"

"Oh, not really, ma'am," the child replied, in a bright voice.

Edge felt it was curious how confident the bit of a thing seemed.

"And one point you are sure of, this is not yours, Merode?"

"Oh no, ma'am."

"The others were not laughing at you, then?"

"Me? I would'nt have bothered."

Edge sat down in the only chair. She picked the doll up, placed it on her lap. Her face took a peculiarly innocent expression. Merode again got the idea that all this had happened once before. But she felt better, now she had seen her aunt.

"Why would you not have bothered?"

"I just don't pay attention to them, ma'am."

—Yet, for all her being confident, Edge felt, the girl seemed never to take her eyes off the doll while this was in evidence.

"And Mary did?"

Merode swallowed, then joined hands behind her back.

"She was so tired, ma'am."

"Tired? What about? I'd like to have seen myself tired at her age."

"It was all the work she done."

"Oh, do speak English, child. But how do you mean? She is quite well on in her work."

"It was the waiting," Merode explained, with a kind of limpid simplicity.

"Waiting for what?" Miss Edge demanded.

"Orderly duties, ma'am."

These words came as a complete, and genuine, surprise to the Principal. So much so that she even doubted her own ears.

"Say that again, Merode. The orderly duties?"

"Yes, ma'am."

A cramp was forming round Edge's heart, or that was how the lady felt. Then a reasonable explanation occurred to her. Mrs Manley must have put the child up to it. Because they all knew that attendance on Baker and herself was an honour for which every one of the girls longed, it was just the little extra to be intimately close to them both. Nevertheless, she saw how the whole thing could be made to look if Mary did not come back soon, how black if this latest fantastic story was allowed to creep around. She managed to bring out a laugh.

"Really, the ideas you children do get hold of," she exclaimed. "Honestly, Merode, I never heard such silly stuff and nonsense in my life. It might even be ill-natured, I am sorry to say, from one aspect. Now, who told you?"

The girl had flushed under Miss Edge's blue eyes. The lady thought —really, in time, she is going to be extraordinarily attractive.

There was no answer.

"Very well, then, we'll leave it. Now, about yourself, dear. Have you written your Account yet?"

"Must I, ma'am?"

"We shall see," Edge answered, affable but, at the same time, at her most wary. "You know what the Regulations are. I am not sure whether we shall have to make a Report, that depends on a number of things, quite a number of things. But until you have written out your story, you understand, I cannot ask questions. Which is to say, there is nothing to prevent me asking, but you are not obliged to respond. I think it very fair of the State. Now then, where were we?"

"I'm afraid I must have been sleepwalking, ma'am." The girl spoke up easily, with every appearance of candour.

"Sleepwalking?" Edge demanded, as if this were the first she had heard of a dishonourable, yet prevalent custom. "I trust you don't often engage in that."

"Me, ma'am? I did when I was a baby."

"Does anyone else know of this?"

"Auntie does."

"Of course," Edge took her up with a heavy irony that was wasted, because the girl did not notice. "But anyone here? Were we told? There is the essential point, isn't it?"

"I told Miss Marchbanks, ma'am."

"When?"

"After I got back."

Edge was stupefied, but did not show a sign.   A pause ensued.

"When she came up to see you after you were locked here?" she tried again.

"Yes, ma'am."

Another silence began to stretch between them.   Then the Principal thought she saw light at last.

"Merode, tell me something," she said in a voice full of hope.   "When Miss Marchbanks asked her questions, did she caution you?   What I mean is, did she tell you as I have done, about your writing an Account and not being obliged to answer before you had written it?"

"Why no, ma'am, I don't think so."

"Well all right," Miss Edge cried out in triumph. "Nothing you told her has any substance.   Indeed you might just as well not have said a word.   That is to say that as far as we are concerned you did not speak."

Thereupon she quickly got up and left the room, locked the door behind.   —At least I have left the whole thing open, she congratulated herself.   We are not committed to any story yet.

For her part Merode was well pleased.   —Really, she thought, old Edge may not be such a bad old stick, when you get to know her.

Evening was drawing in.   Mr Rock had decided willy nilly it would be best to attend the dance.   So he must get back to wash and change.   Only there was Daisy.

He had found the animal once more but she had been recalcitrant, would not be driven, and, when he did catch up, she looked back over a white flank, waited till he was within three paces, then, with a toss of that drooling, over-weighted head, with a flurry of grunts, she trotted off a short distance and halted, to allow the whole business to start all over again. This happened two or three times, until, in making her escape, she was frightened, made off through the reeds with high squeals, and he lost sight of her altogether as he squelched about over soft ground that bordered the water. He stayed to search a little, because he feared she might have sensed the girl's cold, wet, crumpled body. But he did not find a trace, and, by the time he was about to desist, sweat fogged his spectacles and the shirt was plastered to his body.

He chanced to be hard by a dense withy which he thought he would investigate before he gave up both Mary and the pig, when a voice addressed him from the heart of it, in querulous tones which could only belong to the forester Adams.

"What would you say you're after?" the man enquired.

"Who's that?" Mr Rock asked, knowing full well, but put out by the brutal question.

"I know what I know," Adams said. He spoke in a higher voice than usual.

Mr Rock straightened his back to wave a hand at the cloud of gnats which rose and fell before his eyes. He reached for a handkerchief to clean the glasses, and, when he had done so, searched from where he stood for the still invisible Adams, while he put a finger between his collar and wet skin.

"Have you seen my sow?" he demanded.

"She's been gone this long time since," the forester replied.

There was a pause. Mr Rock felt hotter. —Really,

L

amongst the reeds it is intolerably warm, he said to himself. —And what an idiotic situation.

"Where are you, man?" he insisted.

"Where I can remain unseen," the fellow answered.

"Then come out and have done." Mr Rock sternly said, turning slow on his heels, in a circle.

"I've as much right as the next man to ask my question and receive the answer," the man replied. "I'm not the one single one round here," he said. "Ask this, ask that, 'Adams, where were you?', 'Adams what're you doing', ''Ow about your work, Adams?' Well then, perhaps you can tell me, Mr Rock," and he stressed the Mr. "What might you be after?"

The old man was facing the withy again. The insulting lunatic could only be hidden away there. So Mr Rock said not a word.

"I've kept me eyes open this long time to what goes on around," Adams continued bitterly, after a pause. "I may not be educated but I was'nt born yesterday, not by many a year. I saw the shape of things right enough this morning when you asked after my cottage. You people, you, and your granddaughter, and her boy," he said, "you're as mean as wood ashes, every one."

He waited for an answer but the old man said no word, just stood to wipe at his face with a handkerchief in a palsied hand.

A gnat got up Adams' nose so that he sneezed. He scratched at his leg. Then, beside himself, he went on,

"You never intended to give me the wire," he accused. "I saw through that like I look out of my windows, it was clear as day you sought how you might get me shunted, shift it over on to me, while up at the house as they're scheming to lay their hands on your place. Likely enough you or your girl done away with 'er yourselves, for a dark purpose. Because I tell you, from now on you and me is strangers of another country, so we don't pass the time of day even. You and me speak a different language, Mr Rock. You and your sort."

For the last few words, Adams had dropped his voice. The old man could not entirely catch what had been said. So it was with intent to make the fellow ridiculous that he asked,

"Lose the fort?"

The forester began to laugh. "Booze the port" he echoed, to make a mock of his adversary. "Ah, and after every meal I don't doubt," and slapped his thighs. "Living like a lord," he went on. "There you are, back at your lies once again," he yelled. "Makin' out you're better nor the rest of us." He dropped his voice. "Like enough you've forgotten the spot you dug the hole, and you're back to see where you can recollect."

"It was the State gave me my place," Mr Rock, who had not meant to answer these bumpkin idiocies, found himself stung to reply about his general position. This mention of the all-powerful sobered Adams.

There was another silence.

"Time I went," Mr Rock muttered, outraged and confused.

"Ah, slink off like you crept out," Adams said, in as low a voice. "But you won't come up on me unbeknownst, not with me on my guard."

The old man waited. It was intolerable. His granddaughter and he had fallen so low that any lunatic could thus address them, and stay unmolested. He blamed it on Miss Edge and the Baker woman.

"I saw," Adams started once more, but not so violently, "I seen you hold your tryst with that shiner and old Edge. The moment I set eyes on you I knew the game. Put it all on a working man who's alone in this world," he said, tears in his voice.

"For all my weak eyesight I only noticed Baker," Mr Rock announced with triumph.

"Which don't alter facts, that you never come upon what you sought," Adams replied. "It takes more'n glasses to see round your kind," he said.

"I'm an older man than you, Adams," Mr Rock answered at last. "Civility between neighbours is worth a coal fire in the grate, any time."

Conscious that he had hardly, perhaps, said all he might, and with a feeling that he had not heard the last in consequence, Mr Rock walked off and out. For his ludicrous position was, he realised, that whether or no he had been elected, he must hasten to curry favour with those two mewing harlots up above for fear they might listen to this madman's ravings.

"Get on off out," he heard Adams yell after him.

When Baker arrived back in the Sanctum, she found Edge ready to take over.

"I was just going up to change," Miss Edge greeted the lady.

"I know," her colleague said, a little out of breath. "It took longer than I thought. I met the police sergeant with Mr Rock."

Miss Edge accepted the statement without comment.

"In many ways," she said, "I think this has been the most miserable day of my life."

"Why dear? There's nothing fresh, then? No bad news, I mean?" She had been thinking that laugh she heard behind her must have been imaginary. Now she was not so sure.

"No, on the whole, no," Edge comforted her. "But the intentional stupidity, Baker, is what I find so fatiguing. Take Marchbanks, now. Merode definitely admitted, only a moment ago, she had told the woman she was a sleepwalker."

"Well," Miss Baker said, and forgot that laugh once more. "It lets the child out to a certain extent, does'nt it?"

"Yes, until we go further into all this," Edge replied, with a weary gesture. "Up to a point, yes," she agreed. "But wait until we know more tomorrow, Baker. We may have a day of decision there. I dread it."

"Marchbanks is so experienced she's hardly likely to have made a mistake over a man," Miss Baker assented. "Although she may have jumped to the obvious conclusion. But we are at one, now, over the dance, are'nt we? It must proceed. In the present state of our knowledge at all events. We may even laugh at each other, dear, within the next fifteen hours, at having been so worried and upset."

"I feel that is hardly likely, Baker," Edge objected. "For we still may not have done all we might under the circumstances, which is no trifling matter, placed as we are. Still, I am with you that our little Tamasha shall succeed."

"Then let's not say another word now, even to one another, about what's occurred."

"But the way those two girls could, Baker? On the very day before. Our children don't get much fun here, my dear. We have to keep them pretty well to the grindstone. And then these two little wretches, if they do not merit a harsher word, to endanger the whole affair with an escapade, it is hardly credible, is it?"

The sinking sun partitioned their room into three, as it came in by three windows. Miss Edge sat shaded between the first and second, Miss Baker similarly between the second and third windows, so they addressed each other across a thick wedge of colour-bearing sunlight in which motes of dust descended, now day was done. Left of one, and to the right of the other, was a vase of azaleas that had not wilted yet, a brilliant crown, which one of the girls had saved over from the decorations to place between their desks of office. Miss Edge reached out to push this into shadow, and Baker remembered.

"We still have time before we need go," she said, forgetting that she had just suggested they might leave the whole matter alone for the moment. "I wanted to ask, dear. D'you think the anonymous letter yesterday could have some connection with all this?"

"We should not attach the slightest importance, Baker." Miss Edge spoke with complete confidence. "I know I never do. Whoever stoops to send a thing like it deserves immediate punishment, but, above all, to be ignored. When we have cleared this up, we can try to trace the poison pen, if you like. While, for the present, I strongly counsel you to put it out of mind."

"All the same, what did the horrible thing say, Edge? 'Who is there fornicates and the goose'. That's rather extraordinary, surely?"

Miss Edge looked. The door was shut.

"Furnicates, dear," she corrected, in a low voice. "F.U.R.N." she spelled.

"Well, don't let's quarrel over details," Baker said, with a sort of laugh. "But it all does rather point one way, you see?"

"Even then I am not certain you are quite accurate," Edge elaborated. " 'Who is there furnicates besides his goose?' was the charming message, if my memory serves me right."

Miss Baker gave an embarrassed laugh.

"How should we know about anonymous letters, dear," she agreed. "Perhaps we should ask Mr Rock?"

"Yes, what would two old spinsters, which is, I am led to believe, how Elizabeth Rock describes us, know of such a subject? No, Baker, dismiss it entirely from your mind."

"Does furnicate mean what I mean?" her colleague ventured. But she was to remain in ignorance.

"Forget all this, Baker," Edge said with decision. "I do not know, and I care less. What I have determined is, that our dear girls should have their Time tonight. There will be leisure for every kind of tiring foolishness tomorrow, I'm only too certain. But how curious you should bring that unspeakable message back to the disastrous Rock. However, no more of it, please."

"Well, it seemed the only possible conclusion."

"I agree, dear," Edge said. "But do remember. Only this morning you would not have that."

"No, Edge, we never discussed the note, did we? Surely we were talking about Sebastian Rock?"

"Birt, dear. They are not married yet, and if I know much of the young man, they never will, not if he can help. Such a pity, with Winstanley making sheep's eyes at him. But that is the sort of creature he is, to pick on a half crazed woman like the granddaughter."

"I say now what I said then," Miss Baker warned. "Go carefully. We must not exceed our duties."

"You and I are here to protect our girls, Hermione," Miss Edge announced in her strongest manner. "We stand on guard over the Essential Goodness of this great Place. And when we sense a threat, our duty is to exercise the initiative the State expects to avert a danger. Now something, we do not yet know what, has occurred, and it is for us to stamp out the evil, or better still, get rid of it quietly, without fuss, as one does with swill."

"You're reverting to the anonymous note, of course."

"Far be it from me, Baker. I refer to two misguided children who have cast a shadow this year over Founder's Day, probably in a fit of pique. Do you know Merode actually claims she told Marchbanks about the sleep-walking."

"Does she?"

"Yes." There was a heavy pause. And then inspiration visited Edge. She saw the way out in a flash.

"What, after all, can one make of it?" she began right way in a great voice. "Creeping down at dead of night in her pyjamas and then, hours later, to be found comfortably ensconsed within a fallen beech, having made herself a nest, thank you, and not forgotten the coat, which she still had with her. What is one to think? Finally, discovered by Sebastian Birt of all people, well on in the morning, as if he did not know where she was the whole time, oh then she is quite composed, of course. A little fuss at first, naturally, when she finds herself the centre of attention, but no excuses, Baker, mark you. So what is the inescapable conclusion?"

Her colleague got up, began to pace to and fro across a thick shutter of sunlight.

"It's all very difficult," she said.

"Do you think so? And how about Mary, after she turns up, as she will? For she must. But let us not meet her trouble half way. Time enough when the girl returns. Because do you still not see it, dear? At least for Merode. Why, I gave you the answer to our riddle not ten minutes since."

"What riddle, Edge?"

"The quandary in which we find ourselves. How to explain Merode's absence without this horrible rigmarole of Reports. Though we owe it to the Trust, with which you and I have been privileged, Baker, to cast out evil hanging over the heads of our Students root and branch, this we must do, or forfeit all selfrespect. For I have watched the situation grow, and I have held my hand. Rock, who I deeply suspect, his disastrous granddaughter, and a weak young man. You will agree I have given you my views on them many a time the past few weeks. No, they must, and shall, be sent packing. But don't you, even now, see the way to explain Merode?"

Her colleague, in perplexity turned towards Miss Edge, and was blinded by sun. She screwed her face up into a pathetic maze of bewilderment before a hot dazzle of evening.

"My dear," she began, and could not go on.

"Sleepwalking," Edge brought out at last in an even louder voice, jubilant as a trumpet.

"But she . . ." Miss Baker started to object, only to be ruthlessly interrupted.

"Has told three people the same," Edge insisted. "Marchbanks, her aunt, and myself. No doubt Mrs Manley encouraged the child to stick to the truthful account of what had occurred. But I simply cannot understand, now, that I could have been so blind as not to accept it, at once, face value, immediately. Because this is, in an exact measure, sufficient to our purpose, Baker. Of course we do not want the playing truant to be known, for the child's own sake. Not many of the girls have learned. Merode was just Sleepwalking, that's all, and the Dance can go ahead. Of course she will rest in Quarantine, until Mary comes back with her tail between her legs. It is amazing to me, after what has occurred, that I always trusted the girl. Yet in justice to ourselves, we must leave no stone unturned to rid the Precincts of the three persons I have named. That's all."

"But Edge . . ." Baker began once more.

"Not another word, dear," Miss Edge said firmly.

"And will you do me the favour to look at the Time? If we are to be ready we shall have to hurry, Baker."

Miss Edge watched her colleague out of the room. When the door closed on her, Edge's face took on a look of triumphant satisfaction.

Later, Mr Rock and Elizabeth were on their way up to the house for the dance. She wore a trailing black silk dress, with a yellow ribbon in her hair. Both walked in rubber boots because he feared the dew. He carried his shoes, and hers, in a despatch case which went back to the days of his youth.

Daisy was not home yet, or Ted. He had left some milk outside for Alice, but then she spent most of her time these days away at the Institute, currying favour, —as he would, if he were wise, he smiled wryly to himself. And Elizabeth had been too silent, he thought, so quiet there must be something yet to come ; from her poor starved heart, no doubt, under that stained mackintosh hung over the shoulders. She was spent and sad, he knew.

The first blackbird, up on a branch, gave heed that night rode near, the light grew ever softer, rhododendrons stared, air was still, the boots they wore gleamed wet so soon; it was cool, and gnats had departed to the last bars of sun which, high above, slanted from one beech to another that dwarfed the azalea bushes where bluebottles no longer waited, whence butterflies were gone, and whose scent had faded, whose honey was now too late for bees in the hush of sunset preparing in the west that would lie red over the sky like a vast bank of roses, just time enough for lovers.

He saw an empty bird's egg lying on grass and glanced upward to find the nest. He then realised his evening heavens, which precisely matched that blue.

He thought she had said something he was too deaf to hear.

"What is that?" he gently asked.

She, who had not yet spoken, told him then,

"About Sebastian, Gapa."

"Yes dear," he said. He had known it would be this.

"Oh Gapa, I want you to be marvellous to me now. I mean you always have. But there are times, are'nt there? The thing is I'm in terrible trouble. In my mind you understand. About him. And I do so want you to promise."

"You tell me," he suggested, gentle as before.

"But you may not agree, not look at it the way he does. Yet he did'nt ask, you need'nt think, because honestly he never did. In fact if he thought for a minute I was talking to you he would be furious. Really he would. He's so worried."

"Is he?"

"Yes, oh, you would'nt know. About that silly girl who's missing."

"Why, dear?"

She swallowed.

"It's not what you imagine at all," she hurried on. "He's absolutely true to me, you can be sure, and they fling themselves all the time at his head. I don't think they ought to have masters, Gapa, at these places, do you, since they're only children, the girls I mean, and sex is unconscious at their age. It's such a temptation for a man."

He winced, as Sebastian himself had earlier, at the assumption of sexual knowledge.

"Come to your point, Liz," he said firmly.

"I'm so worried for him. It's not what he's actually

mentioned, yet he could'nt help but drop hints, poor sweet; you know, underneath, he's half out of his mind with the torture of it all. Oh, everything's my fault, I should never have met him. They blame it all on Seb, you see. Is'nt that inconceivable, but so wicked, so wicked of them? You were absolutely certain from the first, oh Gapa you really are the most wonderful man. I know when I was all right, and I used to come down to see you, I had no idea, I thought there was just a bee in your bonnet, but you were sure. They're dangerous. The two of them should be behind bars."

"Edge and Baker I presume?" he said.

"You see, when you're young and all that," she went on, "starting in the State Service, because I know, Gapa, I've done it, things have so changed since your day, well then, the slightest bad report he gets and he'll never receive promotion. Never. It is'nt a story, honest. No redress, nothing. And you realise what an Enquiry means, if you appeal against one of these awful Reports. It's the end. Absolutely. Even if you think you've brought it off, it boomerangs back onto you. So I want you to promise you'll lend a hand."

He judged from her tone that she was near tears.

"I'll do what I can," he said for comfort, though he could not but show the bitterness in his voice. She mistakenly took this to be aimed at the two Principals.

"And I do really realise what it costs to say that," she announced, "I understand how you hate to speak to them, even. If you were'nt the most splendid man you'd never have promised to talk to Miss Edge." She brought this out quite naturally, and he did not contradict. "You need'nt do much, Gapa dear. Get her to sit out one dance, just like that, she'll be thrilled, because they truly appreciate you here, the staff does, despite all you speak against them when you get out of bed the wrong side of a morning. Seb's often told me how Miss Edge talks about you," she lied, while the famous old man had to hold himself back in order not to squirm from his grand-daughter, that she should be so transparent. " Get her quietly alone somewhere," then she laughed and it was worse, so that he drew himself away. "Come back, Gapa," she ordered, hanging her whole weight on the arm to pull his old shoulder back to hers, "just take the woman quietly somewhere she can watch her sweet students dance with each other, because they're fiends, those girls, you simply must believe, I'm a woman and I know, they're sincerely dreadful, I could'nt possibly tell. Of course you must not admit to anything, she'd see us at the bottom, she's quite sharp enough for that, but will you? Well, I mean, you have promised, surely? Just tell her you won't under any circumstances report a word of the evasion to Mr Swaythling."

The old man was alarmed.

"In which respect has Swaythling to do with this?" he asked. "In any case, what evasion?"

"Why, that's Seb's word," she answered, almost gay. "I think it's so smart of him, don't you? Two girls who escape, and a couple of old women who, what he calls, evade the whole issue. But you told Seb you were going to send in a report to Mr Swaythling, Gapa."

"I did nothing of the kind," the old man truthfully protested.

"Must have slipped your memory, then," she said, altogether sure of her facts.

"There are times you remind me of Julia," he said, with a grim laugh.

"Did'nt you know a woman will always get her own way," she replied as obviously. She laughed, then grew serious again. "Oh, but Gapa it is so important, this is. You see I'm planning my future on Seb," she said. "If

anything should happen to him, I'd die.   And what chance
has he got, if Miss Edge and Miss Baker turn against Seb,
I mean?   It's his first post, you see.   Oh, was'nt that a
pity we came across the wretched girl?"

"Look Liz, don't lose your head.   What have they
against Sebastian?"

"But nothing, dear, nothing naturally.   What could
they?   It's so difficult to explain.   After all, you've lived out
of things a long time, Gapa.   You see, I'm frightened for
the reprisals.   Don't you understand, and of course, I know,
they're so fiendish, those two old creatures, it must be hard
to believe, yet Seb has studied them, he's told me, the
point is they watch like pussies, they've learned all Seb
and I mean to one another, and he's certain they'll strike
back, if you should do anything, you see, right at your
weakest part, the chink in your armour."

"Which is?" he patiently enquired.   She was biting her
lower lip.

"Why me, of course," she wailed, but he thought she
seemed well satisfied.   "They're capable of anything,"
she explained.   "Oh Gapa, I'm dreadfully worried.   You
will, won't you?"

"What?" he asked.

She stopped dead.   She turned, and stamped a foot.
Unseen, a rabbit, which had come out of its hole fifty feet
away, stamped a hind leg back.

"You know perfectly," she accused.   "Only sometimes it suits to pretend you don't, like often when you
say you can't hear.   No, Gapa, you must promise you'll
never let on to Mr Swaythling about what's happened."

"Yet suppose they just hide it up?" he asked calmly.
"What then?"

"How on earth?" she demanded, searching over his face
with her eyes, as if she feared for his sanity.

"I've some experience," he told her.   "They're caught

in a trap those two, like the cruel weasels they are." He spoke with great patience. "They drove that poor child to this," he went on. "She's been over to me about them. Only because they liked the colour of her eyes they pushed her unmercifully, set her to fetch and carry all day through, 'Just bring my pince nez from the Sanctum'," he quavered, in a horrible mimicry of Miss Edge. "No, Mary will never come back now."

"Did she tell you?" his granddaughter asked him, wide eyed.

"Of course not," he said sharply. "If she had, I'd have known where to look, would'nt I? No, but she has complained, Liz, often and often, the poor girl. All she's got in the world is out in Brazil, she has no relatives besides."

"Oh, Gapa dear," she cried. "You should'nt listen, you really must'nt. They're so deceitful at that age, you can't imagine."

"And do you know how Mistresses Edge and Baker will act next?" he went on. "They'll cover up. They have made one or two gestures today but they're only sitting back, they're saying to each other 'Mary must turn up tomorrow', and when she does no such thing, perhaps she's not in a position to oblige, they'll tell one another, Liz, 'Wait for the next day'. And so on."

"Now, Gapa, they can't hide it altogether, I mean they have their lists, have'nt they, Mary won't simply disappear into thin air, surely, you see?"

He stayed silent.

"They won't, will they?" she pressed him, with rising terror.

"I'm not one to look into their dark minds," he said at last. "But they must find something, a means to put the blame onto her however it turns out. I do know that," he said.

"And then the cottage?" she wailed.

"Don't let yourself get upset, Liz," he said in a loud voice. "Just allow me to handle this my way."

"But it's our whole future, Seb's and mine," she almost shouted, unmasking herself. "When we're married, where are we to go? I did'nt mean to ask you like this, but I've been thinking. Oh Gapa, you would'nt mind, surely now, I mean you'd hardly notice. But I had felt when we're married we could live on here with you, the both of us."

When Mr Rock heard this, he was terrified for his grand-daughter. She could not have them both.

"Dear, you know the Rule," he said gently. "When one of the staff takes a wife the State always moves him to another post."

"Yes, but you could put in a word with Mr Swaythling. You would'nt mind. You see I'd never get over leaving you. It's hard to set these things to words, but you're my life, Gapa, you understand."

He kissed her cheek clumsily. She began to cry.

"So my little girl is going to be married," he said.

"Oh, there's nothing absolutely fixed yet," she replied, stepping back to blow her nose, and sent a sharp look at his face. "I never meant to tell, then I'm such a fool, I get upset at times and bring it all out. You won't breathe a word, will you, Gapa, not to Seb either, because he's funny that way, and of course, if Miss Edge got to hear before we were ready, it would be the end. I mean, I've considered this for ever so long, because I'm sure the only way is to run off one morning, and get it over, almost before you know you're doing it yourself. Get married, you see. All those tremendous preparations are simply no good. Next, soon as Miss Edge saw it was finished, after I'd shown her my certificate, I mean, there'd be absolutely nothing for her to do, would there?"

"It wants thought," he said, reminding himself, if he were to show opposition, that it would drive her into the man's arms and then he would lose her finally. But he was not so blind, he said under his breath, spectacles or no, he could see Birt coveted the cottage, would move heaven and earth to have him sent to the Sanatorium once the ring was on her finger.

"I hardly know that I should bother Swaythling," he said about the cottage, and began to walk away from the house.

"Wrong way, Gapa," she said. He turned without a word, marched up to, and past her. She followed at his heels.

"You mean you won't get on to him, then," she started. "Not one teeny word, when all the time you've sworn if anything happened to this Mary you'd move heaven and earth?"

"I intended nothing of the kind," he lied, over his shoulder.

"No, but that was what you said, did'nt you?"

"We shall be late, Liz."

"Why are you, I mean, what's all the hurry?" she called, unable to catch up.

"Justice," he cried. Looking at his back, she thought —oh dear he's upset.

"What's that? And must you go so fast?"

"Do you really consider I should leave Mary be? Have you any idea what you've said?"

"Oh I just don't understand," she wailed.

"It is a matter of simple justice, Liz."

"Yes, Gapa."

"I'd do as much for any dog I saw maltreated, I'd report it."

—But not for me, she felt. Their skins and hair simply allowed these wretched chits to get away with things.

M

However, she had the sense to say no more. His pace slackened.

"Don't be afraid of life, Liz," he said. "Everything settles itself in the end. I've lived long enough to know that."

"Yes, Gapa," she agreed. Now she could see his face she noted it was red with more than the sunset, and puckered into deep wrinkles, an infallible sign of distress.

"You want me to write to Swaythling about yourselves and the cottage while not mentioning this girl?"

"Oh my dear," she lied. "It's not that at all. I explain myself so badly, ever since I've been ill. You know, sometimes I feel as if I'd something in my head and I simply can't get out the words. Have you ever? No, it's silly to ask. The whole thing, you see, is Seb. He's worried."

"Yes, Liz," Mr Rock encouraged, reminding himself that she must not become distressed, the doctor had been insistent.

"He knows them so well," she was going on. "He lives all the time within sight and sound of Miss Baker and Miss Edge, so he can watch and judge, day in day out, he has to. He really understands, you see. And he's worried for the cottage. Oh, of course, he wants to live there, but he's true, Gapa, you must believe. Because, naturally, I realise you don't like him. But I do know what you don't, that you will in time, you'll come round, there's noone in the world who would'nt, once they'd seen the real person underneath the skin. Still, I do realise, it is'nt a little thing I ask, I do honestly."

"Don't fuss, dear, we'll find a way," he said.

Then, as they came to where the trees ended, and black-birds, before roosting, began to give the alarm in earnest, some first starlings flew out of the sky. Over against the old man and his granddaughter the vast mansion reflected a vast red; sky above paled while to the left it outshone the house, and more starlings crossed. After which these birds came in hundreds, then suddenly by legion, black and blunt against faint rose. They swarmed above the lonely elm, they circled a hundred feet above, until the leader, followed by ever greater numbers, in one broad spiral led the way down and so, as they descended through falling dusk in a soft roar, they made, as they had at dawn, a huge sea shell that stood proud to a moon which, flat sovereign red gold, was already poised full faced to a dying world.

Once the starlings had settled in that tree they one and all burst out singing.

Then there were more, even higher, dots against paler pink, and these, in their turn, began to circle up above, scything the air, and to swoop down through a thickening curve, in the enormous echo of blood, or of the sea, until all was black about that black elm, as the first mass of starlings left while these others settled, and there was a huge volume of singing.

Then a third concourse came out of the west, and, as the first birds swarmed upon the nearest beech, these late comers stooped out of dusk in a crash of air to take that elm, to send the last arrivals out, which trebled the singing.

The old man wondered, as often before, if this were not the greatest sound on earth. Elizabeth stood quiet. The starlings flew around a little and then, as sky faded fast, the moon paled to brilliance, and this moment was over, that singing drooped, then finished, as every bird was home.

"I'm glad I had that once more," Mr Rock said aloud.

Behind them the first cock pheasant gave a challenge.

"We're to have the most lovely night," Elizabeth told her grandfather.

They went on their way again.

"I want you to know," she said, from the heart, "in spite

of everything, whatever happens, absolutely, if Seb asks me to marry him even, there'd be nothing could alter the way I love you, Gapa. I would'nt let it."

"Don't allow yourself to grow sentimental, child," he answered.

She gave a soft laugh.

"And don't you be gruff with me, my darling," she said. "Not tonight of all nights. Listen, I think I hear their music already. They'll have every window wide. Yes, I'm almost certain.

"Good," he said, alone with blank thoughts, in his deafness.

"I'll dance every dance," she murmured happily.

DOWN a dank Passage which led to the Banqueting Hall Miss Winstanley, hurrying at the far end, saw a bunch of students outlined against great, wide opened double doors to the ballroom. They were in their long, white dresses. She smiled through her misery, they looked so serious, and thought, as she watched them wait for music, that one and all were in what she called 'the mood', that, once Edge and Baker had opened proceedings, the first waltz would send each child whirling forward into her future, into what, in a few years, she would, with age, become.

"Could'nt care less," a fair child asserted, "but I won't ever speak to Merode now, it's perfectly rotten of both to upset our whole show. What, we might've had the thing cancelled, thanks to those two."

"I don't know why you gripe, Moira," another objected. "We're to hold it after all, aren't we, or I can't see what we are waiting for, then. Of course there've been whispers. But that is the whole trouble with this academy. A fat lot of talk and no do, in my opinion."

"Will anyone quite say what Merode and Mary have actually done?"

"Need'nt ask me. I don't want a summons to be put through the old mangle in the Holy of Holies. But all the same I do think those two have at least given everyone a bit of excitement."

"Even so," Moira protested, "and you can't be too sure we've heard the last yet, I still think it beastly selfish to have picked on this one date of the entire year. If they let her come down in the end, I'll tell her straight."

"You need'nt worry. She's safely locked away."

"How d'you know?"

"Because I've been to look. But I heard someone I shan't mention got through to her all right." Moira took this without the slightest sign.

"How d'you mean?" she asked.

There was no reply. And all the girls listened.

"You realise, probably, they've still not gone so far as to put telephones along the bath corridors?"

"I thought everyone knew how, Moira."

"Some people are certainly bent on having a mystery at any cost these days," the girl said.

"It's only there's a grating right through to the floor above. Whoever this was must have used it," a student informed them all, unaware that she was telling the girl who had first found this out.

Then Marion protested.

"I'd just like to say, I think it's beastly to deliberately plague poor Miss Edge and Baker, and get into touch with Merode in spite of what they said. Because they're not too bad considering."

"All right, Marion, but who put the whole dance in danger herself? After all, you did tell them both that Mary had gone to Matron, did'nt you?"

"Oh? Then what would I be doing down here now? You can't suppose they'd have let me come if I was in disgrace, surely to goodness."

There was rather a pause. It began to seem probable that Marion, in some way, had bought permission to attend, had tendered treachery over the counter.

"If anyone wants to know what I think, in my opinion you were decent to cover for them as long as you might," a girl volunteered.

"Just you wait till I catch Merode," Marion commented.

"But need there have been all the embroidery with that silly doll business?"

"Who did anyway?" Moira joined in.

She was given no answer. Everyone feared her tongue.

"Well, I shan't lose a night's sleep," a girl, who had been yawning, informed the company. "Praise be that a couple of us rustled up the gumption to do something in this dead-alive hole."

Moira took her on.

"But have you got the latest?" she demanded. "Right before the finish, pipped at the post, one minute before the whistle, two seconds left for play, guess what? Liz has hooked him. He's buying the hoop Saturday, and they'll be married in September."

"Who's he?"

"Why Sebastian, naturally, old 'Cause and Effect'. Or have you been asleep till now? Is'nt it splendid for Mr Rock, though." And it was plain from her voice that Moira meant this. "He might be a great grandfather extraordinarily quick. Only nine months, and what's that in his lifetime?"

The news was taken reflectively. Then someone asked, by way of fun,

"I wonder what Edgey'll give for a present?"

"A stuffed goose."

"One of those lucky cat charms."

"Or a black and white china pig money box."

"No, listen, Baker is not too bad really, you know. I bet she even signs them a fat cheque."

"However he could. Why, Liz's a million."

"Pity does it, dear. That's the way to get a man. Go weak up top."

"But she must be years and years older."

"D'you imagine the proper reason's that husband and wife may'nt give evidence against one another?"

"If you really believe what you've just said then all I can

say is, you've been having a sight too much of old Dakers in class."

"Plenty of time for slips betwixt cup and the lip, between now and September, in class and out."

"What d'you mean, because they won't wait six weeks. They'll be wed at the end of a gun."

"Only what you said, Moira, was'nt it, not till the autumn?"

"I say, is'nt everyone confusing, in white dresses for once? I'm frightfully sorry, I'd never have spoken to you if I'd seen you were a senior."

"That's all right. This is your first summer term, I expect. Else you'd know that tonight of all nights we're all in the party together. You can even ask Edge for a hop round if you want."

"Oh her."

"Don't be too sure. She does it divinely. You simply can't tell just by looking at people."

"Or their dolls," someone else put in.

"Oh, shut up."

"But I could never have imagined about her dancing. Anyway, it's awfully decent of you not to mind when I spoke."

"Well, my point is, Mary's a curse."

"Can you imagine? Mrs Blain does'nt know even yet."

"You suppose she'll go into hysterics when she does find out? My dear, the whole of that ancient stuff about her favourites is simply my eye and that Betty Martin. It's just she can't cook without she must make an almighty fuss of someone."

"Lord, things are slow. When on earth is it all due to start?"

"No hurry. I've been sick of the whole business for days."

"Well, there might just be some more on downstairs, remember."

"Watch your step, Melissa," Moira warned. "It would'nt do, now, for everyone to learn."

"I tell you," a girl said from the back, "I agree with Marion. This making blue eyed well-done-girl stuck up posters out of those two is perfectly crazy."

"Who has?"

"You, only this morning. When you promised us all they were wonderful. And started to cry even, as you thought of what might have happened to Mary."

"Oh I did, did I?"

"Stop squabbling, children. But please, I mean it. In another minute I shall be saying 'oh my poor head'."

This was a tolerable imitation of Marchbanks.

"How will Ma manage?" one of them asked. "That sinus of hers's been really bad."

"How could she ever dare not? We'll have a laugh over the love birds anyway. Someone might cut in a bit on S. just to make her wonder."

"Good for you, duck," another greeted Moira over this last remark. She was an unpopular girl.

"Anyway three cheers for the old State Service."

"Nobody's to touch the crab sandwiches if they know what's good for 'em. They're poison."

"We made the lemonade too sweet again, for that matter."

"There won't be much downstairs, you know where."

"For the third time, Melissa! Shut up, will you?"

"So what about downstairs?"

"There you are, all of you."

"Nothing."

"Oh, for the love of Mike, tell her."

"That's just one item. Because is it right we're to look after pigs now? Are'nt pigs rather the end?"

"Old Mr Rock will be in charge," Moira assured them confidently. "I've already told him," she lied.

"Why, what are pigs to him?"

"Pearls before swine."

"Well, of course, he would'nt like competition for Daise. After all? Can you imagine his precious darling set down in the middle of a hundred sties?"

"It'd be company. I feel Daisy's so alone."

"Anyway, I think Mr Rock an old sweet."

"He's afraid for her most of the time with this filthy swine fever," Moira explained. "If I was to be a vet I'd do something about it. Perhaps I'll wed one and make him."

"I did'nt expect you of all people to poke fun at Mr Rock, Moira."

"I'm not. I meant every word. After all, it's always the end for the poor pigs."

"And the waste when they die. 'A drain on the whole economy of the State'."

"I say, Midget, you do take S. off beautifully. Will you give us a star turn later?"

"Why, do they allow turns at the dance?"

"Not up here, we don't."

"Everyone this evening seems to imagine other people are poking elaborate fun. But swine fever's a true waste, is'nt it?"

"So what?"

"Oh, you're hopeless."

"I'm sorry to say, children, I don't fancy Mr Rock will be here much longer."

"Oh, not another death, Mirabel?"

"There's been nobody died off of late, has there, or if so, then I've not heard."

"He'll be shifted, you'll see."

"Lucky old, old man."

"But they can't. It would be the finish. Being with us is everything for him."

"Why? Has he told you, Mirabel?"

"Anyone knows just by looking in his sweet old face."

"At least be sure of this. If they are to get married Edgey will slide all three out one way or another."

"But why on earth?"

"Jealousy."

"Oh no. You can't be so absurd."

"Can't I? But it's right enough, mark my words. She won't have anyone wed just under her nose. And if the old man is broken hearted it will be that silly Elizabeth's fault. Honestly I've got now so that I loathe my own cloth, I hate all women."

"Not if we have the pigs, Edge won't. Why, there's noone else but Mr Rock."

"You're dappy where he's concerned, Moira. He's too aged to look after a fly even."

"How can you say that, when he's made such a success of Daisy and Ted?"

"What about Adams?"

"You don't include the granddaughter, I notice. No, he's nursing the viper in that woman, all right."

"You're all of you crazy," Moira said.

At this precise moment, and out of sight of these girls, Miss Inglefield, without warning, started the gramophone just once more to see if it would work. The loud speaker was full on so they could even hear the conductor, dead these many years, tap his stick at a desk some thirty summers back, and the music, with a roll of drums, swayed, swelled into a waltz. The girls, each one, gave a small sigh, moved, as one, each to her long promised partner, took her by the hand; they held hands as women but in couples, what had been formless became a group, by music, merged to a line of white in pairs, white faces, to the flowers and lighted ballroom, each pair of lips open to the spiralling dance. Then it stopped sharp into silence when, satisfied out of sight round the corner, Miss Inglefield lifted the needle. At once these students broke away disappointed, years younger once again.

"False alarm," someone commented severely.

A single pigeon, black in thickening sky, flew swift and on past the Park.

It was dusk.

Light from wide open windows increased by strides, primrose yellow over a dark that bled from blue.

With a swoop an owl came down across and hooted while Mr Rock and his daughter crept up the last stone flight when, unheralded, unannounced, and they could not see inside for the windows were yet too high above their heads, the gramophone crashed out once more, so loud now the old man halted entranced by the first bars of another great valse of drums and strings which, a second time however, was no sooner begun than cut off again by Inglefield.

"False alarm," Mr Rock said in a loud voice, and was about to elaborate with an attack on Edge for not keeping the instrument in proper order, when he was silenced, made mute, because, through his deafness, he had caught the last echoes of this music sent back by the beeches, where each starling's agate eye lay folded safe beneath a wing.

"We've started well," he then contented himself by suggesting.

"He said we'd meet out here," Elizabeth remarked. "To unlock us the side door."

"Better not," Mr Rock answered. "I'll ring the bell at the main entrance and be decently announced, or not attend at all," he said.

"Now Gapa," she wailed. "Who promised he'd be good?"

They slowly advanced across the last Terrace.

"Liz," he said, "in this world one should do a thing right, or leave it. If I'm to help as you've asked, you must give me credit for being able to see into their minds. I tell you they are dazzled by the position they hold here. We have to make our impression."

"Yes, Gapa," she agreed, not to upset him.

"They behave like the Begums of British India in my young days," he continued. "Besides there is noone need creep like a thief, particularly in our circumstances."

"Very good, Gapa. But will they let me see myself in a mirror, if only for a moment, then?"

"I'll be bound they gaze at their reflections on the glass at all hours," he replied. He was invigorated at the prospect of a strange, difficult night ahead.

"You will speak all right?"

"You can be quite sure I'll get you your chance to prink."

"Oh, you know I did'nt mean that. About Seb and me, I was trying to tell?" she asked.

"If their Byzantine obliqueness will allow, I might," he answered gaily, when a man hailed low and soft. "Liz," he called.

"There he is, oh at last," she exclaimed.

"Birt, can that be you?" the old man cautiously raised his voice. "And if so, don't skulk."

A dark, short figure rose, almost from under their feet.

"This is not Guy Fawkes night, after all," the sage commented.

"Sorry, sir, but you know the way things are," Sebastian

excused himself, adopting the hearty voice of a junior who was there to report present.

"Have they found my other child, then?" Mr Rock asked.

"Good Lord sir, not yet," Birt replied, still the shy, deprecating junior.

"Then you may lead us to the front entrance, for me granddaughter and I to be announced like civilized beings," he said.

The younger man was struck silent at this effrontery. He felt that Mr Rock should on no account so flaunt himself.

"It's this way, Gapa," Elizabeth prompted, resigned to disaster.

They turned, and at once became aware of the new powered moon, infinitely more than electric light which, up till then, had seemed, by a soft reflection from whence it cut into the Terrace, pallidly to surprise by stealth these mansion walls. For their moon was still enormous up above on a couch of velvet, blatant, a huge female disc of chalk on deep blue with holes around that, winking, squandered in the void a small light as of latrines. The moon was now all powerful, it covered everything with salt, and bewigged distant trees; it coldly flicked the dark to an instantaneous view of what this held, it stunned the eye by stone, was all-powerful, and made each of these three related people into someone alien, glistening, frozen eyed, alone.

"I'll leave you now," Sebastian said, as if to announce the moon had found him out.

"Thank you, I don't fancy that," Mr Rock objected. "They shall not come upon us unawares in this light." He also had on his mind the winking pairs of silvered eyelashes, still unseen, there might be watching from out black caverns of unlit, shadowed upstair casements.

"Oh, is this wise?" Elizabeth half wailed.

"He's to escort us in good order," the old man explained of Sebastian who had no torch.

"Well sir, I'd really rather not," Sebastian attempted to insist.

"Nonsense. Never try to duck when you're in the open."

Thus it was they came, one hydra-headed body to the enormous, overhanging portals, and Mr Rock pressed the bell which, by the moon, shone like a pearl on a vast hunk of frozen milk. To do so he had to enter and be lost, as if by magic, in a cube of impenetrable shade.

Elizabeth almost cried out after him, until his dead hand came forth to stab the bell a second time.

"Did it ring before?" he asked, out of his deafness.

"The girls are off duty," Sebastian said. "Tonight."

"Then we'll stay on notwithstanding, till we are made welcome," the old man answered, sure of himself, from the dark.

Steps made themselves heard within, at the advance. And, with a fearful creak, the great door was opened. Miss Baker stood silhouetted. It was Elizabeth she saw first, and she mistook the girl.

"Mary," she cried, in a small voice.

But she did not take long to come back to earth.

"Oh do enter in," Miss Baker said, bright as the light behind, to three silent people.

Mr Rock took time to dry his gum boots after which, through what to them was blinding electric, copper illumination they followed Baker, without another word, the short distance down this corridor on into the sanctum.

Each of these two Principals thought the other had invited Mr Rock and his granddaughter, yet, while Baker did the honours, and Edge rose to greet them with the words, "How kind to have troubled," this lady had twin notions at one and the same time; that Sebastian, since he was a member of the staff, had no business unsummoned in the Sanctum; and also that, on no account, must this sudden rush of guests mar Baker's and her own triumphal entry, by which the Dance was ever opened. Thus she observed, while shaking hands,

"You are rather late, you know." And added, "which is naughty," as she received Mr Rock, letting the smile die when she came to face Sebastian.

The old man bowed with the servile courtesy that he could assume at will.

"The pleasure is ours, ma'am," he announced, attentively serious. He was aware how, washed and brushed, he made a fine figure. Not so Elizabeth, for all her effort to seem at ease, while Sebastian could look noone in the eye, had even to shift his weight continuously from one foot to the other.

"I regret we have nothing in the way of light refreshment," Edge lied. She was not to put herself out for these people. "It does seem absurd on a Great Night like this, but there things are, we have to abide by our Regulations," she went on. "And if we were to make an exception the once, then we would do no more than to give rise to a Rule, should we not, in a contrary sense?"

"We are not here to eat and drink," Mr Rock pronounced stoutly. "It is just that Elizabeth would like to change her shoes."

"So kind . . . sorry . . . such a nuisance, I fear," the younger woman stammered.

But, although it was now more than time for the Principals to declare the ball open by making a personal appearance, Miss Edge, who had not wanted to give them more, did not seem able to leave her guests.

"And what is your news?" she asked of Mr Rock.

N

"At my age, ma'am," the old man answered, "one day is much like another. Which is what renders tonight memorable," he added, with a gleam in the huge eyes behind spectacles. "Because, on this occasion, I must insist that you allow me a dance."

"Oh Mr Rock, how splendid," Baker warmly said.

"But I always do dance with you, whenever you ask. What about last year? You remember?" Miss Edge put in at random, almost whinnying with nerves.

"I have not attended these three years past," Mr Rock, who had never been to one of their dances, announced with a small bow. "The year before I was indisposed, and on a previous occasion, I remember, I had hurt my leg."

"Twisted his knee . . . sprained his ankle," Elizabeth supplemented.

"Yet what I feel is, it only seems like yesterday," Edge announced, with a wee inclination from the waist. "And Sebastian," she ordered, turned on him for the first time, "you are not to shrink now. Not sit out continually."

"He won't. I promise," Elizabeth shrieked.

"These special Occasions mean so much to the Girls," Baker added.

"Because, while we're here, and if you permit, of course, I have a small suggestion I might offer," Mr Rock said to Miss Edge.

"By all means," she agreed. "And let it be now rather than later. Otherwise we could seem to be sharing secrets, putting our heads together before the children, and that, even at our age, might seem curious," she added with a sort of sneer.

"You flatter an old man," he said.

"My dear Mr Rock," Miss Baker cried, delighted, unaware.

"It was only, ma'am, it came to me I could, perhaps,

render a small service. But, naturally, this is a mere suggestion."

Edge felt the urge to consult her wristwatch, then restrained herself.

"I'm positive my colleague and I would be more than willing . . ." she faintly encouraged him, all the less enthusiastic because of her pressing anxiety to get the Dance begun.

"I thought I might lecture, say once a week, to your older girls, ma'am," Mr Rock brought gravely out. His granddaughter and Sebastian were astonished, as also the two Principals.

Miss Edge could recollect little of the subject in which he had made his name great so very many years ago, but her first determined thought was, —not suitable for younger Students, even nowadays.

"Well now," she said, as she believed cordial to the last. "This is generous indeed, is it not, Baker? You have quite taken away my breath."

"Why, Mr Rock," Miss Baker assented, wondering at last.

"We shall ponder this. Believe me I am truly Grateful," Edge went on, and experienced the most acute impatience. "Is that not so, Baker?" Then showed her hand. "Yet it just does occur to one . . . Oh I know, living as you have the best part of a lifetime with your great Discovery, at this late hour it must seem plain as day. Yet I cannot but put the question, would it be quite right for our dear Girls?"

Mr Rock found himself literally choked by momentary rage. How could these two dastardly trollops for a moment imagine he would ever so demean his nature as to discuss the Great Theory before children? He felt it so much that he reeled, and bumped into Sebastian, who had taken shelter. He controlled himself.

"We are at cross purposes, ma'am," he said. "What I had intended," he went on, in the self-absorption of old age, and a pathetic kind of dignity which they took for mere insolence, "was this. In fact a brief weekly homily on the care of pigs."

"You did?" was all Edge could bring out for the moment, while Baker gasped. Elizabeth took her young man by the finger of a hand, but, from the misery of his embarrassment, Birt shook her off.

"By the time they're older, one or more might be encouraged to have a go at this filthy swine fever," Mr Rock surmised, at his most bland and serious.

"Not many of our Students enter the Veterinary Service," Miss Edge said, in a distant voice. She began to move off. "Baker," she commanded. "We must not keep the girls."

"Now run along, Sebastian," Baker urged. He did not have to be told twice.

"But of course," she went on coldly, to the Rocks, "how thoughtless. I think you had both better come this way, to our washroom. You'll find a mirror for yourself, dear."

"Do hurry, Baker," Miss Edge called.

So the old man came upon himself alone with his granddaughter in front of a white enamelled door.

He was silent for a minute. Then he said severely,

"Barbarous of them to mix the sexes."

"You go first," Elizabeth commanded. As he fumbled with the handle she caught at his sleeve.

"Oh Gapa," she exclaimed, "you did'nt . . . I mean, what an extraordinary idea . . . to keep the cottage for us all, was'nt it . . . oh, are you sweet."

"I'll leave your shoes inside," he answered, shutting her out.

When the music began a third time, eighteen children waiting in the corridor lifted heads from their confabulations but did not immediately move off towards the Hall because of two previous disappointments. Then the valse continued, on and on, and they could see couples circle into view, their short reflections upon the floor continually on the move behind swinging skirts over polished wax, backwards and forwards, in and out again as each pair swung round under chandeliers. And at the sight these others walked on the lighted scene, held white arms up to veined shoulders, in one another's arms moved off, turning to the beat with half shut eyes, entranced, in a soft ritual beneath azalea and rhododendron; one hundred and fifty pairs in white and while,—equally oblivious, inside their long black dresses, Miss Baker and Miss Edge lovingly swayed in one another's bony grip, on the room's exact centre, to and fro, Edge's eyes tight closed, both in a culmination of the past twelve months, at spinsterish rest in movement, barely violable, alone.

Above, locked safe into a sick bay, curtains close drawn against the moon, Merode's infant breathing told she was asleep.

Still farther off, in their retiring room, unaware that the dance had opened, the staff sat to make scant conversation. They were embarrassed; and, out of sympathy, perhaps, for the lovesick Winstanley, had chosen to pretend, by ignoring him, that Birt, who seemed most ill at ease, was not present in fat flesh amongst them.

All over the Institute hardly a word more was now spoken, not one down the Hall where Inglefield had taken up her stand to drive the deafening music. Then, suddenly at a doorway, there loomed unheralded the figures of Elizabeth and the old man. Both were dressed as black as those two Principals.

His great white head nodded to rapt, dancing students.

"The first will have to be with me, then," he announced to the granddaughter loud under music, for Inglefield had turned the power full on and because, as he looked around, he had seen no sign of Sebastian. Then Moira whirled past, hair spread as if by drowning over Marion's round, boneless shoulder. He let his arms, which he had held out to Elizabeth, drop back as he followed the child with carefully expressionless, lensed eyes. And Liz gave a gasp of disenchantment as she bent to raise the old hands from his sides; after which they launched out together onto the turning, dazzled floor. But not for them, as with the others, in a smooth glide. Because Mr Rock went back to the days before his own youth, was a high stepper.

He stepped high, which is to say he woodenly, uproariously lifted knees as if to stamp while he held the granddaughter at arm's length, but did not cover much ground. Still the one man on that floor, they made a twice noticeable pair because they were alone in paying heed to where they went, in his case to avoid a fall when he might break a hip, certainly fatal for a man his age, and she for the boy who remained, at the moment, her one hope of continuing to live.

"They are here," Baker, who kept an eye half open, murmured to Miss Edge. The news came to this lady as though from a distance.

"Let all enjoy themselves. They must," she mumbled in return.

There was just one note might have jarred at the outset, though it passed unnoticed. Mrs Blain had, as was natural, been amongst the first starters. She'd grabbed hold of an orderly, and was saying while she blindly danced,

"Oh, we're champion."

"You do waltz beautifully," her girl replied.

"Soft soap," the cook answered. "But I've one matter on my mind. Why my Mary's not here to enjoy things. I can't make out the reason she never phoned." Mrs Blain panted, because puffed.

"Perhaps she could'nt," the child lazily suggested.

"Oh, are'nt we all dancing?" Mrs Blain enthused. "Just look at us," she said, from closed eyes. "I do wish she could be here, though. She might've given me a ring. Mind now, will you look how you go? This night's for all to enjoy, is'nt it, bumpin' into people? Yes, I'd've liked to get a word. Illness in the family can be a terrible upset."

"I hardly think it is," this vague girl told her, after they had danced some more.

"There, you're only dizzy, a bit. What do you know?" Mrs Blain demanded.

"I don't fancy she's home," the child softly insisted.

"Then where is she?" Mrs Blain cried out, and opened green eyes rather wild. It seemed they danced like a whirling funnel.

"She's gone, you'll discover."

"Nowhere to be come upon?" the cook wailed, and pushed that spiralling orderly away at arm's length until, she felt, the girl revolved about her like a wisp of kitchen paper. "Lost?" she yelled, but it was drowned by music. "What's this? So that was it, then? Oh, you wicked things."

"Not to do with me, Mrs Blain," the orderly gently protested, given over to her shivering, glazed senses.

"Wicked deceivers," the woman said, in a calmer voice. "I'll have my enquiries to make on that, all right."

"We think it's pretty rotten of her to want to spoil this heaven evening."

"Well then," the cook said, quietened at once, and folded

the child to an enormous bosom. Upon which both gave their two selves over, entire. As they saw themselves from shut eyes, they endlessly danced on, like horns of paper, across warm, rustling fields of autumn fallen leaves.

Quite soon, girls began to cut in. While Inglefield kept the instrument hard at it, the original partners began to break up, to step back over the wax mirror floor out of one another's arms, moving sideways by such as would not be parted yet, each to tap a second favourite on a bare, quiet shoulder. Then the girl so chosen would give a little start, open those great shut eyes, much greater than jewels as she circled and, circling yet, would dip into these fresh limbs which moved already in the dance, disengaging thus to leave her first choice to slip sideways in turn past established, whirling partners until she found another who was loved and yet alone.

Less satisfactory was the crush of fortune hunting children, with more fabulous gems for eyes, round Baker and Miss Edge, both of whom affected to ignore their riches as, oblivious yet well aware, they danced out together the dull year that was done. One after the other they would be tapped on a hard, black garmented back. But, as was traditional on these occasions, they lingered in one another's orbit, until at last Edge had had enough. When that moment came she simply opened eyes, from which long years had filched the brilliants, said "Why Moira", in simulated wonder, and so chose this child who, of all the suitors, was the first she saw in her hurried tiredness.

"Oh, ma'am," the girl said, delighted, while they drifted off on music, Moira leading.

"Is'nt it wonderful?" the child asked, when she proudly noted the Principal had once more closed her eyes.

"I could go on for ever," she murmured further, when there was no response.

Then, as was usual at these Dances, but which came, as it always did, in all parts of the room at one and the same time because it occurred to almost everyone at once, there was mooted the project of a gift to their Principals.

"Why don't we get up a sub for Edgey and Bakers?"

"I think we ought to do something for both.   They're sweet."

"This is too marvellous.   We must manage a present in return."

"Ma'am," said Moira to the dreaming guv'nor like a black ostrich feather in her arms.   "You're wonderful. So good."

The music was a torrent, to spread out, to be lost in the great space of this mansion, to die when it reached the staff room to a double beat, the water wheel turned by a rustling rush of leaf thick water.   It was so dispersed and Winstanley, seated alongside Sebastian, could, for the conversation of her fellow teachers, hear no breath, neither the whispering in the joists from a distant slither of three hundred pairs of shoes, nor the cold hum of violins in sharp, moonstruck window glass.   She did not know until Sebastian, who could not tell why, other than that he was restless, got up to open a door, when at once she realised the house had come to life, and recognised the reason.   —He would never listen for me, she accused Elizabeth.

It came to all the staff along the outside passage, first as a sort of jest, a whispered doublemeaning almost, then as a dance master's tap in time with music.   After which, at any rate for the women, a far rustling of violins once recognised called as air, beaten through stretched feathers, might have spoken to the old man's goose, that long migratory flight unseen.   So they rose, as Ted had never yet, and, with a burst of nasal conversation, made haste toward their obligations in the excitement of a year's end;

not without a sense of dread in every breast which, in
Sebastian's case was even more,—for him it was the violin
conjured, sibilant, thin storm of unease about a halting
heart.

While they hurried closer the whole edifice began to
turn, even wooden pins which held the panelling noise-
lessly revolved to the greater, ever greater sound. Thus
they almost ran to their appointment, so giddy they were
fit to tumble down; but, once in the room, paired off
quietly, decently as best they might.

Sebastian stood against a wall, Winstanley could only
take on Marchbanks, and Dakers was left with the last
woman he would have picked.

"He's here," Miss Rock said to her grandfather, but he
did not catch on.

"Care? Of course I care," he replied, in the deepest
voice. Yet she took her hand out of his, was slipping
from his arms.

She detached herself and, not unnoticed, made her way
to where the young man waited. As for Mr Rock, when
he saw himself abandoned, he moved clumsily over to the
dais. Moira steered past with Miss Edge, whose eyes
were tight closed. The child's lips sent "Later," at him,
and he read them. Then, when he reached the sort of
throne he had picked out, he climbed up and sat himself
heavily where none but the Principals had a right to be
seated. He was proud.

It was such a grand sight Mr Rock was almost glad he
had attended.

Miss Winstanley noticed Elizabeth make for Sebastian,
and it turned her sick as she circled about Marchbanks.

"How are you, dear?" she asked the older woman,
thinking of herself.

Miss Marchbanks danced with great concentration,
and the little smile of a martyr.

"Thank you, my shoulders are broad enough," she replied.

"There is something presumptuous in all this," Winstanley said of the evening with what was, for her, an unusually sad voice. She was watching Elizabeth give herself over, dance as one with Sebastian, deep in his arms. They moved as though their limbs had mutual, secret knowledge, were long acquainted cheek to cheek; the front of their thighs kissed through clothes; an unconscious couple which fired burning arrows through gasping music at her.

"Our dear girls must have a marvellous time," Marchbanks volunteered, with conviction. "But if you spoke of Mr Rock, the uninvited guest, then you knew of this fresh honour, that he is to be elected? I expect he feels sure of himself now."

The repetition of the beat, and her lazy misery about Sebastian, began to make Winstanley drowse.

"How goes your head?" she asked again.

There was a silence between them. Then Marchbanks murmured,

"I'm so used to my heads I don't notice."

"There's anaesthesia in a valse."

"But I do wonder time and again, dear," Miss Marchbanks dreamily answered. "Do we not meet this modern music the same way, in the old days, as they used to go to fairs? You will have read of it. People plunging into the hurly-burly to forget their miserable condition, their worries."

"Ah, they were'nt fools, then, they seldom are," Winstanley said at random, and shut her eyes tight. Through a blinding headache Miss Marchbanks guided the younger woman, who still had hope.

"Darling," Elizabeth said to her young man, out of shut eyes also, "I spoke to him. He'll do it."

"Oh Liz," he answered, looking over his shoulder. "But you should neither of you have come."

She smiled the little smile of satisfaction.

"Are'nt you glad we came?" she asked.

He did not answer. Still from her closed eyes she thought how the hand she had on his shoulder must seem to him like his heart's white flower.

"I'd have imagined you'd be glad," she said, still satisfied.

Moira had long been succeeded in Miss Edge's arms by other partners, but Mr Rock had forgotten the girl in his wait for the Principal to be vacant. He sat on alone, a monument, determined to buttonhole Edge the first moment he might. But she was too popular. Even when he saw Moira come crabwise through the serious, frantic dancers, he did not imagine she was after him. As he concentrated on the guv'nor, he did not notice the child again until she stood below his chair, to make the usual offer of herself, to present, as she always instinctively did, the endless prize of her fair person.

"Are you ready?" she asked.

"Hullo," he said. "I've danced enough."

"Mr Rock, d'you mean to say you've forgotten?" she protested. "I was to show you," she lied. "Now, don't you remember?"

He did not wish to appear confused in a crowd, or by this music.

"Where do we go, then? Lead away," he said, blithe, and got up with difficulty.

"Over here," she told him, took the little finger of his right hand.

Once they were outside, the passages seemed quite deserted, although there was one girl yawned alone in the pantry.

"Not many down yet, Moira," she greeted, unlocking a door which opened onto a steep flight of stairs that led to the depths. There was no hand rail, only a length of rope looped to some rusted stanchions. Mr Rock's courage failed.

"Have I to negotiate these?" he pleaded aghast, unwilling to admit his disabilities. "I don't think I can manage."

Meantime, the other girl bolted the door through which they had entered.

"Oh, but you must," Moira said, calm but firm.

"You might tell them to hurry my relief," the first child suggested.

"It's my eyes," Mr Rock confessed, and put a foot forward as though about to enter an ocean.

"Come on," Moira begged, started to descend in front, still holding his finger. "We don't want to get caught, do we?"

When he thought over the episode a day later, Mr Rock felt this last remark, with its suggestion of conspiracy, had been the prime factor, squalid as it was to have to admit it, which induced him to embark on the first venture.

"Wait," he said, abandoning himself to the descent.

As soon as he was fairly engaged on these stone steps, the other child locked the door above, and, with it, shut away a last murmur of the dance. So they haltingly crept down into blinding silence, lighted by dirty bulbs festooned with cobwebs.

"Where are you taking me?" he demanded, and awkwardly pulled the rope.

"Wait. You'll find out," she answered.

—Age made a man very dependent, he thought, for this was like the pretty child that led the blind. Indeed his eyes were adequate, even if thick lenses distorted edges of vision, but it was his feet were blind, which fumbled air. Then, with a great feeling of relief, he had arrived; he stood on a level cellar passage, but nevertheless, still groped forward, with the forefingers of his free hand brushing a wall, and picked up more cobwebs. —He was on the way to wet wine and dry coke, he thought, for this was the region of bins and boilers, and also, presumably, of somewhat else.

Moira, in order not to dirty her frock, led the old man as if they had to pass through a tall bed of white and black nettles. She walked sideways, delicately, held his other hand high which seemed to protest in the traditional manner of the sightless.

"Is'nt it awful?" she exclaimed.

"Now look, my dear," Mr Rock said, "All this is very flattering, I don't doubt, but we have to get back upstairs, some time. Surely we've done enough."

Then he saw the bare corridor turn to an upended empty crate and a green baize door.

"Stay two minutes," she said, going round one and through the other, to leave him alone.

"What foolishness is this?" he pettishly demanded aloud of his solitude, hard of hearing, yet with an idea he could catch whispers, even more the other side. Then she was back, and had closed the door. She looked sad, listened a moment. But she climbed onto the crate, so that the rajah's hoard of her eyes was on a level with the old man's spectacles.

"We're too soon," she said. "You must'nt look before they're ready. Come here," she demanded. He went up. She laid a cheek against him, and, before he knew what she was at, had rolled her face over until soft lips brushed his that were dry as an old bone.

"Stop it," he muttered, and stepped violently away

until his back became covered with powdered whitewash. He rubbed a hand over his mouth, left a cobweb on the corner.

"You're mad, Moira. You did this for a bet," he said frightened.

"Yes," she lied. It was only part of the routine; also she had wanted to make up to him, of course, for the fruitless journey.

He hurriedly started off towards the stairs. Her eyes, as they turned to watch, hung out more diamonds.

"Come on at once, my poor girl," he ordered, and did not look for her. Mopping at his face with a handkerchief, as Dakers had at breakfast, he set the pace out of it. He trod high again, as though afraid of a wire that might trip him. She followed obediently, in immodest silence.

When Inglefield allowed the instrument its first interval, the usual twenty minutes, and that Banqueting Hall spun down to a flower hung cavern of still white couples, Elizabeth had the sense not to make at once for moonlight with Sebastian, but joined a sideways drift which had begun to the buffet next door. In front of the willow pattern, hand-basin of lemonade, however, they became quite a centre of interest. For word had gone round that at last they were engaged; the students, one and all, were in a giving mood; and the idea, which seemed to each gently panting chest to be unique, the possessor's very own, took shape, flowed spontaneously into a project of the wedding gift. But not so loud that it could be expressed, not yet at least, not all at once.

"Careful with the lemonade," they said to her. "It's poison. I ought to know, I made it."

"Is'nt your grandfather wonderful? I'm so proud he came."

"Sweet for us that Edgey asked you."

"Do try one of these."

Elizabeth simpered at the girls about, accepted all they offered with small cries.

"What of your Daise," a student began. "Will she like company?"

Liz took this up.

"What does one, I mean it is'nt possible, is it? Animals you know. There's no way, can there be? But you see all I'm trying to say is, you may never tell, and not only with pigs when everything's told, you can't be sure of human beings, either?"

Sebastian hurried to the rescue.

"Surely this much could be assumed," he said, unaffected and serious, in his lecturer's voice. "That where waste occurs, and, mark you, waste as such, in normal times, is not so bad a thing, it can represent no more than the effect of a high standard of life, then, in those conditions, is'nt it better that what waste may naturally exist should be diverted to a guise in which those who cause the self same waste may employ it to replace what has been wasted? I'm afraid I've got a bit involved, you know. In other words, if you are in a position to be able to afford not to eat potatoes in their jackets, why not feed the peelings to pigs?"

"But that's what happens, surely, Mr Birt," one of them objected.

"Daisy does'nt have all," he said. "The rest goes to pig farms, I agree, but here we touch on what might be termed the ethics of political economy. I would'nt exactly recommend your using this in exam papers, but I do put it forward that, if there is waste, then you should keep your own pigs. Clean up so to speak, behind."

"Then what are they going to eat on pig farms?"

"But, surely, that is the affair of the State?" he asked. "A mass feeding of swine should not be haphazard. The surplus of a hundred thousand State factories must be made up into balanced pig foods."

"And what if the pigs don't like?"

"They will. That is the purpose of the State," he said.

"But how can you tell, which is my whole point, don't you see?" Elizabeth rushed in. "You never know with animals, or anyone."

"Yet, Liz," he explained patiently, "the one goes thin, the other complains aloud, and both go thin."

"Oh it's not only food, I would'nt be so silly, there's lots of things people are as silent as animals over. In what way is any single person sure how a certain matter will turn out?" She told him this with such intensity that he grew cautious. "Whether they will like it, or no?" she explained, about their sharing the cottage with Gapa.

"I'm not sure I follow," he said, as well he might.

"Would'nt you say that was like a man, all over?" she exclaimed, favouring the girls about with a delighted smile. "Why it's quite simple." Then she sheered off again. "If you had to cook for someone, you'd soon learn," she said. "There need be no question of waste in the least. What does count is what's available. Don't you see how? Suppose I know my grandfather likes prawns and I can only get shrimps. As a matter of fact," she elaborated to the students, "he adores a prawn tea," pretending that she invariably arranged his meals every day. "But very likely I can only manage the other. What's the difference? Why, shrimps give him a pain." Then she had an urge to be open with them. "As a matter of fact," she went on, "I had a breakdown at work, you

O

may have heard, and I have'nt seemed able to do a great lot lately. Oh, Gapa's been marvellous, has'nt he, Seb? He's cooked for all of us," she said, to underline the special, though as yet unpublicised, relationship between her and the young man. "Of course, it's not a mere matter of food and cooking. There's everything comes into this. Someone wanted to know whether Daisy would like all the other pigs on either side. Well, what about us? Who can say if we shall like? D'you see what's back of my mind?"

She gave Sebastian a piercing glance. Some of the students had already had enough, were discussing other topics.

"My point was, dear, you would feel better if what you had to support was nourished on your left overs," Sebastian said.

"That's not so," she cried. "How about children?"

"When they're nursed, it exactly bears out my point."

"I don't think we need go into biological details here," she said. "Anyway, after six months or so they're weaned, surely? No, but when children are growing up. You don't give them your leavings then."

"We were on the subject of pigs," he insisted.

"You will, sometimes, be so dense, well pigheaded," she archly complained. "Oh my dears, what must you think of us?" she asked the girls who, for the most part, had long ceased to pay attention. "You know Gapa's notion, about what he might decide to do," she said with a loaded look at everyone, which even Sebastian did not seem to understand. "The last one, of course. What he suggested to Miss Edge just now? Well, could anything be better?" She referred to Mr Rock's unexpected offer to give talks on pigs. "To hold you know what," she ended, to make it doubly plain she meant their cottage.

"Is'nt it splendid Mr Rock's to teach about Daisy," one

of the students took her up, innocent as the day, obviously under the impression that she was opening a fresh topic.

"Why whoever told you that, then?" Elizabeth asked, delighted at what she took to be confirmation.

"Oh everyone knows. Don't they, girls?"

"Sebastian, did you hear? Is'nt it marvellous?" Miss Rock crowed. "You see? It means Miss Edge must have thought of our plan first." In such a way the granddaughter both claimed the idea for her very own and assumed Edge's acquiescence, thus wilfully ignoring the heights, or depths, of gossip prevalent amongst these children.

Miss Edge, when the gramophone stopped a second time, once more found herself the centre of a slightly panting group plying her with invitations. She shooed them off towards the buffet, and stalked to the dais that she might rest herself. She had not gone far before she perceived Mr Rock up there again, alone, as though lionised. She paused. But, after all, it would be too absurd if the man's presence hindered one of the Principals taking her rightful place. So she glided over despite him.

With an acute struggle against his old joints, he rose to this approach.

"My congratulations, ma'am," he said. "A memorable sight we have tonight."

"My dear Mr Rock. Sweet indeed to bother."

"I trust your exertions will permit, later, your partnering an old man."

"My dear Sir, how could I forget? I shall hold you to it."

In no time they were seated side by side, Miss Edge delicately inclined towards the sage. Her eyes roved over the Hall of her girls, in stiff pairs as if bereft at this interruption of music. He, for his part, looked on the old fashioned dancing pumps he wore, while he leaned in her direction to minimise the deafness.

"Takes me quite back to my young days," he persisted.

"And mine, if you please," she countered.

In this he lied, however. It was true the more distant past now made a sharper picture; the time at school, hard work, then six months chasing girls and finally the signal triumph; but he was concentrated now on his granddaughter, on how best to approach Miss Edge.

"I do know a little about these things. It is your powers of organisation, if I may say so, which I especially applaud," he said.

"You understand our Tamashas are traditional," the lady condescended. "They run themselves. All Baker and I must do, is to watch that there are no departures."

—Departures? Escapes? Was this a reference to poor Mary, he wondered?

"Ah, the sudden, the unexpected," he tested her.

The sudden, she asked herself? Could he be aiming at that unfortunate child? The whole trouble really was, too many knew about Merode and Mary.

"The odious deviations from what is usual," she corrected, dashing him a glance. "One of the things we should provide here is memories, which is why I strive for the repetitive. It is a minor function, of course, in a great Place like this, but we must send them out so they can look back on the small pleasures shared. I dare say there are several reunion parties to celebrate Founder's Day in many a State Recreation Room this self same moment. You know, it is not long since that Baker and I were privileged by the State to create the Institute out of a void. Believe me, Mr Rock, it was a vacuum indeed when we first came. But already our old girls would be distressed to hear of change in any shape."

"It is a sadness in old age," he agreed. "One's contemporaries die. One can no longer share one's youth."

"Ah, you have lived the lonely life," she said.

—Now what could she mean? He wondered. He waited.

"But there have been compensations, surely?" she continued. "Of course, noone can speak for another, life has at least taught me that, I hope. Yet to remain on in this beautiful Place, as a reward for great work well done, must be a remarkable privilege I cannot help feeling."

"One has a pride in achievement," he answered, to show that he, at any rate, need not be modest. "Still, old age is a lonely condition, as you'll find in due course, Miss Edge."

—What could the wily old man be hinting, she impatiently asked under her breath?

"Yet you do have company," she insisted.

He reminded himself to be careful. Doubtless she intended a sly reference to his habit of speech with certain students when they strolled down to the cottage.

"Not the life shared, memories in common," he brought out, conscious of his deep, pathetic tones.

"But your granddaughter?"

"She's only here when ill."

"I have noticed, Mr Rock, how much improved she seems in herself."

—Now, what was she after? Was this to be the clean sweep, to rid herself of Elizabeth and him at the single, Machiavellian stroke.

"I wish I could think so, ma'am," he said, with anxious care.

"Just look at Moira," Miss Edge then changed the subject without warning. The old man wildly raised his head, in guilt. "Really she stares out of those great eyes of hers as though she were going to be ill."

He said not a word. Did these two blockheaded Principals never have any idea of the strains and stresses, he wondered? And what was all this about sickness? He kept his face a blank for the child's sake.

"Yes, I'm sure she's ever so much better."

"Moira, ma'am?"

"No, your granddaughter Elizabeth, naturally. Tell me, what are your plans for her?" This was to come out into the open with a vengeance, he thought.

"It is in the hands of the doctor, of course," he replied, with a sidelong glance.

"Sick notes seem quite to govern all our decisions these days," Miss Edge agreed, to abandon the subject. She fell silent, the better to watch her girls at rest.

This silence made the old man increasingly nervous.

Then, with no further word exchanged, the Principal made a sign to Inglefield, who at once restarted the gramophone.

The crowd of girls in white poured back. Even before they were in one another's arms they twirled in doorways.

This music was heavy, stupendous for Mr Rock.

"May I have my honour now, ma'am?" he enquired.

"How kind," she answered. "But I wonder if I might rest a little."

"I never knew you had trouble with your eyes, ma'am," he said. 'How blind', was what he had heard.

"Kind," Miss Edge shouted, with a brilliant, fixed smile at her circling throng of children. —It will be such a tiresome bore if I have to try to make him hear above this perfectly heavenly valse, she thought.

"You did not catch what I said. Only Tired, want to Rest a minute," she explained in a great voice.

—Why must Moira watch him like it, as if he had done her injury, he asked himself? The foolish little intriguer. She was perilous. Because Edge who had noticed already, might end by getting it into her narrow skull.

Then, at that precise moment, Elizabeth came just below, dancing, as he thought, in a manner which could not be permissible in any era, so as to flaunt the fact of Sebastian no doubt. He assumed an idiot look of pride, in the way he could the swill man's cry, and turned towards Miss Edge to note her reaction. He saw she had not bothered to see them, which was a relief, though at the same time he resented the culpable blindness. —Perhaps she is really having trouble with her eyes, as I with my ears, he wondered.

Edge may have sensed he watched, because she swung her head round with a dry smile.

"The dears," she said. "They must and shall enjoy themselves."

Now the music was in full flood he could not be sure of what he heard. When he thought he caught what had been said, he was often wrong; and the few times he was confident he had the sense, he still knew he hardly ever did have it when, as now, under a difficulty. So he assumed she was speaking of Liz.

"Thanks to you, the time of her life," he assured Miss Edge.

—Why cannot the sad man realise I will not be bothered tonight with individuals, she asked herself?

"There must not be a child who does not take a happy memory of this away in her, for the rest of her days," she answered.

"And so they ought," he agreed stoutly, leaving the Principal in ignorance as to whether he had heard.

Another silence fell between them. But there was a deal he had to tell her yet. He was determined to have it out.

Accordingly he tried to bring the conversation back some-where near the more immediate topics.

"Is this correct, what I hear about pigsties, like mush-rooms after rain, over the magnificent grounds?" he asked.

"Why, whoever gave you that idea, Mr Rock?"

"A flat idea? I don't quite follow, ma'am."

—Really, the man was intolerable. It was indeed time for him to go where he could be properly looked after with his deafness and everything, she thought.

"I never question a decision of my Superiors," she reproved. "No, I asked how you had learned?" She yelled this at an ear. He took it in.

"Amazing the way things get about a community such as ours, ma'am," he replied. She wondered at his effrontery, that he should claim kinship with their Work. "No," he went on, "of course I have given a hand with the swill in the past, and now, I suppose, you will want all of it for yourselves? But to tell you the truth, ma'am, time has lain a bit heavy on my hands. In fact I don't know that I've been pulling my weight. It is a privilege to lead my existence," he said with an irony just sufficiently controlled to escape her notice. "What I had wondered, since you don't seem to be too keen that I should give them a few plain talks on pigs, was whether I could not, after all, work up a little course of lectures on what I may have done. Something along the lines of the joy, and reward, of achievement," he ended in great bitterness, effectively disguised behind a mandarin smile.

—Of all bores, Miss Edge moaned to herself, the per-sistent ones are worst. He could not have appreciated, then, what she had told him on this very subject in the Sanctum.

"Well," she said genially. "Well! That will need thinking over. But how lucky for the Girls."

"No trouble at all," he lied at random.

"Shall we leave it till tomorrow, Mr Rock?" she suggested. "I hardly feel, just at the crux of our little Jollification, that we can give your project the attention it deserves."

"Whatever you say, ma'am," he agreed. —At least Elizabeth could hardly now make out that he had not explored every avenue, he told himself.

Soon after, he got up and left Miss Edge. The lady was so obviously lost in happy contemplation of her charges. And he felt he had done enough. Honour was satisfied, he thought.

Perhaps forty minutes later, Edge was joined on the dais by her colleague who declared she could dance no longer, and sat herself heavily down, to fan a cheek with a lace bordered black and white handkerchief.

"It is excellent, dear, quite excellent," she cried.

"I think so, Baker," Miss Edge answered, in an exalted mood again.

"What a good notion of yours, Mabel, to ask the Rocks," Baker, full of enthusiasm, gaily cried above the music. "It will give those two so much pleasure later, when they get home," she added.

"I did no such thing," her colleague said, but did not seem to pay attention.

"The old man really cuts quite a distinguished figure," Baker insisted, to all appearances not having taken in Edge's negligent reply, perhaps because of this great spring tide of music.

"Nevertheless," Edge enquired, "what was it led you to ask them, Hermione?"

"I?" Miss Baker demanded. "I never invited anyone, dear."

Edge leaned over her colleague in one swift movement, as though to peer up Baker's nostrils.

"Then you mean they are here unasked?" she hissed. "Oh no, Hermione, not that, for it would be too much."

"I did'nt," Baker promised. They looked wildly at one another. "Now careful, Mabel," she went on. "We don't wish to make ourselves conspicuous."

"But this is preposterous persecution. It could even be wicked."

"Mabel don't, I beg of you. Just when we were so enjoying ourselves. If you could only catch sight of your expression, dear. We shall have everyone look our way in a minute."

"Hermione, they shall leave at once," Miss Edge proposed.

"To brazen themselves like this," Baker hastily agreed. "Why, it's wrong."

In time, however, both ladies gained sufficient control to be able to look straight out over the Hall with a glare above the dancers. But when Elizabeth came by once more, still in Sebastian's arms, hair still disarranged, still dancing as though glued to him, they both deflected their vision through the degrees necessary to take in this orgiastic behaviour, which they had not previously bothered to notice. They then followed the couple with palsied indignation, rooted to valse trembling chairs.

"You saw?" Miss Edge brought out at last.

"Yes, and alas I still do, Mabel."

"Well, whatever else we may decide, dear, their little display of animalism must be stopped at once."

"Whatever you think," Miss Baker agreed. But seemed hesitant.

"Yes, Hermione, and why on earth not?"

"Is it always wise to bring matters of this kind out in the open? The thought just flashed through my mind, that's all."

"Hermione, I wish I could follow your reasoning."

"It's just I can't quite make out that any of the children appear to have caught on, particularly. You see?" Miss Baker asked.

"Should we wait for the girls to copy this themselves?"

"It does seem a most ambiguous style to dance, I must admit, Mabel."

"In a moment, when the first flush of this glorious music has worn off, I'm very much afraid the cat will be out of the bag, Hermione."

"Where has Mr Rock got to, then? I don't see him," Miss Baker said, to draw a red herring across the trail. She was a cautious woman.

"Oh drinking, undoubtedly drinking outside," Miss Edge proclaimed.

"But there's no more than lemonade, dear."

"He had a flask, Hermione. I saw the bulge myself, in his pocket."

"You appal me."

"Ah, if it were only that."

"Oh surely, Mabel?"

"I insist he is far too close to some of the girls."

"Be that as it may," Miss Baker sternly said, pulling herself together, "I do beg you to take this fresh affront in a Christian spirit."

"Why should I?" her colleague demanded. "When he flaunts our authority?"

"You know how deaf Mr Rock is. Perhaps he misheard some time this week. Thought you had invited him?"

"Oh no, no, that simply will not wash. You must realise all he misunderstands is just what he does not wish to hear.   Besides I have not said two words to the man in months."

"Of course there may have been . . . but I don't think . . . wait, I'm trying to remember," Miss Baker said.   "He might have thought, when I mentioned, when we met by the Lake," she delicately hinted, to scale down Mr Rock's offence.   "But of course I'm in no two minds. A member of the staff has no business whatever dancing with the misguided woman.   If we don't pull together on occasions of this sort, what good are we, after all?   And to go about it in that disgraceful way is too bad of Sebastian.   As to her, I cannot believe she can be responsible for her actions.   Oh no, don't think I don't agree with you, dear."

"Then, Hermione, I am going straight onto the floor. I shall simply tap him on the shoulder, gesture him Off. I shall not say a word," Miss Edge announced, and made as though to get down from her chair.

"But Mabel, is this wise?" Miss Baker asked, in a sort of shriek to pierce the double basses which, at the moment, held the recorded melody.

"There is more to our duties than a kind of still-born native caution," Edge complained, but stayed seated.

"Yes, dear," her colleague comforted, satisfied that she had, at least, held off immediate action.

"If we see another woman ridiculed before our very eyes, are we to sit by without a word?" Miss Edge demanded.   "There is a double obligation on us, surely. To call Elizabeth Rock to order, for she is leading him along to make a fool of her, to compromise herself with him, Baker; and, second, to show our girls we shall not turn a blind eye upon wrongdoing, which this disgraceful behaviour most surely is."

"You are right, Mabel, of course.   But how will Mr Rock react?"

"He should be eternally grateful. You cannot tell me he wants his girl compromised with Sebastian Birt."

"No, Mabel. But you know the way he is. He might take our reproof for an affront."

"And if he did?"

"My dear, he is such friends with Mr Swaythling. This can hardly be a moment to invite publicity, the attention of the Supervisor, just when we are face to face with the enigma of Mary, not to mention Merode."

"Yes, but there must be some justice in our affairs, Baker. If we are to harbour the informer in our midst, let us have nothing to hide, at least."

"Leave sleeping dogs lie, Edge."

"And what have we done? My conscience is clear. Can you point to any single circumstance under which we could possibly be said to have countenanced the girl's disappearance?"

"Of course, this whole thing's absurd," her colleague answered. "At the same time, I did'nt quite care for Mrs Manley's attitude. After she had seen Merode she rather made capital out of Mary's being such a favourite of ours."

"I trust, whenever we make friends with one of the Students, that will not be considered sufficient justification for the child concerned to make off at dead of night, and in her pyjamas."

Miss Baker laughed elegantly at this sally.

Just then Sebastian bumped Elizabeth, through careless-ness, into another couple and she opened hers to find herself gazing into the Principals' four eyes.

"Look out Seb," she said. "They're glaring like a couple of old black herons down in the meadow, over the daisies."

After this, they danced with more circumspection.

"It is a matter of elementary justice, Baker," Edge insisted, but in so much calmer a voice, now Elizabeth was no longer dancing cheek to cheek, that her colleague could be satisfied the danger of an open breach was past. "If one sees wrong done, one cannot sit idly by, dear."

"Of deportment, or behaviour? Even on a special occasion?" Miss Baker asked.

"But really, sometimes you astound me," Edge said, mildly warming to the subject. "That sort of thing is like an infection, surely? I refer of course to the way those two have been dancing. If you find scarlet fever in a community, you isolate it. There is the fever hospital."

"I dare not look at Winstanley," Baker replied.

"Then I will do so for you," Miss Edge offered. "There she is, with a look on her washed out face of weariness, and disgust, poor child. I do not know if we should not get rid of her as well," she ended, but in an uncertain voice.

"No really, dear, there must be limits."

"It is the risk of Infection again," Edge explained, all at once rather magisterial. "Jealousy is an epidemic, can even lead to crime."

"Now, Edge, I really should . . ."

"Yes, Baker, but there is so much which is unexplained. That is the reason I feel we must have a clearance, a real spring clean," Miss Edge interrupted. But, now the tension was relaxed, she spoke in almost languishing tones.

Miss Baker became unusually confident. The music, the dance, the air of festivity had loosened her tongue.

"So long as we ourselves don't get swept up into the dust pan along with the wet tea leaves," she said.

"Baker, surely that is rather fanciful," her colleague reproved, in an idle voice.

"This is hardly the time and place to discuss it," Miss Baker admitted. "Why, look at Mr Rock and Moira."

"Where? Dancing?"

"No, Edge, over in the doorway. Really he imagines he has particular manners, to use the Institute idiom."

"So long as they do not sample moonlight," Edge exclaimed.

Miss Baker laughed, then she said, "Of course if there was really anything of the sort I'd never hesitate. Out they'd all go, neck and crop. But until we have cleared Mary up, and got quite to the bottom of Merode, we may'nt be absolutely sure, you know. Even his turning up tonight with Elizabeth looks suspicious from a certain angle, I agree. Yet there's Mr Swaythling, not to mention Hargreaves. Both are old friends, remember."

"The way to handle all matters of this sort is to act in the name of the State at once, then congratulate the State on what has been done afterwards," Edge propounded, with a sudden dryness.

"My dear," Baker replied. "Those tactics may have served when we had to have another corridor of bathrooms, but I venture to think this an altogether different problem."

"I must have that cottage," Edge goodhumouredly insisted.

"And so you shall," Miss Baker promised, in the voice she would have used to a little girl who was wanting more chocolate, in the one day, than was proper. "Now, shall we postpone all this until tomorrow?"

"Very well," Edge agreed, content on the whole to let things slide this night of nights. "But I must just mention one thing, Baker," she added, as a last gesture, and in a rising voice, as though to yell defiance. "They can go too far," she shouted under the music, but kept her face expressionless. It was like a prisoner, confined with others to a workshop in which talk is forbidden, and who has learned to scream defiance as an unheard ventriloquist beneath the deafening, mechanical hammers. "They can outstretch themselves," (she was working herself up), "there is a Limit, and this," when, at that precise moment, the music stopped dead into a sighing silence, "this Rock" she continued, and could only go on, in a great voice, heard throughout the Hall, "upon which our Institute is Built," she recovered, and beamed at the Students.

"My dear, magnificent," Miss Baker approved, in praise of the recovery.

Mr Rock had had a grand time, so close surrounded by children that he was protected even from Moira's pressing attentions.

Very likely because, on this occasion, it would be one way a girl could draw attention to herself, or, at any rate, that was how he explained it, he had been deluged by pretty, laughing invitations to be amongst his partners, all of which he had known how to refuse. It was enough that he had danced with Liz, would be ready again for Edge when the spirit moved her, and that he should be at hand if Liz lost her Sebastian even for a moment. One or two carefully done evenings like this, and she'd come right in no time. Nevertheless he was charmed with the fuss these children were making.

"Why don't you, Mr Rock, this once?"

"You might, you know. It's rather particular, with me I mean."

"We need'nt finish the whole thing out. Come on, just three times round the floor."

After the dancing there had already been, these children were hot despite windows wide open onto sky-staring white Terraces, and, as several tugged at his old hands, Mr Rock could feel their moist fingers' skin, the tropic, anemone suction of soft palms over rheumatic, chalky knuckles.

"You do me honour. But no, I think not," he was saying.

"Why can't you leave the man be?" Moira demanded, on the outskirts.

"Well, it's not fair for you to have all," one objected.

"If I were fifty years younger," the old man fatuously said.

"I'll bet you were terrific, Mr Rock."

"Then what I say is, I wish I'd been about at the time," another cried.

"Now, will you let him alone?" Moira objected.

"All right, my dear, I'll call for help when I'm in need." Mr Rock told her.

"But you know you promised," she lied.

"What? Did I?" he asked, contrite at once. These last few years he had been nervous regarding his memory.

The others began to drift away, at this uncalled for intrusion of privacy.

"I wish poor Inglefield would'nt hesitate so long between," one said.

"I'd something particular I wanted you to see below, now d'you remember?" Moira told him. She spoke right into his good ear, having to stand on her toes to reach.

"I'll not have that nonsense a second time," he said in a low, gruff voice.

"Oh I'm so sorry, and if you don't want, of course you shan't," she answered.

"Well, what is there?" he relented.

"Come and see."

"Certainly not."

"Then I'll never tell," she announced with a voice of authority, as she turned away.

"But need we go just the two of us?" he weakly asked.

P

He considered the suggestion that another might come along must provide the impediment he sought.

"Naturally not.   Whoever said?"

He misunderstood what he heard of this last.

"That's that, then," he concluded, much relieved.

She immediately caught hold of his hand once more.

"All right, come with me, tag on," she laughed.   "Here, Melissa," she called, and lugged both off.   "For better or worse," she ended.

"Where are we going?" he appealed, as soon as he was led into the pantry.   A different girl stood guard.

He was ignored.

"Never those stairs again," Mr Rock weakly protested.

"Not much doing yet," the new child said, as she locked up behind.

"Why you managed last time like a bird," Moira said, with greater authority.

"Must I?" he pleaded, horrified at the thought that he could only make a fool of himself a second time on the scramble down.   At his age it was a sort of rock climb.

"Yes," Moira insisted, Melissa laughed, and they began to whisper.   As he painfully negotiated the steps, he thought his children were rough with him, but was too confused to protest.   He could not understand, nor hear. When at last the thing had been managed, he was hurried along that dead silent, underground passage until, once again, they came to the green baize door and the upended case.   As soon as Melissa had clambered up on this, he was so muddled he did not connect the action with what Moira had previously done, perhaps because neither of the girls had yet gone through the door.   And he was painfully out of breath because he had been bustled.   So, when the child said, "Come over," and Moira gave him a great shove in the back, he went forward, an old lamb offered up.   Exactly the same recurred.   Melissa laid a cheek against him, then rolled it over until her lips brushed his. "Stop," he demanded, stepping back, but not so far that he got whitewash on his clothes this time.

"Oh please don't be so dreadful, Mr Rock," Moira laughed. "It's only our Club rules and regulations. I must now enjoin you to silence," she recited.

"Mum's the word?" he asked like a fool, ashamed, blaming his deafness that he had been let in for this, afraid.

"You can talk all you want, you know, once we're inside," Melissa said as she jumped off the case. "Quiet a moment, just the same." She knocked on the door, which was opened forthwith. She gave what must have been the password. Upon which a child opened it wide, and all three came forward into a quick flicker of candle-light.

The first thing that arrested him was a notice, "INSTI-TUTE INN". The next he knew he was warmly surrounded by six or nine children, who clapped their hands, giggling. Then Moira stepped through them.

"My job's to welcome you," she said in a loud, formal voice. But she grew embarrassed, poor old Mr Rock did look pathetic. "Make yourself at home," she added on a much weaker note, at the verge of helpless giggles.

Melissa handed the old man a glass, as though it were a goblet.

"What is it?" he enquired, glad to be able to ask the familiar question.

"Will you be initiated now or later, Mr Rock?"

"You have to drink this down. The Club Special," Melissa told him.

"I'm not sure if you realise a single thing," a girl severely said. "But you're the first outside one has come down here. When we voted to ask you tonight, it was most particular."

"Yes, and when I'm caught, as will doubtless happen, I'll be the last," Mr Rock dryly said. He was recovering.

"That would be an honour," the child approved. "Oh, for us too," she corrected herself. "How idiotic."

"You're perfectly sweet," Moira assured him. "And we've our guard up top. They change every three quarters of an hour so they can get some dancing. She's got a bell up there. The moment the alarm goes, look here it is, we just lope out the back way. Though we've never had to yet, thank goodness."

"I see," he said, and at last sat down. He sipped what was in the glass. He judged it to be a kind of medicated syrup.

The girls having begun an argument, he was left to himself for the while. He looked around. He felt rather flattered. At the same time he began to have a gross feeling of immoderate amusement, such as had not come his way in years.

—What would those two idle, no good, boasting spinsters say to this, he wondered of the underground passage, widened here like a green bottle from its neck, and blocked off at the far end by a blue rug. More coverings in faded canvas had been hung to cover the walls. Pinned up in a continuous and beautiful arabesque, were single sprays of azalea filched from above stairs. In the light from a row of candles, on a trestle set back, so he found, too close for safety to the canvas, these flowers, laid flat against tarpaulin, cast each one a little shadow by which it was outlined from above; a medieval fancy, he thought; the sweet tented furnishing for a campaign the women followed, a camp in Flanders in an old war of bows and arrows, he opined, and smiled.

The children had come to an end of another of their discussions.

"Lord, it is slow, is'nt it? Could'nt we have our music?" one demanded.

"Something's the matter with the thing. Margot's gone to fix that."

"Why don't we all go off, then?"

"Outside? Why Melissa, whatever for?"

"Have'nt you heard, even yet?"

"Shut up," ordered another girl.

"Do you relay the music from above down here?" the old man enquired, and thought to identify himself with youth by the question.

"That ancient stuff?" Marion demanded. "You must think us properly out of date. Lord no. We get on to . . ." and she mentioned a source of which he had no knowledge. And he could not be sure he had caught the name.

"I do wish Mary might be with us," he remarked, suddenly regretting the child, ill at ease.

"Oh she's all right, don't you worry your head," Moira answered. Unseen by him, she pouted with jealousy.

"But where is she, then?" the old man persisted.

"I thought just everyone had a very good idea," Moira replied. "I'd not trouble myself if I was you. She's not worth it."

"She never bothered much where we were concerned," one of the others elaborated. "She put the whole show in danger. You wait until I catch Merode."

"No, but what has happened to Mary, please?" Mr Rock begged. He was frightened again.

"That's a secret. We're bound to silence, don't you realise?"

—How could one be certain these children were not simply prevaricating? Because he felt some true friend of Mary must get to her if she was hidden.

"Not an entirely intelligent mutism in that case," he tried, one more.

"It's the way it is," was all he got for his pains.

"Many of you see much of Adams, nowadays?" he next enquired, across the chatter they kept up at each other.

"Him?" Moira said, and laughed. "We call that man the answer to the virgin's prayer."

"Now Moira, duck," Melissa protested. "Who's gone too far this time?"

"Well, a person has only to look, have'nt they? He's enough to bring on anyone a miscarriage."

"You're crazy."

"Am I?"

"What is the matter with Adams, if you will excuse my persistence?" Mr Rock tried once more, floundering after information.

"Look. Some of the girls in East block go out at night to find him."

"Oh no, Moira, it's too much," protested another.

"Not Club Members, of course," Moira admitted.

"But anyway, how are you sure?" the same child asked.

"Because I can afford to save my beauty sleep up, thank you, until I need. I mean, I don't have to go hogging it the whole night through in case I get pimples next morning on account of I stay awake," she proudly answered.

"Careful the stable clock does'nt toll midnight and catch you making faces at the horrid Adams, then. Under a new moon."

"Me?" Moira demanded. "I would'nt be seen dead beside him."

Mr Rock was less than ever at ease. He began to ask himself how it would look if he were caught down here.

"But you do claim you have a lot on him," the first child insisted.

"Why should'nt I? Who's to prevent me?" Moira demanded.

There was rather a pause at this last remark.

"After all's said and done, we're only young once," she

said, with a trace of malice, at Mr. Rock. But when she continued, it was after she had correctly interpreted the lines of distaste that had formed about his mouth. "Oh, you need'nt pay attention, please," she said directly to the old man. "This is only a lot of talk. Fun and games," she added, as though to explain everything.

Upon which a couple of atomic cracks sounded from the amplifier up in an angle. Immediately followed, crescendo, by a polka which had been out of date even in the days when the old man had had his few months dancing. So he waited for a howl of protest from the children.

When none came, he looked up, and was amazed. With rapt expressions on their fair faces, they were already rocking to the ancient music.

"Is'nt it marvellous?"

"Sh . . . Melissa. How can anyone listen if you . . ."

For the second time, Mr Rock was moved to suppress a smile despite his fears.

Then the apparatus stammered a few notes, gave out, broke down.

"Oh, is'nt that just like this beastly hole?" Moira wailed.

"She's hopeless. She'd never repair a thing."

"Perhaps you'd like to go up and have a shot, then?"

"If I did, I would'nt stop by the old apparatus, thanks. I'd find somewhere else, I expect, a little farther out."

"Will you shut up, Melissa, and for the last time?"

"I say, Mr Rock," Moira said. "If I asked, would you be dreadfully angry?"

"I can't say until you have tried, can I?" he answered.

"Oh, so you will. No then, I'd better not."

"Come on out with it. Get along with you," he said. He had not the slightest suspicion, was even beginning to be thoroughly amused again.

"We've all been so thrilled," Moira began. "In fact we

don't know if it will be announced some time upstairs. And if she does, you might send word down, won't you? I mean we'd hate to miss that, through being stuck in the Inn, would'nt we, girls?"

"What is this?" he demanded, at his most assured.

"Why, your granddaughter's engagement, of course. Don't pretend you have'nt kept that dark from us when . . .", but his face so clouded over that Moira bit her fat lower lip. "Oh, Mr Rock, have I said something awful?" she meekly asked.

"Never heard such arrant nonsense in all my born days," he blustered. "Why, Elizabeth's a sick woman."

"I'm frightfully sorry, Mr Rock," Moira apologised, while the others watched, mouths open.

"Just gossip," Mr Rock thundered, rather white. He was furious. "Not a word of truth."

"Yes, Mr Rock," they said.

"And if you catch anyone repeating what you've just told I'd be glad if you would deny it, once and for all," he continued, trembling. Then he struggled up. "I'm tired. I shall go back home to bed."

"Oh, Mr Rock, it is'nt anything we've said, surely?"

"We live in an ungrateful world," he replied. "I'm sorry, but there are times I have had enough."

He stalked off with dignity, and, for a short while, left behind a silence.

Then someone said, "oh Gosh," and laughed.

Mr Rock came away in a flustered rage. He banged on the stair door and a new girl immediately opened. She, also, was chewing. He thrust straight past, shambled off uglily and at speed to where they danced.

A white bunch of children, stood in the doorway, fell open to let him through like a huge dropped flower losing petals on a path. Then the thunderous, swinging room met him smack in his thick lenses, the hundred couples sweating glassily open-eyed now it was late; each child that pulled at her partner's waist to speed it, to gyrate quicker, get much more hot, to keep pace.

Elizabeth saw him. She considered if she would hide, but knew it might be wicked. Accordingly she yelled, "See Gapa, darling." Even then, Sebastian, cheek to her mouth, barely caught what she said. In any case, he paid no heed.

At the same moment the old man had a dark sight of them both. He made such an immense gesture to summon Liz, he almost smashed off his nose the spectacles that reflected reeling chandeliers. "In a minute," her lips shaped back across the shattering valse. He did not take this in, misunderstood it for impertinence.

But when, inevitably as tumbled water, the dance delivered them over, two leaves that touch beneath a weir, caught in the eddies, till they were by his side, she awoke Sebastian as she drew off from the young man's arms. He said,

"Why hullo, sir?"

"We must go. We are not welcome," the grandfather told Liz.

"Hush, Gapa," she said. But he walked away, they followed, and a second time that group of children opened, reclosed behind the couple trailing after, having parted as another vast bloom might that, torn by a wind in summer, lies collectedly dying on crushed fallen leaves, to be divided by one and then two walkers, only for a strain of wind to reassemble it, to be rolled back complete on the path once more, at the whim of autumnal airs again.

The three left music.

"Hush," she at last repeated, when he could hear.

"There is no use. We are not wanted," Mr Rock announced, in a low voice.

"Why? What? I insist, has anything happened?"

"We need never have demeaned ourselves," he said.

"Oh do say," she wailed. "Was it dreadful? But Gapa, you're making me nervous."

"No. We have to get out, that is all," he explained. "D'you hear?" And came to a halt.

"Don't go now, sir," Sebastian cravenly protested.

They stood, a miserable trio in black cloth, in the dank dark; music at their heels.

"What?" Mr Rock demanded.

"I said why just yet?" Birt asked, pale and obstinate.

"I've seen enough," the old man proclaimed. "Miserable children that they are. Too much freedom here. Lack of control. All they have to do is chatter," he ended.

"Was it about your lectures, then?" she enquired.

"They're downright illnatured," he replied, at a tangent. "And inclining towards a dangerous mentality in which I shall take no lot or part. I hope a man of my years would know better. Come out."

"But Gapa, don't you think, I mean might'nt it all look rather odd if we simply just walked off? Ought'nt we at least to say goodbye, you must agree?"

"Everything comes if one can bide one's time," Mr Rock said, to ignore her. —He's certainly waited long enough, Sebastian considered.

"Whatever you say, of course," Elizabeth consented. "But we must at least offer thanks, surely? And I'm sure I don't know where Miss Edge's got to, do you Seb? I've a notion I have'nt set eyes on her this last half hour, have you?"

"I don't like it, I don't like any of it. I'll shake the dust from my feet," the old man insisted. He was very upset.

"Yes, Gapa, but at the same time, after all, when we're merely uninvited, I mean you can't just come in and out as you please, can you? We should thank them. Don't you feel we'd better? Come on, of course you . . . you know you do."

"Well then, where is Miss Edge?"

"Powdering her nose to pretend she's what she's not," Sebastian brought out in his parson's voice, to cheer them.

"Well, you can't chase after her in there, however you feel," Elizabeth protested, almost contemptuously, to the old man.

"Might I make a small suggestion?" Sebastian proposed, his own self again at last. "Could Liz and I finish this dance? We'd keep our eyes skinned for the guv'nor all the time."

—The old man seemed visibly deflated, he thought. He wondered what had punctured him. No more than some second-hand foolery about Mary, he decided, satisfied Mr Rock was now in such a state of tired confusion that he would swallow, entire, any ancient guff the girls chose to hand out.

"They're fiends," Mr Rock protested all at once. "Fiends. Every single one."

"It's the girls are, Gapa. You listen to a woman," Elizabeth said of herself. "Miss Baker and Miss Edge are'nt so bad."

He glared. But he was not going to admit he agreed. "So you won't come?" he challenged.

"Why, of course. Anything you want," she answered in a rude, spoilt voice. "But one must say thank you, surely?" she wheedled.

—You know full well I'm afraid outside, alone in the dark, the old man accused Liz, in his heart. Her carelessness for his feelings made him tired and sick, twice over.

"Then I'll seek Miss Edge for myself," he replied, and stamped off towards the sanctum. Sebastian made as if to follow.

But Elizabeth put a hand on the young man's arm.

"Let Gapa be," she said. "It's his pride. Don't I know, oh so well, so often. I can tell you what's happened. One of those horrid children, and they're out to simply ruin our lives, darling, yours and mine, has mentioned something about his lectures. But tonight I don't care, I'll just not allow anything to come between. Let's nip back for a minute. Oh, this heavenly tune. He'll cool off. He does'nt mean to go."

So they slipped back into the whirlpool to forget, to join in again. But she soon found she could not put Mr Rock out of mind, not yet, not all at once at all events.

Edge had retired for the treat of the day, a cigarette. Because one of these made her feel she had both feet up on mantelpiece, she usually kept herself to the one, night and day. It was delicious, so bad for her heart she even had the sensation she was drunk, and this evening, in the Sanctum, as a special, exceptional indulgence, she had started on another immediately the first was finished. And had no sooner done so before she heard leather shuffled outside. Upon which, while she could hardly get so far for that heavenly lassitude she inhaled, she went over to the door, pushed it wide, and came face to face with the sage.

Light was dark in the passage. He must have had difficulty to get along it to collect the rubber boots. And, as she swayed at his unexpected appearance, she found, without surprise, she now had nothing but pity for the old man.

She leant, a lightweight against a doorjamb, he brittle and heavy against the wall over on the side away from her.

"I'm off home," he announced abruptly, curious, for his part, to find he no longer seemed to hate the woman, all the go gone out of him.

"Why so soon, Mr Rock?" she asked, the butterfly gently fluttering in a vein at one of her temples, from the cigarette.

"Passed my bedtime," he lied.

"Won't you come in for a minute?" she invited, by the entrance to the Sanctum, then took another long draw at the weed to exquisitely drain more blood from her thin limbs.

He made no move however.

"Can't help but worry about my cat," he replied, at random.   "If I don't get her in she'll be out all night."

"Ah yes," she said, "the splendid creature."

"She comes over here such a deal," he added, rather petulant.

"So sweet," the Principal agreed, still with no trace of irony, speaking as though from another existence.   Mr Rock was amazed.   He had never known the woman so amenable.   And then he himself could hear so well, away from the music.

"And has your granddaughter enjoyed it?" Edge enquired.   —Ah well, he thought, day is done, this is a truce.

"Liz?   Of course she is older than the others."

"I saw her take the floor with Sebastian," the Principal said, in an approving voice.

"Those two are great friends," Mr Rock agreed, cautiously.

"I'd much like to have a little chat with you one day about that young man," Edge suggested, gentle, undangerously soft.   The sage was not yet to be drawn, however.

"Yes?" he asked, to gain time.

With a languorous gesture, Edge took one more anaesthetising puff.

"I would really appreciate your advice on Sebastian," she said, in the laziest voice he had heard her use.

"You would?" he countered. He almost surrendered then.

"My dear sir," she murmured. "Need we be too formal the one night of our Founder's Day Ball? I don't really fancy so, do you?"

There was a pause. The old man struggled with a lump in his throat. Then he let go, gave way.

"She's all I have," he said, given over to self pity.

"She loves you," Miss Edge dispassionately stated.

Mr Rock swallowed twice.

"But I can't care for him, ma'am," he admitted, still as if in spite of himself.

"Nor me," the lady answered readily. They looked at each other with great understanding.

"I can't stomach parlour tricks," the old man elaborated, stronger.

"So curiously unwise," Edge agreed. "A word which is out of fashion nowadays," she added. "The girls don't seem to know the meaning, but there, I bless them," she ended.

"Liz has been ill . . ." Mr Rock began, mistaking the object, prepared to take offence at once.

"Why I declare, after all," she soothed him. "I spoke of the man, the tutor, the untutored tutor, please. I trust you would not think . . ."

"My deafness," he explained, to cover the slip.

"D'you ever have treatment?"

"What's the good. I am too old."

"Never that, good heavens no," she countered, through a film of weakness.

"Well, there you are. I have to lump it," he said, and smiled.

"You of all men," she murmured.

"I've been most fortunate in my life," he admitted, weak as water yet again. All this sympathy was so unexpected.

"Look, come in, please. I can't tell what we are standing here for, could you?" she invited. "As a matter of fact, if you will keep our little secret, we've some sherry in the cupboard, Hermione and I."

He suddenly wondered if she could be drunk. He was not to connect the cigarette with her mood, because he had never previously seen the lady smoke. Yet it seemed he should be on guard. Nevertheless this was now a remarkable opportunity, he had to admit. He made up his mind. "And I, for my part," he said, for better or worse weakly entering the sanctum, "would appreciate if I could have two words with you? A domestic matter."

"My dear Mr Rock I make it my rule never to interfere." This was on the assumption that he could only be referring to Elizabeth.

"To do with your students, ma'am," he announced.

"Ah yes."

"They talk so."

"They do indeed," she languidly assented.

"There must be limits, after all," Mr Rock argued. She slumped quickly down, in an elegant attitude, to hold her cigarette like a wand.

"Where would you draw them?" she asked, at ease.

"Where would I draw the line?" he echoed, but without conviction. Then he pulled himself together. "Yet there must be human decency," he said in a firmer voice. "The give and take of a civilized community," he said. "Justice," he ended.

"Of course," she admitted. "Naturally, of course." This time with her first trace of malice which, however, was lost on him.

"Yes," he said, in a muddled way of the girls below. "I mean, they can go too far, can't they?" He was desperate.

"Yes?" she enquired.

There was a pause. Came again the lump in his throat. Once more he surrendered.

"I love her. She's all I have," he said. He could have sobbed.

Edge was so distant, so absent that she had forgotten Mary and Merode. What she could do, and did without the slightest sense of shock, was to ask herself if he had meant Moira all along.

"My dear," she murmured. "As time goes on one clings to what one has."

"She's all I have," he repeated, still about his grand-daughter, secure in self pity.

"But is it wise, or fair, to foul the nest you have built?" she archly enquired.

"In what way?" he demanded, at a loss.

"Were'nt you complaining of the child's behaviour?"

"Never," he protested, of his granddaughter.

She remembered she had not brought out the sherry, but let this go. She was too tired.

"Believe me, I think sometimes you are inclined to mis-judge us, Mr Rock," she said. "We have eyes in our grey heads. And we prize your friendship for the child," she lied, a white lie.

"I don't follow," he said.

"Why, Moira of course," she patiently explained.

"We are at cross purposes, ma'am," he concluded with pride, suddenly and finally disgusted. Then he noticed that she had finished the cigarette. He offered another from his case, as a matter of course.—She knew it to be madness, but how was she to refuse? So she lit up, as though this were the last action she would have strength for in life.

"We are just two old women trying our best, but we do have eyes in our heads," she repeated, obstinately gentle, unaware of the effect she had produced.

"Well, I don't think this Birt is up to any good here, either," the old man said, angry and tart. He had gone back to the doorway, so as to make good his escape, if need be, at a moment's notice.

"Where are you? I can't tell," she demanded.

—And only an hour since, she would insist she had no trouble at all with her eyes, joyfully he reminded himself.

"Are you sure you feel all right?" he asked, after he had narrowly regarded her. He almost hoped she would fall sideways, flat on an ear.

"I'll let you into a little secret," she said. "It's these smokes. My one small indulgence. They make me rather giddy. But it's true I had a nasty turn this afternoon."

"How was that, ma'am?"

"Where on earth have you got to, man?"

"Here," he replied, and came forward a second time, betrayed by curiosity, only to sit, without thinking, in her own place, behind the great desk of office.

She did not notice.

There was a pause.

"You had a fainting spell?" he hazarded. He had long since learned all about it. He thought, —perhaps she drinks all day.

"Oh, I've forgotten. Don't bother me," she said.

"Was it about this sorry disappearance, ma'am?" he persisted.

"Whose? Why, we've got to the bottom of Mary and Merode," she lied. "That did not take long. Absolutely nothing in their storm in a little teacup."

"Thank God," he said, anxious, of course, to learn about Mary.

"Why?" she dreamily wanted to know. "Can these children truly mean much to you?"

Q

"Whatever occurs round this great place affects us all," he covered himself.

"Just one or two small points still to clear up," she emended, for, truth to say, she was superstitiously ashamed. "Believe me, Mr Rock, but now and again, at the end of a long day, I do get sick and tired of these girls. At their age they are terribly full of themselves, terribly."

Edge was being so revealing that Mr Rock once more decided he could not lose a minute of her present mood.

"Have you ever considered the fellow Adams?" he enquired.

"I had to see him this forenoon. Yes?"

"I thought he was hardly himself when we last met." —Like someone else I could mention, he added under his breath.

"I could'nt get sense out of him at all. But I meet so many, so many," she said. "There was a Mrs Manley," she added.

"It seemed as though he had something on his mind."

"Yes?" she airily replied.

"A widower who lives alone in his cottage," Mr Rock suggested.

There was a pause.

"Why, so he does," she said. Mr Rock could see the gray light begin to dawn within the woman.

"It had just occurred to me, that's all," he said.

"And so he does," she repeated, but not with quite the conviction for which he listened in her voice.

A silence fell.

"Then tell me," she demanded, back to her more usual tones. "We do so value your counsel." —And how often have you asked it, he commented to himself? "What would you propose?" she insinuated.

"I'm only an old fellow who's well passed his bedtime," Mr Rock countered. He had gone far enough. Yet he found that, if one tried, one could forgive this woman, and he wanted to bring the conversation back to himself.

"Oh, I'm tired too, deathly so," she idly agreed.

"I'm older than you. I'm older," he repeated.

She let this pass.

"I'm not much longer for this world," he said, on his dignity.

"Don't talk like that, Mr Rock, please. Tonight of all nights."

He sat, looking straight ahead.

"They will fiddle faddle so about themselves," Miss Edge went on, about the children. "It makes for such a deal of bother. I get no help from Baker, none at all," she ended.

He said no word.

"Strictly in confidence we are not certain of much about Mary yet," she went on, again in a most languid voice. "But we shall be tomorrow. I've had experience. Believe me. They will worry over trifles, but it all comes out in the wash, in the end."

He stayed silent. Contemplating his own death with disinterest, he did not catch what she said.

For her part, she felt so queer she hardly knew what she was doing, but found herself, somehow, committed to the following,—as though on top of a hill in a dream on a bicycle with no brakes. "Mr Rock," she began,—then experienced a last titter, or wobble, before it was too late. She threw the cigarette away which had been burning her forefingers. She missed the fireplace. Falling on a State Kidderminster rug it began to glow, unnoticed. "Mr Rock," she said, a second time. For she knew now she could not go back. "You really should have someone to take good care of you. Marry again," she said.

At this she giggled, once. —What a desperate expedient to gain possession of a cottage, she laughed to herself,

almost completely out of control.   She must be mad.   But
then, oh well, what harm was there?   Things would all
come out in the wash, be utterly forgotten come daylight.

"Why yes, yes," he said from the vast distance of his
final, cold preoccupation, not having taken in the drift.

She dreamily excused herself to herself by thinking
that, of course, he would not listen any more than he did
now, which was not at all.   This only proved, so she
thought, that the kindest was to pack him off forthwith to
an Academy of Science.

"I don't believe you bother with me," she rallied.

"How is that, then?" he asked, coming back to earth.

"I said, you must marry again."   She spoke out with a
slow simper which allowed of no misinterpretation.   This,
he at last saw, was an offer, and unconditional at that.   He
took it in his stride as entirely understandable; unthinkable
of course, but not, in her pitiable circumstances, in the
least surprising.   He proudly ignored it.

At the same time he wished to let her down lightly, the
safer course.   He cast about him how to encompass this.
And almost at once proceeded to discuss his health.

"I've been quite well the last few years.   But there's
none can dodge Father Time.   Yet I sleep remarkably
sound.   I take care, naturally.   Regular exercise every day,
fetching Daisy's swill and so forth.   No, it's just anno
domini."

She despised him for not, as she thought, having heard.
Or had he?

"What age are you really, then?" she asked.

"Seventy six next month."

"You don't look it," she lied.   For she considered he
looked more. —Too old, too old, she admitted, in another
part of her head.   But now it was up to him, she knew.

"Not bad for an old fellow," he said, pleased.

Oh, she must have lost her sanity just then, she thought,

realising he did not intend to take her up. She would never, as long as she lived, ever indulge in so many cigarettes again. But was that, could it be, a smell of burning? And what had he meant, when all was said, discussing his health as he had?

"I keep a deal healthier, even, than she does," he remarked of Elizabeth.

"The child looks ever so much better," Edge agreed, dreamily, but with anguish. She still thought he referred to Moira. In a dazed state, she began to imagine larger and longer flames, as that smell came through.

"I am tired. I should go home," he said.

"In that case, goodnight," Edge answered from her deep chair, coldly, more of an enemy than ever. She had finally decided there would be nothing. "Look after yourself," she added with tired venom, while he dragged his body out of the Principal's rightful place, to take leave. She did not, of course, get to her feet when the old man came over. He, for his part, ignored the taste of burning. "Goodbye," she ended, gave him a slack hand. He turned his back to leave.

"Gracious," she remarked, as though to make conversation, having seen the cigarette at last. "Quite a blaze," she said, rose up in no haste, and stamped it well out.

Either he did not catch that, or could not be bothered, but he just stepped outside, closing the door behind him.

In the passage he gave one short, sharp laugh.

She heard.

Elizabeth, her thoughts on Sebastian, waited for Mr Rock outside the Principal's lavatory under a lighted bulb.

She was watching a moth dab its own shadow up above. "It kisses," she said inside her.

When the grandfather came along, he remarked, "There you are, my child;" Mr Rock's calling her his own as much as the old man allowed himself to show of how surprised and touched he felt that, after all, she should have spared time off to see him home. She gave no answer. She continued to watch the moth while he went past. She was concentrating on Sebastian.

Mr Rock bolted the door, sat on a seat, and laboriously took off those oldfashioned pumps. Then eased his toes. But when he got up to step into rubber boots, he trod right on the torch, which, so that he might not lose it, he had slipped down to a heel in one of the legs at the start of the evening. At once he remembered another time that same thing had occurred, when Julia was still alive and, for a further moment, was sorry for himself, heavy and bleak.

Then the old man sallied out, said "Come," and went to open the front door. It had two catches so that, for some minutes, he fumbled between his torch and door-handles. She did not lift a finger.

When, at last, the sage had it wide, the moon was so full and loud, that stored light he used fell altogether dimmed. What had been a round pat of yellow over brass knobs and keys became oval at his moonlit, shovel feet, but like cream on milk, a skim of one colour over something the same, and so faint he was able to switch the torch off at once. Indeed, he thought he could now see tolerably well, and was almost sorry he'd begged for her company. —Not that he had, in actual words, ever asked her to come along, but at least he'd not, once again, denied what she knew perfectly, his age-long fear of the dark. Because, now they had left the house, his relief caused him to forget the pitch black between trees at night, which they were yet to meet in the ride leading to their cottage.

He even turned round to view the hated mansion which the moon, plumb on it, made so tremendous that he spoke out loud the name, "Petra".

Elizabeth followed in silence, struck into herself by the man she had left, deeply promising she would come straight back. She had no eyes for what was lavished from above, nor ears for what her grandfather expressed, astonished at the sight.

Lovesick, she walked as someone will who, in a dream, can find herself on frozen wastes where the frost is bright then black, but will still keep warm with the warmth of bed, although that imagined world outside stayed cold, dead cold.

Her grandfather, again in difficulty on account of the treacherous light, but glad of his escape, waded much as though the moon had flooded each Terrace six inches deep. For the spectacles he used seemed milk lensed goggles; while he cautiously lifted boots one after the other in an attempt to avoid cold lit veins of quartz in flagstones underfoot because these appeared to him like sunlight that catches in sharp glass beneath an incoming tide, where the ocean foams ringing an Atlantic.

So much so, that when he came to the first flight of stone steps Mr Rock turned completely round and went down backwards.

Upon which a faint cry came from those beechwoods he had been facing. The great crescent of the moonlit house received and gathered the sound, sent this back in a girl's voice, only deeper. "Mar . . . eee," the gabled front returned.

He was halted by it between two steps, "What was that?" he asked, peering over a shoulder at moondrenched trees, starched, motionless in the distance he had yet to traverse.

When his granddaughter did not deign to reply, Mr Rock assumed it must have been a noise in the head from his old heart, the sudden twang on a vein. He sighed. He began the climb once more, down his cliff face, grabbing at the balustrade each step he took.

Next he sneezed. Fumbled after a handkerchief. "Careful you don't take yourself a chill, dear," he called. But she ignored him. She warmed herself at the blaze in her heart for Sebastian.

As he struggled forward once again, he blamed the girl for what he took to be a fit of sulks because, after all, she was not much company if she would trail five foot behind, and never open her mouth. Upon which the cry came a second time, "Mar . . . eee." The house received this, drove it forth louder, as before, and twice.

"Could someone be calling from the Institute?" he asked in his deafness.

When she paid no heed, he sharply demanded, "Well, is it?"

"Oh I don't know, you know," she answered in a pre-occupied, low voice. "I expect that's only some of their girls out amongst the tree trunks."

"But it came from behind," he objected.

"The echo did," she replied, as languid as Miss Edge.

He hesitated onward, silent in his turn.

"Would they be after Adams, then?" he enquired at last, and received no answer. The stars above were bright. She was vowing herself to Birt.

The trouble Mr Rock had with his eyes, under a moon, brought him back to where he left off with Miss Edge, to health. Had he tried, he would have been unable at this precise moment to remember more of his latest talk with the Principal. He slowed up, to let Elizabeth draw level.

"I keep well in myself for a man my age," he boasted. "Of course I have difficulty with my eyesight, and I wish I'd thought to bring the stick along. You might have reminded me when we started."

She made no comment.

"No, I have been very fortunate," he went on. "Few men of my years could conscientiously boast of health like mine. I enjoy my food, I get my sleep all right in bed, I have few of the usual aches and pains. Noone asks me if it will rain tomorrow, which I always consider the ultimate insult to a man's white hairs. True I'm a bit deaf, naturally. That can't be helped. No, I've a deal to be thankful for. And if they would only trouble to pronounce, or even sound, their consonants, I'd hear as well as the next man. Too much, even, on occasion," he added, half remembering the girls below.

There was a pause.

"Your grandmother always did say there could be no deaf people if those who condescended to open their mouths away from a plate would bother to be distinct."

She received this in silence. He started on another tack, as he painfully began to negotiate steps down to the third Terrace.

"Have you seen Alice?" he asked.

She did not answer.

"I said, had you run across my cat?" he insisted.

"No, Gapa. Why?"

"Because I'm worried about the animal, of course," he explained. "I would not put it altogether past those two dangerous fanatics to do away with Alice. You know how foully underhand they are. A pet could be fair game. Damn this moonlight. I can't see where to put my feet."

—How frightfully unreasonable he is, she thought. Just when it was light as day. —Quite the sort of thing Seb would'nt ever believe, if he still resented her seeing Gapa home, when she got back. Oh Seb!

"Daisy still out. Noone can tell what's become of me Ted. What a day. Too long by half."

"But they've been off before," she protested. "I mean,

there's nothing new . . . this is'nt the first time, Gapa, after all, on their own, is it?"

"I would'nt know about that, of course," he said, tart.

"You'll find them when you get back."

"You surely do not propose to leave me walk through the woods all by myself?" he cried out. Indeed, these were now much nearer.

"Why Gapa dear, how could you think? Of course not."

"Work one's fingers to the bone and fat thanks in return," he grumbled.

She said not a word.

"Pay no attention, Liz," he said, at last.

"I got hot up there. I'm glad of a breather," she lied, to meet him half way.

"The ludicrous female would have upset me if I had'nt kept control," he went on, suddenly remembering Miss Edge at last.

"Then you did speak? Oh, you are good." Elizabeth was dreamily enthusiastic. "And what did she . . . you know . . . was it, I mean did you smooth things out?"

"Smooth what out?"

"Why, everything."

"How can I tell yet?" he demanded, in an exasperated voice. "But I swallowed my pride," he muttered. "Yes, I had to do that," he said, to make all he'd done into sacrifice. Then he at last entirely recollected the proposal Edge had just made him. He gave one more short, sharp laugh. He'd nothing other than contempt for the half crazed harpy. "The trouble with drunkenness is that it will not realise the other party can be sober," he added, aloud.

This last remark did not make sense to her. She could only guess.

"What?" she asked, alarmed. "Miss Edge pretended

you'd been . . . oh Gapa, was there more trouble, then? Because you have'nt . . . that's to say, there could be no question . . . but this is awful." The fact was, the old man might, on occasion, get muddled drunk.

"Liz," he said sternly. "Don't be a fool."

"Then what is it?" she cried, rather wild. She looked close into his moon brown face. The forehead was corrugated.

Mr Rock knew he had gone too far. If he told her of this last, ludicrous development she was sure to repeat it to Sebastian who, not later than next day, or even the same night, would be all over the place imitating his idea of his Principal's idiom while she proposed marriage. And, in any case, the suggestion, from every point of view except Edge's own, the old man considered, was tantamount to an insult offered by the woman. Mr Rock next experienced a wave of panic. He would have liked to get rid of his granddaughter, in case, somehow, she learned. Then he recollected the black ride that was almost on them. Indeed, raising eyes from a treacherous path, he saw the beeches like frozen milk, and frozen swimming-bath blue water, already motionless in a cascade, soundless from a height, not sixty yards in front.

"Peace, child," he said.

"Oh, what did you mean before?"

"You misunderstood. No more of this."

"Then, had the new bother anything, at least, to do with Seb?"

"Liz, of course not."

"You must remember I have'nt been well," she subsided. "I get so terribly worried, you know." He had realised that before, but wondered how dark the ride would be which was beginning to gape at him, narrow and black.

The cry came a third time, directly on them, from somewhere amongst the trees. But now they had come so far that even though he waited he could barely catch the echo's answer, the house singing back in a whisper, and he just heard it thrice; "Mar . . . ee," " mareee," ". . . eee."

"You must have heard," the old man accused his grand-daughter, as though she had missed the call three times.

"Oh don't pay attention, dear, I told you. That's only their Club they think is so secret, and everybody knows. They go and whoop round the place at night."

"I've never noticed."

"Well, you see, perhaps you would'nt."

"I may be a trifle hard of hearing but I trust I could never miss a shout such as we've just heard."

She left his remark alone.

"No Liz, they're out to comb the undergrowth for poor Mary."

"They might have, you know, this morning. I expect you did'nt listen but it was just after you set off. I mean, they were round the cottage, and you had gone by that time. Still, they are'nt looking now, Gapa, you can be sure."

"Is there any news, then?"

"News? Not that I've learnt. Don't you remember I told you? They're simply fiends."

The old man and his granddaughter had come to the beginning of a ride. Every twenty yards or so there was a separate marsh of moonlight, but the way looked lonely to him.

"Wait a moment for me to light my torch," he ordered, as though he had to strike a match for this. He fumbled.

When he had the thing on, he shone around him. Immediately there came a string of startled grunts. He shuddered, then waved the small megaphone of light here and there through a black shadow of trees till he lit on his pig. Daisy was caught looking full in their direction, until she turned, began to make off, squealing. There was somewhat round her neck. He switched the light away and called his pet. She seemed to have halted. He slowly brought round the long cone of daylight, very quiet in great, open stealth, so as not to alarm her. He picked out a white leg, held it quivering while Daisy's tail flickered to and fro, and, once uncovered again, the pig began to grunt. As, with gentle patience, he gradually turned his wrist to bring his dunce's cap of moonlight on all of Daisy, she grunted crescendo, but held firm. Till he saw a slipper in white satin had been tied round her white neck.

"They'll have been torturing her," he cried in the swill man's tones at once, upon which the animal squealed twice, then stayed dumb. He switched his light out. There was utter silence.

"Oh, you don't know what they're like, you can't, you're a man," Elizabeth announced, lazily, at last, from the morass of her thoughts.

"I shall not overlook it," said Mr Rock, in his deepest voice.

She again began to be made nervous. She dreaded this sort of intervention on his part. But she just had enough sense to keep quiet.

"Should I take the thing away immediately?" the old man demanded, afraid Daisy might run off if approached.

"Try if she will follow," Elizabeth said, coming to earth. "I told you we should find them when we got back, don't you remember?"

Accordingly Mr Rock shone the light once more, but this time at his toes. As they set out along the ride he called encouragingly to Daisy. He kept it up, and was answered, every so often, by a squeal of unease. From which he judged that she followed, like a cat, in fits and starts.

The old man maintained outraged silence. He was oppressed by the dark, by the next dirty trick that might be played.

He did not have long to wait.

When they were in the centre of the second pool of moonlight which was let through by a break in trees, and Daisy skirted this, keeping to black shade, Mr Rock heard Ted, his goose, burst into sharp cries of alarm not sixty yards in front. He halted dead. Next there was a rush out there towards him, a rising string of honks like an old fashioned bicycle, and the goose, which had never flown before, came noisily by at speed six foot off the ground, while Daisy grunted. The granddaughter stepped to one side. But the old man knelt, trembling.

He feared a collision.

Then Ted was gone.

He listened, intent for giggles. He heard no hint of such.

"Are they at the bottom of this, too?" he asked.

"Have you hurt yourself? Oh Gapa I mean, what are you doing?"

"Really, Elizabeth, you can be very absurd. She came straight for my spectacles. And now where is Daisy?"

"It's all right, dear, take my hand, she's not gone, there, at last we're on our feet again. I suspect Daisy's only too glad to be led home. My goodness, but did'nt Ted come by in a rush."

"I'm a bit stiff about the joints these days," the old man admitted, dusting off his wet, cold trousers. "No, but even you will agree, this is too much, Liz, altogether. Noone has to keep silent under persecution, except dumb animals of course. Tomorrow I shall have it quite thoroughly gone into."

"All's well that ends well," the young woman comforted.

"How d'you know they have'nt even put Alice in a sack to drown," he asked, in quavering tones. He called "Daisy", in the swill man's voice, and was at once answered with a grunt, close.

Once more they started on their way. Mr Rock did not speak. He was wounded at having been made to look ridiculous, profoundly disquieted for what might come next.

Elizabeth said no word. It would not be long now before she got back to Seb. Meanwhile she gave herself over to the young man once more.

So they came at last to the outskirts of their cottage, by which time Mr Rock had almost recovered. The first outpost, or guard house, was Ted's kennel. As this was in full moonlight, Mr Rock switched off the torch. And he would never, for the rest of his days, be able to explain why, but he bent down to put a hand inside. He was answered, slowly, by the bird's low hiss.

"Good God," he said. "Ted's home."

She paid no attention.

"We shall never know the truth," he said.

"Gapa," she broke in. "Now we're here, I'm going back. I don't suppose I'll stay long. You won't be nervous, will you?"

"Nervous? How many times have I to tell you I am never nervous. It's only my eyes, can't you understand. Very well, then, not that anything I can say will make much difference, I suppose."

She moved off at once. Then he remembered.

"Wait," he called. "Where's Daisy?"

"She ran into her sty," the young woman sang over a shoulder, stepped out of moonlight, and disappeared.

Mr Rock moved across to shut the gate on his pig. What with the torch, the case he carried, and that latch, he fumbled a good deal. Then he listened for, and heard,

Daisy's heavy breath. He leant inside, felt about. The moment he touched her, she squealed terribly. But he got hold of the slipper and jerked it from her neck. She yelled as though about to be stuck and then, as soon as he moved off, she stopped. He hurled the shoe away. Once it was no longer in moonlight it disappeared, the thing might have flown. He did not, of course, hear it fall. Upon which he realised he still had Elizabeth's shoes in the despatch case. She could scarcely dance in rubber boots. He thought to call her back, but decided against. —Gum boots would not help Birt, he considered, not realising they would force her to take the young man outside.

He entered the cottage, switched on a light, began the routine he carried through each bedtime, set things to rights. When he was just about done he heard a cat discreetly yowl. He went to the door. It was Alice. After getting her in with some milk, he climbed the stairs to bed.

On the whole he was well satisfied with his day. He fell asleep almost at once in the yellow woollen nightshirt.

THE END